PRESIDENT ELECT

(A LUKE STONE THRILLER—BOOK 5)

JACK MARS

ISBN: 978-1-63291-918-2

BOOKS BY JACK MARS

"Death is softer by far than tyranny."

- Aeschylus

Two years later…

CHAPTER ONE

November 2
2:35 a.m. Eastern Standard Time
Near the Tidal Basin—Washington DC

"Okay," the man said, his breath drifting away in plumes of white. "What are we doing here?"

It was late, and the night was chilly with a light rain falling.

The man's name was Patrick Norman, and he was talking to himself. He was an investigator, a man accustomed to spending long periods of time alone. Talking to himself was part of the job.

He stood on the concrete path along the water's edge. There was no one else around. A moment ago, what looked like a homeless man had been sprawled under some newspapers on a bench about fifty yards away. Now that man was gone, and the newspapers were all over the wet ground.

From where Norman was, he could see the Lincoln Memorial far to his right. Directly in front of him and across the tidal basin was the dome of the Jefferson Memorial, lit up in shimmering blue and green. Lights glinted on the water.

Norman had been in this line of work a long time, and these were the kinds of meetings he relished. Late at night, in a secluded place, with someone who was hiding their identity—risky, but this exact type of thing had paid off for him in the past. If it hadn't, he wouldn't be here now.

A man slowly walked along the path toward him. The man was tall, wearing a long raincoat and a wide-brimmed hat pulled down over his face. Norman watched the man approach.

Suddenly, there was movement behind him. Norman turned, and two more men were there. One of them was the homeless man from before. He was black, in ripped workpants and a heavy winter parka. The parka was wet and stained and dirty. The man's hair stood up in odd tufts and curls on the very top of his head. The second man was just another nondescript nobody in a raincoat and hat. He had a bushy black mustache—if Norman had to describe him later that was the best he was going to do. He was too startled at the moment to absorb a lot of details.

"Can I help you gentlemen?" Norman said.

"Mr. Norman," the tall man said from behind him. The man had a very deep voice. "I think I'm the one you want to speak with."

Norman felt his shoulders sag. They were playing a game. If these men wanted to hurt him, they probably would have already done so. That relieved him a little—these were government people. Spooks. Spies. Intelligence operatives, they would probably call themselves. That also annoyed him a little. There was no mysterious source with information for him. These guys had dragged him out here in the middle of a rainy night to tell him... what?

They were wasting his time.

Norman turned around again to face the man. "And you are?"

The man shrugged. A smile showed just below the shadow from his hat. "It doesn't matter who I am. It matters who I work for. And I can tell you my bosses are not pleased with the caliber of your work."

"I'm the best there is," Norman said. He said it without hesitating. He said it because he believed it. Much was open for debate. But one thing that was never called into question was the quality of the job he did.

"That's what they believed, too, when they hired you. I think you'll agree they've been patient. They've been paying you for a year with no results. But suddenly, all this time has passed, and it's very late in the game. They're forced to go in another direction, one they had hoped not to take. The election is five days from now."

Norman shook his head. He raised his hands, palms upward, at his sides. "What can I tell you? They wanted me to find evidence of corruption, and I looked. There isn't any. She may be many things, but corrupt isn't one of them. She has no ties to her husband's business interests, formal or informal. Her husband no longer even manages the day-to-day affairs of his company, and the company has no government contracts, here or anywhere else. All of her premarital assets are managed in a blind trust, with no input from her—a measure she took when she first won a seat in the Senate fifteen years ago. There's no evidence of pay-offs of any kind, not even a hint or a rumor."

"So you failed to find anything?" the man said.

Norman nodded. "I failed to—"

"You failed, in other words."

A flicker of light appeared inside Norman's mind, something he hadn't considered because it had never been asked of him before.

2

"They wanted me to find something," he said. "Whether it was there or not."

The men around him said nothing.

"If that was the case, why didn't they just tell me so from the beginning? I would have told them to stuff it, and we never would have had this misunderstanding. If you want to invent bad news, don't hire an investigator. Hire a publicist."

The man just stared at him. His silence, and the silence of his two henchmen, was unnerving. Norman felt his heart begin to pick up the pace. His body trembled the slightest amount.

"Are you afraid, Mr. Norman?"

"Of you? Not a chance."

The man glanced at the two men behind Norman. They grabbed Norman without a word, each putting a painful armbar move on him, one on either side. They wrenched his arms backward behind his back and forced him to his knees. The wet grass instantly soaked through his pant legs.

"Hey!" he shouted. "Hey!"

Shouting was an old escape technique he had learned in a self-defense class many years before. It had come in handy a couple of times. When under attack, scream as loud as you possibly can. It startles the attacker, and often brings people running. No one expects it because regular people rarely raise their voices. Most victims never do. It was a painful truth—many people in this world had been mugged or raped or murdered because they were too polite to scream.

Norman gathered his air for the loudest shriek of his lifetime.

The man wrenched Norman's head upward by the hair and stuffed a rag in his mouth. It was a big rag, wet and dirty with oil or gasoline or some other noxious substance, and the man rammed it in there deep. It took the man several violent thrusts to push it all the way in. Norman couldn't believe how deep it went, and how it filled his entire mouth. His jaws opened as wide as they would go.

He couldn't force the rag back out. The foul smell of it, the taste, made Norman gag. His throat worked. If he vomited, he was going to choke to death.

"Guh!" Norman said. "Guh!"

The man slapped Norman across the side of his head.

"Shut up!" he hissed.

The man's hat had fallen from his head. Now Norman could see his fierce and dangerous blue eyes. They were eyes without pity. They were also without anger. Or humor. They betrayed no emotion of any kind. From inside his coat, he pulled a black gun. A

3

second later, he pulled out a long silencer. Slowly, carefully, in no rush at all, he screwed the silencer onto the barrel of the gun.

"Do you know," he said, "what this gun will sound like when it goes off?"

"Guh!" Norman said. His whole body shook uncontrollably. His nervous system had gone haywire—so many messages flooding it at once, trying to move through the infrastructure, that he was frozen in place. All he could do was shake.

For the first time, Norman noticed that the man was wearing black leather gloves.

"It will sound like someone coughed. That's the way I usually think of it. Someone coughed, one time, and tried to do it quietly so as not to disturb anyone else."

The man pressed the gun to the left side of Norman's head.

"Good night, Mr. Norman. I'm sorry you didn't get the job done."

* * *

The man gazed down at what remained of Patrick Norman, former independent investigator. He had been a tall, thin man wearing a gray trench coat with a blue suit underneath. His head was ruined, the right side blown out in a large exit wound. Blood was pooling around the head on the wet grass and running onto the path. If the rain kept up, the blood would probably just wash away.

But the body?

The man handed the gun to one of his assistants, the one who had pretended to be homeless earlier this evening. The homeless man, also wearing gloves, crouched by the body and pressed the gun into the right palm of the dead man. Meticulously, he pressed each one of Norman's fingers onto the gun in various places. He dropped the gun about six inches from the body.

Then he stood and shook his head in sadness.

"A pity," he said in a Londoner accent. "Another suicide. I suppose he found his work stressful. So many setbacks. So many disappointments."

"Will the police believe it?"

The Englishman offered a ghost of a smile.

"Not a chance."

CHAPTER TWO

Luke Stone did not move at all.

He crouched perfectly still on a rooftop, behind a low stairwell outbuilding made of slapped together cement. The night was warm and heavy—hot enough that the sweat had soaked through his clothes. He breathed deeply, his nostrils flaring, but he did not make a sound. His heart beat inside his chest, slow but hard, like a fist pounding rhythmically on a door.

Boom-BOOM. Boom-BOOM. Boom-BOOM.

He peered around the corner of the outbuilding. Across the way, two bearded men waited with automatic rifles on their shoulders. They stood at the building's parapet, watching the harbor below them. They chatted quietly, laughing about something. One of them lit up a cigarette. Luke reached to his leg and slipped the serrated hunting knife away from the tape holding it to his calf.

As Luke watched, big Ed Newsam appeared, coming into view from the right, walking almost casually.

The big man approached the guards. Now they spotted him. Spotting Ed Newsam was an alarming proposition. Ed put his empty hands in the air, but continued to walk toward them. One of the men growled something in Arabic.

Luke burst around the edge, knife in hand. One second gone. He raced toward the men, his heavy footfalls crunching on the gravel roof. Three seconds, four.

The men heard him, turned to look.

Now Ed attacked, grabbing the closest man by the head, twisting it viciously to the right.

Luke hit his man chest high, knocking him to the rooftop. He landed on top and plunged his knife hard into the man's breastplate. It punched through on the first try. He clamped a hand over the man's mouth, feeling the bristles of the man's beard. He stabbed again and again, in and out, fast, like the piston of a machine.

The man struggled and squirmed, tried to push Luke off, but Luke slapped his hands away and kept jabbing. The knife made a liquid sound each time it penetrated.

The man's arms drifted down to his sides. His eyes were open, and he was still alive, but the fight had left him.

Finish. Finish it now.

Luke tilted the man's head up, free hand pressed hard against his mouth again, and swiped the serrated blade across the man's throat. A jet of blood pulsed out.

Done.

Luke kept his hand pressed against the mouth until the man was gone. He stared up at the black night sky, letting the life quietly ebb from his opponent.

"Look at your man," Ed's voice said. "Look!"

"I don't want to," Luke said. He just kept staring up at the sky, the great sweep of the Milky Way galaxy filling his vision. Millions of stars were visible. It was... he had no words for it. Beautiful was the only thing that came to mind. He wanted to gaze at those stars forever. He knew what he would see if he looked down—he had looked too many times already.

"You have to look, man," Ed said softly. "It's your job to look."

Luke shook his head. "No."

But there was no choice. He cast a glance at the body beneath him. The black beard of the jihadi was gone. The rugged face was replaced by the pretty features of a woman. The curly black hair was now long and soft and light brown.

Luke was covering the woman's mouth with his hands. Her dead blue eyes stared at him, unseeing—the eyes of his wife, Becca.

Ed whispered now. "You did it, man. You killed her good."

Luke snapped awake.

He sat bolt upright in the deep darkness, his heart hammering in his chest. He was nude, and his body was soaked in sweat. His hair was a long, matted tangle. His blond beard was as thick as that of any Islamic holy warrior. With his hair and his beard, and his weathered skin, he could easily pass for a homeless man.

He was wrapped in a mummy sleeping bag—rated for extreme cold, twenty degrees below zero. Outside his small tent, the wind howled—the tent's skirt flapped madly, a sound so loud he could barely hear the wind itself. He was alone above 16,000 feet on the western slope of Denali, and the mountain was already deep into its winter. A snowstorm had blown in two days ago, and hadn't stopped blowing.

He hadn't had a fire since the storm came in. He hadn't left the tent except to urinate in forty hours. He was 4,000 feet below the summit, and it looked like he wasn't going to make it there. Some people might say he wasn't going to make it anywhere.

He had come up here woefully unprepared—he realized that now. He had brought enough water for four days—it had run out two days ago. He was eating snow and ice for water at this point. That was okay. Worse was food. He had brought a stack of dried meals-ready-to-eat. They were mostly gone now. When the storm came, he had started rationing the food. He was eating less than half the daily calories he needed—luckily, he had barely moved in two days, and was conserving energy.

He hadn't bothered to bring a camp stove. He didn't have a radio, so he had no idea what the weather report was. He had choppered in with a private pilot, and hadn't filed an itinerary with the park service. No one had any idea he was out here but the pilot, and he had told the guy he would call him when he was done.

"Am I trying to kill myself?" he said out loud. He was startled by the sound of his own voice.

He knew the answer. No. Not necessarily. If it happened, okay, but he was not actively trying to die. You might say he was daring it to happen, taking foolish risks, and had been doing so ever since Becca died.

He wanted to live. He just wanted to be better at it. If he couldn't do that…

He was a failure as a husband. He was a failure as a father. His career was over at forty-one years of age—he had walked away from government work two years ago and hadn't looked for anything else. He hadn't checked his bank accounts in a while, but it was reasonable to assume that he was almost out of money. About the only thing he'd ever been any good at was surviving in harsh and unforgiving environments. And killing—he was good at that, too. Otherwise, he had been a total, abject failure.

He could die on this mountain, but the prospect of it held no terror for him.

He was blank, empty… numb.

"Gotta start thinking of a way out of here," he said, but he was just making conversation—he could leave, or not. It would be an okay place to die, and an easy thing to do. All he had to do was… nothing. Eventually—soon—he would run out of food. Drinking snowmelt wouldn't sustain him for long. He would become gradually weaker, until it was impossible for him to make it back down the mountain by himself. He would starve. At some point, he would drift off to sleep and never wake up.

How to decide? How to decide?

Abruptly, he shouted, unaware he was going to do it until he did.

"Give me a sign! Show me what to do!"

Just then, his phone did something it hadn't done in a long time—it rang. The sound made him jump, and his heart skipped a beat. The ringer was on as loud as it would go. The ring tone was a rock song that his son, Gunner, had put on the phone two years before. Luke had never changed it. More than not changing it, he had kept it on purpose. He cherished that song as the last link between them.

He looked at the phone. It reminded him of a living thing, a poisonous viper—you had to be careful how you handled it. He picked it up, glanced at the number, and answered it.

"Hello?"

The sound was garbled. Naturally, the thick tent was blocking the satellite signal. He was going to have to go outside to take this call—not a cheerful thought.

"I have to call you back!" he shouted into the handset.

Even moving quickly, it took several minutes to assemble the layers of clothes he needed and get dressed. It was too cold outside to do it halfway. He unzipped the tent, crawled through the tiny foyer, and pushed out into the weather. The wind and the stinging ice hit his face at once. He'd better make this quick.

He hung a beacon lamp on the tent frame and stumbled away from the noise of the flapping material into deep snow. He carried a powerful flashlight with him, turning back every few feet to mark the location of his camp. There were no lights out here, and visibility was about twenty yards. Snow and ice swirled around him.

He pressed the button to make the call and brought the phone inside the hood of his parka. He stood like a statue, listening to the beeps as the phone shook hands with the satellite and the call tried to go through.

"Stone?" a deep male voice said.

"Yes."

"Hold for the President of the United States."

It was a short wait.

"Luke?" a female voice said.

"Madam President," Luke shouted. He couldn't help but smile when he did. "It's been a long time."

"Much too long," Susan Hopkins said.

"To what do I owe this honor?"

"I've got trouble," she said. "I need you to come in."

8

Luke thought about that for a moment. "Uh, I'm a long way from anywhere right now. It's going to be a little hard to—"

"Doesn't matter," she said. "Wherever you are, I'll send a plane. Or a helicopter. Whatever you need."

"A big friendly Saint Bernard would be good for starters," Luke said. "With one of those little whiskey kegs around his neck."

"Done. He'll bring you a sandwich too, in case you're hungry."

Luke nearly laughed. "Hungry is one way to describe it. And when I'm done eating, I really will need that chopper."

"Also done. Before we hang up, I'll give you to someone who can take your coordinates and send someone out to get you. We go the extra mile around here. We believe in door-to-door service."

Luke had to admit he felt a quick flash of relief. Just moments before he had seen no way off this mountain, no second chance at life. Now, he had one. He hadn't known before whether he'd wanted to die or live—but now he knew for sure. He could tell by the quickening of his blood when she mentioned a way out of here. Intellectually, he still didn't know, but viscerally, his body told him.

He wanted to live.

Despite all the hell he'd been through, somehow, he wanted to live.

"What's going on?" Luke said.

She hesitated, and her voice shook the smallest amount. He could hear it even through the wind whipping around him. "Yesterday was Election Day."

Luke considered that. He had been off the grid for so long, he had no idea what the date was. Somewhere far away, in another world, people still campaigned for office. The wheels of government ground on. There were policies to argue about and important decisions to be made. There was media coverage, and talking heads shouting at each other. He hadn't thought about any of these things in some time. In fact, he had almost forgotten they existed.

A long pause passed between them.

"Luke," Susan said. "I lost the election."

CHAPTER THREE

8:03 a.m. Eastern Standard Time
The Oval Office
The White House, Washington DC

"That evil bastard," someone in the room said. "He stole it, plain and simple."

Susan Hopkins stood in the middle of the office and stared at the large flat-panel TV on the wall. She was still numb, almost in shock. Although she watched intently, she was having trouble forming clear thoughts. It was too much to process.

She was very aware of the suit she wore. It was dark blue with a white dress shirt. There was something uncomfortable about it. Once upon a time, it had fit well—in fact, had been tailored to fit her perfectly—but it was clear today that her body was changing. Now the suit hung wrong. The shoulders of the jacket were too loose, the slacks were too tight. Her bra straps pinched the flesh of her back.

Too much late-night food. Too little sleep. Too little exercise.

She sighed heavily. The job was killing her anyway.

Yesterday at this same time, just after the polls opened, she was among the first people in the United States to cast her vote. She had come out of the booth with a big smile on her face and a fist in the air—an image that had been caught by the TV cameras and photographers, and had gone viral all day long. She had ridden a wave of optimism into Election Day, and the polls yesterday morning pegged her support at more than sixty percent of likely voters—a possible landslide in the making.

Now *this*.

As she watched, her opponent, Jefferson Monroe, took the podium at his headquarters in Wheeling, West Virginia. Although it was eight in the morning, a crowd of campaign workers and supporters were still there. Everywhere the cameras panned in the crowd were tall, red, white, and blue, Abraham Lincoln–style hats—they had somehow become the emblem of Monroe's campaign. That, and the aggressive signs that had become his campaign's war cry: AMERICA IS OURS!

Ours? What did that mean? As opposed to who? Who else would it belong to?

It seemed clear: minorities, non-Christians, gay people... you name it. In particular, it was clear it meant Chinese immigrants to America, as well as Chinese-Americans. Just weeks before, the Chinese had threatened to call in their debt and potentially bankrupt the US. This, indeed, had allowed Monroe to ride a wave of Chinese fear in the final days of his election. Monroe thrived on fear—Chinese fear in particular. According to Monroe, these people were acting as a secret cat's paw for the imperialist ambitions of the government in Beijing, and the Chinese oligarchs who were buying up vast swaths of American real estate and business interests. According to Monroe, if we didn't get tough, the Chinese would take over America.

His people ate it up.

Jefferson Monroe's archenemies, and the enemies of his supporters, were the Chinese. The Chinese were America's great nemesis, and the airhead former fashion model in the White House either didn't have the eyes to see it, or was a bought and sold Chinese collaborator.

Monroe himself stared out at the crowd with his deep-set, steely eyes. He was seventy-four years old, white-haired, with a lined and weathered face—a face that seemed much older than its years. Judging by his face alone, he could have been a hundred years old, or a thousand. But he was tall, and stood erect. By all accounts he slept three or four hours a night, and that was all he needed.

He wore a freshly starched white dress shirt open at the throat with no tie—another signature of his. He was a billionaire, or close to it, but he was a man of the people, by God! A man who had come from nothing. Dirt poor, from the mountains of West Virginia. A man who, despite his newfound wealth, despised the rich all his life. A man who, more than anything, despised the liberals, especially Northeasterners, and New Yorkers in particular. No fancy pants, Washington, DC insider suit and power tie for him. He somehow managed to conveniently overlook that he himself was the ultimate Washington insider, that he had spent twenty-four years in the United States Senate.

Susan supposed there was some modicum of truth to his affect. He'd had a hardscrabble upbringing in Appalachia—that was common knowledge. And he had clawed his way up and out from there. But he was no friend of the common man, or woman. To orchestrate his climb, he had always, from his earliest days— aligned himself with the most backward elements in American society. He had been a Pinkerton thug as a young man, attacking

11

striking coal miners with clubs and ax handles. He had spent his entire career in the back pocket of the major coal interests, always fighting for less regulation, less workplace safety, and fewer workers' rights. And he had been rewarded handsomely for his efforts.

"I told you," he said into the microphone.

The crowd erupted into raucous cheers.

Monroe tamped it down with a hand. "I told you we were going to take America back." The cheering started again. "You and me!" Monroe shouted. "We did it!"

Now the cheering changed, gradually morphing into a chant, one with which Susan was all too familiar. It had a funny awkward sort of cadence, this chant, like a waltz, or some kind of call-and-response.

"AMERICA! IS OURS! AMERICA! IS OURS! AMERICA! IS OURS!"

It went on and on. The sound of it made Susan sick to her stomach. At least they hadn't started in on the "Kick Her Out!" chants that had become popular for a while. The first time she had heard it, it nearly brought her to tears. She knew a lot of the people involved were probably just showboating. But at least some of these lunatics really did want to hang her, supposedly because she was a traitor in league with the Chinese. The thought of it left a hollow place inside of her.

"No more empty factories!" Monroe shouted. Now it was his turn to raise a triumphant fist in the air. "No more crime-ridden cities! No more human filth! No more Chinese betrayals!"

"NO MORE!" the crowd answered in unison, another of their favorite chants. "NO MORE! NO MORE! NO MORE!"

Kurt Kimball, crisp, alert, big and strong as always, with a perfectly bald head, stepped in front of the TV and used the remote control to mute the sound.

It was as if a spell had been broken. Suddenly Susan was completely aware of her surroundings again. She was here in the sitting area of the Oval Office with Kurt, his close aide Amy, Kat Lopez, Secretary of Defense Haley Lawrence, and a few others. These were some of Susan's most trusted advisors.

On a closed-circuit video monitor, Susan's Vice President, Marybeth Horning, was attending. After the Mount Weather disaster, security protocols had changed. Marybeth and Susan were never supposed to be in the same place at the same time. And that was a shame.

Marybeth was a hero of Susan's. She was the ultra-liberal former senator from Rhode Island who had lectured at Brown University for more than two decades. She seemed mousy and frail, with a bob of gray hair and round-rimmed granny glasses.

But looks, in this case, were deceiving. She was also a thunderous firebrand for workers' rights, women's rights, the rights of gay people, and the environment. She was the mastermind of the successful healthcare initiative Susan's administration had launched. Marybeth was at once an unassuming genius, a student of history, and a vicious political infighter with sharp elbows.

Another sad thing: Marybeth lived in Susan's old house on the grounds of the Naval Observatory. The house was one of Susan's favorite places on Earth. It would be nice to go there once in a while.

"This is a problem," Kurt Kimball said, gesturing at the silent TV.

Susan nearly laughed. "Kurt, I've always admired your gift for understatement."

Jefferson Monroe had made a campaign promise—a promise!—that he would go to Congress and seek a Declaration of War against China on his first official day in office. In fact, and most people had trouble taking this seriously, he had implied that the American military's first move would be tactical nuclear strikes against China's artificial islands in the South China Sea. He had also promised that he would erect security walls around Chinatowns in New York, Boston, San Francisco, and Los Angeles. He said he would demand the Canadians do the same in Vancouver and Calgary.

The Canadians, quite naturally, had balked at the idea.

"The country has gone insane," Kurt said. "And Monroe is expected to call for your concession speech again, Susan."

Kat Lopez shook her head. As Susan's chief-of-staff, Kat had matured and come into her own these past couple of years. She had also aged about ten years. When she came in, she had been a surreally beautiful and youthful thirty-seven—now she looked every minute of thirty-nine, and then some. Lines had appeared on her face, gray was invading the jet black of her hair.

"I advise you not to do that, Susan," she said. "We have evidence of widespread minority voter suppression in five Southern states. We have the suspicion of outright polling machine fraud in Ohio, Pennsylvania, and Michigan. The counts are still too close to call in many places—just because the TV stations have called these states for him, doesn't mean we have to. We can make this thing drag out for weeks, if not months."

"And cause a presidential succession crisis," Kurt said.

"We can weather it," Kat said. "We've seen worse. The inauguration isn't until January twentieth. If it takes that long, so be it. It buys us time. If there was fraud, our analysts will discover it. If there was voter suppression like we think, there will be lawsuits. In the meantime, we're still governing."

"I'm with Kat on this," Marybeth chimed in through the monitor. "I say we fight until we drop."

Susan looked at Haley Lawrence. He was tall and heavyset, with unkempt blond hair. His suit was so wrinkled it was almost as if he had passed out in it. He looked like he had just awoken ten minutes ago from a fitful sleep full of nightmares. Except for their shared height, he and Kurt Kimball were near opposites in appearance.

"Haley, you're the only Republican in this room," Susan said. "Monroe's in your party. I want your thoughts on this before I decide anything."

Lawrence took a long moment before answering. "I don't think that Jefferson Monroe is really a Republican. His ideas are far more radical than conservative. He surrounds himself with gangs of young thugs. He spent the past year appealing to the most backward and basest notions of angry and resentful people. He is a danger to world peace, the social order, and the very ideals that this country was founded upon."

Haley took a long breath. "I would hate to see him and his ilk occupy this office and this building, even if it turns out that he really did win. If I were you, I would obstruct him as long as possible."

Susan nodded. It was what she wanted to hear. It was time to gear up for battle. "All right. I won't concede. We're not going anywhere."

Kurt Kimball raised a hand. "Susan, I'll go along with whatever you want to do, as long as you realize the potential consequences of these actions."

"Which are?"

He began to tick them off on his fingers, in what seemed like no particular order, as if he were ready to describe each one as it occurred to him.

"By not voluntarily surrendering the seat, you are breaking with a two-century tradition. You will be called a traitor, a usurper, a would-be dictator, and probably worse. You will be breaking the law, and you could eventually be brought up on charges. If no evidence of election fraud arises, then you will look vain and foolish. You could hurt your place in the history books—at this moment, you have a sterling legacy."

Now Susan raised her hand.

"Kurt, I understand the consequences," she said, and took a deep breath.

"And I say bring them on."

CHAPTER FOUR

November 11
4:15 p.m. Eastern Standard Time
Mount Carmel Cemetery
Reston, Virginia

A single red rose, just cut, lay on the brown grass. Luke stared at the name and the epitaph carved into the gleaming black marble.

REBECCA ST. JOHN

To Live, to Laugh, to Love

The bleak overcast day was already fading and night was coming on. He felt a shiver go through him. He was overtired from the long trip back east. He was also clean-shaven, with short hair— no longer protected from the chill by his shaggy mane. He looked away from the stone and stared out at the cemetery, row upon row of gravestones covering rolling hillsides in a quiet part of suburban DC.

He gazed up at the gunmetal sky. When they married, Becca had taken his last name. Apparently, she had chosen to go to her grave under her maiden name. That burned him, all the way deep inside. Their rupture had been complete. He almost shook his fist at the sky, at Becca, wherever she might be now.

Did he hate her? No. But she made him very, very angry. She had blamed him for everything that went wrong in their marriage, right up to and including her own death from cancer.

On the cemetery road, just down the hill and about a hundred yards away, a sleek black limousine pulled up in front of Luke's nondescript rental sedan. As he watched, a chauffeur in black jacket and cap opened the back door of the limo.

Two figures emerged. One was young and male, growing tall like his father. The boy wore jeans, sneakers, a dress shirt, and a windbreaker jacket. The other figure was old and female, stooped a bit, wearing a long heavy wool coat against the damp autumn air. Luke didn't have to guess who they were—he already knew.

Luke had cheated. Of course he had. Fifteen minutes ago, he had been tailing that same limousine. When he guessed where it was going, he decided to beat it here. The two people working their way slowly up the footpath now, arm in arm, were Audrey, Becca's seventy-two-year-old mother, and Gunner, Luke and Becca's thirteen-year-old son.

Luke looked away for a moment as they approached, scanning the horizon as though something interested him out there. When he turned back again, they were nearly here. He watched them come. Audrey moved slowly, carefully studying her own feet as they touched the ground—she seemed older than her years. Gunner stepped awkwardly along with her, supporting her. The slow pace seemed like it would make him lose his balance—he was like a young colt trapped in a stall, all frustrated energy, desperate to unleash his own speed and power.

Gunner stared quizzically at Luke, but only for a few seconds. It had been nearly two years since last they'd met—an immense amount of time at the boy's age—and for a brief moment, it was clear he didn't know who Luke was. His face darkened when he realized he was staring at his own father. Then he looked at the ground.

Audrey knew who Luke was right away.

"Can we help you?" she said before they even reached the grave marker.

"*You* can't," Luke said. Audrey and her husband, Lance, had never accepted him as their son-in-law. They had been a toxic influence on his marriage since well before he and Becca exchanged their vows. Luke had nothing to say to Audrey.

"What are you doing here, Dad?" Gunner said. His voice was deeper now. His throat had the cleft of an Adam's apple—that hadn't been there before.

"I was called here by the President. But I wanted to see you first."

"Your President lost," Audrey said. "She's holed up inside the White House like a lunatic, refusing to admit defeat. I always knew there was something suspect about her. Now it's on full display for the world to see. Was she hoping to become Emperor?"

Luke looked at Audrey, taking his time, soaking her in. She had deep-set eyes with irises so dark, they seemed almost black. She had a sharp nose, like a beak. Her shoulders were hunched, and her hands were impossibly frail. She reminded him of a bird—a crow, or maybe a vulture. A carrion eater, in any case.

"She lost," Audrey said again. "She needs to get over it and prepare to hand over power to the winner."

"Gunner?" Luke said, ignoring Audrey now. "Can we talk?"

"I told Rebecca in no uncertain terms not to marry you. I told her it would end in disaster. But I never could have imagined that it would come to this."

17

"Gunner?" Luke repeated, but now the boy was looking away. Luke saw a tear slide down Gunner's face. The kid swallowed hard.

"I just want to apologize."

The words came out wrong. An apology? That wouldn't nearly cut it. Luke knew that. It was going to take a lot more than an apology to set this situation right again, if that was even possible. He wanted to tell Gunner that. He wanted to tell him he would do anything, everything, if only he would let him back into his life.

He had made a terrible mistake. He would spend the rest of his life on this. He would fix it.

Gunner looked at him, openly crying now. The tears streamed down his face. "I don't want to talk to you." He shook his head. "I don't want to see you. I just want to forget about you, don't you understand?"

Luke nodded. "Okay. Okay, I can respect that. But know that I love you and I'm always open to hearing from you. Do you still have my number? You can call me if you change your mind."

"I don't have your number," Gunner said. "And I won't change my mind."

Luke nodded again. "In that case, I'll leave you alone."

Audrey's voice followed Luke down the path. "That sounds like a good idea," she said. "Leave the boy alone." Then she laughed, a mad cackle that would have sounded almost like a coughing fit if Luke didn't know better.

"Leave us alone with our dead."

Luke made it to his car, put it in gear, and was almost to the cemetery gates before he started crying himself.

CHAPTERR FIVE

4:57 p.m. Eastern Standard Time
Bubba's Lounge
Chester, Pennsylvania

No one remembered who Bubba was.

The small tavern had sat there on a street corner in the southeast end of Chester, near the river, since sometime after World War II. Ten different people had owned it at one time or another, and it had always been called Bubba's, as far as anyone knew. But no one knew why.

"I guess she's going to throw in the towel," one man at the bar said.

"About time," said another.

Marc Reeves was working the stick today. Marc was an old-timer, sixty-seven years of age. He had poured beer at this bar, off and on, for the past twenty-five years, outlasting three owners in the process. He had watched the whole town go down the tubes right from this bar. In a city where damn near everything was boarded up or about to be, Bubba's was a success story. Even so, nobody kept it for long.

The place broke even—that was the problem. It didn't lose money, it didn't make money. You were better off working there, or drinking there, than owning it. At least you got something for your trouble.

There was a big old box color TV set mounted on an iron rod behind the bar. This time of the afternoon, the place had four or five daytime drinkers lined up along the rail, wasting their Social Security checks and whatever was left of their livers. Usually the television was set to whatever game happened to be on. Today was different, though. Today the President was holding her first press conference since she lost the election.

Marc had been skeptical of her when she first came into office, especially considering the circumstances, but she had grown on him. He thought she had done a pretty good job, all in all. She, and the country, had weathered a lot of storms. So he had done something yesterday that he rarely did—he had voted for her. He hadn't stepped inside a polling place in twelve years before that.

Not everyone agreed with his decision.

"I like the new guy," a fat man along the rail said. Everybody called him Skipper. He'd probably never been on a boat in his life. "What has Susan Hopkins ever done for Chester, Pennsylvania? That's what I want to know. Anyway, it's about time somebody put a stop to all these Chinamen flooding the country."

"And bring back our jobs while you're at it," a man named Steve-O said. Steve-O was so thin he was like one of those man-like pipe cleaner sculptures. He came in here and drank beer and bourbon every single day. Marc had never seen Steve-O eat even a bite of food. He seemed to survive on alcohol alone.

Marc was drying pint glasses that had just come out of the washer. "Steve-O, you've been on disability for twenty years."

"I don't mean bring *my* job back," Steve-O said.

A few people laughed.

On the TV, an empty podium appeared. It was flanked by American flags.

"Ladies and gentlemen," a hushed voice said, "the President of the United States."

Susan Hopkins walked onto the stage from the right. She wore a tan pantsuit, her hair in a short blonde bob. Beautiful. Marc remembered her from her modeling days, in particular a certain *Sports Illustrated* swimsuit issue from twenty-five years ago. He had been middle-aged then, married with kids. There was something heartbreaking about her photo shoot—she was ethereal, unattainable, from another world. He didn't have the words for what she was. And if anything, she looked even better now—more down to Earth, more mature. Marc liked a woman with a little mileage on her.

"Take it off, baby!" Steve-O said, eliciting some giggles from the others.

Marc had served Steve-O six shots and six beers in the past couple of hours. He'd say Steve-O was visibly intoxicated by now. And he was starting to pluck Marc's nerves. "You're about to get cut off, Steve-O."

Steve-O looked at him. "What?"

"Shut up or go home. That's what I'm saying."

Marc turned back to the TV screen. Hopkins still hadn't said anything yet. She seemed to be choking back some emotion. This was it, then. She was going to concede the election. She had seemed popular, but in the end she had been a one-term President—and not even a full term.

"My fellow Americans," she said.

The bar was silent. The room where she spoke was almost silent—Marc could hear the whirr and click of cameras taking photos.

"I'm going to keep my remarks brief. This was a hard-fought campaign between two very different visions of America. One vision is of optimism, understanding, and pride for what we've accomplished as a nation. The other is a dark vision of anger, despair, resentment, and even paranoia. It sees our nation as a ruined landscape, which can only be saved by the efforts of one man. And it promises violence—violence against our most important trading partner, as well as violence against our own communities, our neighbors, and our friends.

"I'm sure you know which vision I embrace. I cannot accept a worldview based on racism, prejudice, and mistrust. And yet, despite my misgivings, under normal circumstances my task now would be to congratulate the apparent victor in this race, and welcome the President-elect, graciously preparing for the peaceful transfer of power that is a hallmark of our democracy."

She paused. "But these are not normal circumstances."

Marc stood up straight. He felt a tingle along his spine. He looked along the bar at the men lined up. Every single one of them was glued to the television now. Every one of them was suddenly alert, like animals before an approaching thunderstorm. What was she saying?

"My campaign has discovered evidence of Election Day irregularities in at least five states, including voter suppression, but also including outright tampering with and potential hacking of election machinery. We have reason to believe that the election was stolen, not just from our campaign, but from the American people. We have already contacted the FBI and the Justice Department about our concerns, and we look forward to a full, impartial investigation. Until such an investigation is completed—however long it takes—I cannot and will not recognize the results of this election, and I will continue to perform the duties of the President of the United States, carrying out my oath to protect and uphold the Constitution. Thank you."

On the TV, President Hopkins moved to the right and off screen. There was a babble of voices as reporters shouted, competing with each other for her attention. Flashbulbs popped. The TV station switched to a different camera, one focused on the President as she was hustled out a side door behind a sea of very large Secret Service agents. She hadn't taken a single question.

"What does that mean?" Steve-O said. "Can she do that?"

No one said a word.

Marc just kept drying pint glasses. He didn't know the answer to that himself.

CHAPTER SIX

5:48 p.m. Eastern Standard Time
34th Floor
The Willard Intercontinental Hotel, Washington DC

"Are we a nation of laws?" the man shouted into the telephone.

He sat with his feet up on his wide desk of polished oak, gazing out the floor-to-ceiling window at the lights of the Capitol. It was dark out—the sun set early this time of year.

"That's what I want to know. Because if we are a nation of laws, then that woman, the current occupant of the White House, needs to start packing her bags. She lost, and Jefferson Monroe won. Jefferson Monroe is the President-elect of the United States. And come inauguration day, if the current occupant is not out, we are going to evict her, like the sheriff evicting a deadbeat tenant."

For a few seconds, the man paused, listening to the reporter on the other end of the line.

"Oh yeah, you can quote me. Print every word of it."

He hung up the phone and slid it onto the desk. He checked his watch and breathed deeply. He had been on the phones with reporters for nearly an hour, ever since Susan Hopkins had run off the stage and darted out of the room at the end of her silly press conference.

The man's name was Gerry O'Brien. At age fifty, he was very tall and rail thin. He was balding, and his face was all angles and jutting cliffs. He weighed the same as he had the day he graduated from college. He was a marathoner, a triathlete, and in recent years, he had gotten into doing mud runs and survival runs. Anything hard, anything tough, anything extreme where people dropped over sideways, or puked up their guts, or fell down a hill and tore open their knees, it had his name on it.

The son of Irish immigrants, he had come up on the streets of Woodside, Queens. His father was a prison guard. His mother was a maid. Hard people, and they raised him to be hard. You wanted to grow up in Woodside, you had to fight. Okay? He didn't mind. He'd go toe to toe with anybody. He was so fierce, so remorseless, that kids in the neighborhood called him the Shark.

He was the first person in his family to go to college, and then—uncharted territory—law school. He made his first million before he was thirty, chasing ambulances—personal injury law.

He'd gotten a photo taken of himself looking very angry (and few people had the ability to look as angry as he could) and paid for small poster advertisements placed throughout the subway system.

Injured? You need somebody tough to stand up for your rights. A real lawyer. A real New Yorker. You need Gerry O'Brien. You need the Shark.

Almost instantly, he became Gerry the Shark. Everyone who rode the trains in the five boroughs knew the name. He used to ride the subways himself just to look at his own ads—and he hated the subways.

The more he made, the more ads he could afford. And the more ads he ran, the more he made. Soon he was running ads on late-night TV, then mid-afternoon TV. It was a jackpot. He had three lawyers working for him, then five, then ten. Then twenty. By the time he sold the business ten years ago, he had thirty-three lawyers and more than a hundred support staff.

He retired for a few years. Wandered. Drifted. Traveled the world. Did too many drugs. Drank too much. Did too much... of everything. Getting into radical right-wing politics probably saved his life. He had swapped out all the bad stuff for personal discipline and a vision of America that he discovered he shared with a lot of people—a return to an earlier, simpler time.

A time when the supremacy of white people wasn't questioned. A time when marriage was between a man and a woman. A time when a young guy could walk out of high school at eighteen, walk into a factory job, and spend the rest of his working life there, making all the money he needed to support his family.

There was more to it, of course, a lot more. Darker things, things you needed a strong stomach for, things that were not for wider consumption. He had big plans. They were going to clean this country up, once and for all. But that wasn't something you put right out there in public, was it? Not yet.

Gerry the Shark got up from his desk and moved through the suite of rooms. A few secretaries were here, but mostly people worked out of other places. Gerry was here not only because he was the head strategist, but also because he was the body man to the chief—he didn't like to let the old man out of his sight.

They had flown up here from Louisville this afternoon. His boss owned this... what would you call it? An apartment? Sure, an apartment with ten bedrooms, twelve bathrooms, and half a dozen offices with a conference room and a staff dining area. It took up an entire floor in one of the most storied and most expensive hotels in the world. This hotel was where American history happened. This was where John F. Kennedy took his many afternoon trysts. This was the place.

They would spend the night here. They had important business here in DC early tomorrow morning.

Gerry breezed down a hallway, slapped his key card against a sensor, and passed into the living quarters. The front sitting room was furnished in opulent old-world style, like the drawing room in a Victorian mansion.

A man with white hair stood at a tall window, the curtains pulled aside. He stared out at the night. The man wore a three-piece suit despite the fact that he was home and had no intention of going out. The open-throated dress shirts were a shuck, of course. The man liked to play dress-up as much as anyone.

He held a martini in his hand. The martini glass looked tiny. The hands were the thing—despite the man's elegant dress, and his obvious wealth, he had the big gnarled hands of someone who had grown up doing manual labor, and lots of it. The hands said: *What's wrong with this picture?*

It was a raw night in the nation's capital, and the wind howled outside the window, just a little bit. The old man stared out at the backdrop of the great urban sprawl and the lights of the city. Gerry knew that even after all these decades the country boy inside the old man was dazzled by city lights.

"How goes the war?" Jefferson Monroe, President-elect of the United States, said in his soft Southern lilt.

"Beautiful," Gerry said, and he meant it. "She's on the ropes and she doesn't know what to do. Her statement today makes that clear. She's not going to vacate the Presidency? It plays right into our hands. She's isolating herself—public opinion is going to go our way. If we play it right, we might be able to get her out of there sooner rather than later. I think we want to ramp up the pressure— get her to hand over the Presidency early, long before any voter fraud investigation concludes. Then we cancel the investigation ourselves."

The old man turned from the tall window. "Is there any precedent for a President handing over power early?"

Gerry the Shark shook his head. "No."

"Then how do we do it?"

Now Gerry smiled. "I have a few ideas."

25

CHAPTER SEVEN

6:47 p.m. Eastern Standard Time
The Oval Office
The White House, Washington DC

She was alone when they showed Luke into the room.

For a moment, he thought she might be asleep. She sat in the sitting area, slumped in one of the armchairs. She looked like a broken rag doll, or a high school kid showing contempt for the teacher by slouching.

The new Resolute Desk loomed behind her. The heavy drapes were pulled, blocking the tall windows. On the floor, around the edge of the oval carpet, there was an inscription printed:

The only thing we have to fear, is fear itself—Franklin Delano Roosevelt

The words went all the way around the carpet, finishing right where they began.

She wore blue slacks and a white dress shirt. Her jacket was hung on the back of one of the chairs. Her shoes were off and lying askew on the carpet.

Despite her posture, her eyes were sharp and alive. They watched him.

"Hi, Susan," he said.

"Did you watch my press conference?" she said.

He shook his head. "I stopped watching TV over a year ago. I feel a lot better since I did. You should try it."

"I told the American people I'm not going to step down."

Luke nearly laughed. "I bet that's going over well. What happened? You like the job so much you don't want to give it up? I'm pretty sure it doesn't work that way."

A small smile appeared on her face. The smile, barely there, reminded him of why she had once been a supermodel. She was beautiful. Her smile could light up a room. It could light up the sky.

"They stole the election."

"Of course they did," he said. "Now you're going to steal it back. That sounds like a plan." He paused. Then he told her what he honestly thought. "Listen, I think you're better off without this job. Now they won't have Susan Hopkins to kick around anymore. Let them find out how bad it is without you. They'll beg you to come back."

She shook her head, the smile growing brighter. "I don't think it works like that."

"I don't think so either," he said.

She shook her head. A long exhale escaped from her.

"Where have you been, Luke Stone? You should have stuck around. We had a lot of fun in here, once the chaos died down a little. We did a lot of good. And you were going to teach me to shoot guns once upon a time. Remember?"

He shrugged. "Yeah. You wanted to shoot the Chairman of the Joint Chiefs. I remember. But I haven't fired a gun in nine months. I was going to the range once in a while, trying to keep my skills up. Then I decided why bother? I don't want to shoot anyone. And even if one day I have to, I feel pretty sure it'll come back to me."

"Just like riding a bicycle?" she said.

He smiled. "Or falling off of one."

She sat up and indicated the chair across from her. "You really don't know what's going on?"

Luke settled down in the chair. It was an upright chair, neither comfortable nor uncomfortable. "I heard a few rumblings in the distance. The new guy is hard right. He doesn't like the Chinese. He's going to bring the manufacturing jobs back. Not sure how he's going to do that—fire all the robots? Either way, if that's what people want…"

"Ignorance is bliss, I guess," Susan said.

"Not exactly bliss, but—"

"The man's a fascist," she said. "He's a billionaire, a robber baron, who has funded white supremacist groups for decades, apparently even when he was in the Senate. He plans to go to war with China on his first day in office, possibly with tactical nuclear strikes, although I'm not sure how many people really believe that. He wants to build security fences and walls around Chinatowns in American cities. His remarks suggest hatred for minorities, gay people, disabled people, anyone who disagrees with him, as well as contempt for the independence of the judicial branch of government."

Luke wasn't sure what to think about all that. He had been out of the loop for a long time. He trusted Susan, and he could tell that she believed what she was saying. But he had trouble believing it himself. He had served in the military under conservative Presidents, and on the Special Response Team under liberal Presidents. Yes, they were different from one another, but radically different? White supremacy, security fences around minority

27

enclaves different? No. Not really. No matter who was in charge, there was always something you might call the American Way.

"And you're saying that people voted for this?"

She shook her head, emphatically now. "We believe that there was widespread voter fraud and voter suppression in at least five states, all of them swing states. That's why I say they stole the election."

Luke was beginning to see the puzzle, but there were pieces missing. "You want me to investigate this?" he said. "Is that why you called me back here? It seems like there would be a hundred other—"

"No," she said. "You're right. There are a hundred other people. We've got data analysts looking at the voting machines. We've got investigators out interviewing people about voter suppression, especially in black districts across the rural South. And circumstantially, anecdotally, the evidence is already pretty strong. We really don't need you for the investigation."

He was confused by her reply, and maybe a little annoyed. He had been alone, high in the mountains, working on his own issues. Challenging himself. Challenging God to kill him. Maybe even finding some clarity.

Now he was back in Washington, DC, getting yelled at by his son and smirked at by his former mother-in-law. He was sitting in bumper-to-bumper traffic and undergoing security checks. He had shaved his beard off and gotten his hair cut. He was back among regular humans and their interests and their worries. When he was a soldier in combat, they used to call it "back in the world"—a place he really didn't want to be.

"So what am I doing here?" he said.

"I'm not sure yet," she said. "But I know I need you. I did something unprecedented by refusing to hand over power. It's never been done before in American history. Things could get hot around here very quickly, and I don't have many people in my administration that I trust. I mean completely, one hundred percent, without a doubt. A few, yes, but no more than that."

She pointed at him. "And you. Early in my tenure as President, you saved this country again and again. You saved my life. You saved my daughter. You might have saved the world from a nuclear war. Then you disappeared just when things got good. I've never met a man like you, Luke. You're built for bad weather, to put it mildly. And it feels to me like a storm is brewing."

Built for bad weather.

He had never heard it put quite that way before. But of course it was true—she had him pegged, better than Becca ever had. Better than he had ever pegged himself. Not only was he built for it, it was what he lived for. When the weather was nice, he grew bored. He wandered off. He went and looked for a hurricane to get lost in.

"So what do you want me to do?"

"Stay close. Live in the White House Residence for the time being. We can give you an official title—personal bodyguard. Intelligence strategist. It's a little funny, but that doesn't matter. Chuck Berg is still head of the Secret Service home security detail. He knows you and respects you. There are plenty of rooms to stay in. You can have the Lincoln Bedroom if you want. We've had a few celebrities stay in there. The singer from the rock band Zero Hour and his wife slept over just a few weeks ago. Nice people— the guy's nothing like his stage persona. He's been doing a lot of charity work in Africa, paying for water filtration systems and so forth."

She stopped for a breath before going on. "Obviously, the White House was completely rebuilt two years ago, so Lincoln himself never really slept in the new Lincoln Bedroom, but…"

It seemed to Luke that she was babbling now. She was like a little girl trying to explain something important to an adult, without ever saying what it was.

"You want a security blanket," he said. "That's why I'm here."

She nodded. "Yes. I had one when I was a child. It was soft and had a friendly dinosaur image woven into it, which over time faded away to a green blur. I called it Little Cover. God, I miss that thing."

Now Luke did laugh. It came out like the sudden barking of a dog. It felt good to laugh. He couldn't remember the last time it had happened.

"Little Cover, huh?"

"That's right. Little Cover."

Was there something more to what she was asking him? He couldn't tell. Heck, the White House Residence? That had to be an upgrade from the room at the Marriott they'd given him last night.

"Okay," he said. "I'll do it."

CHAPTER EIGHT

"Okay," Kyle Meiner barked. "We're about to hit them. So listen up!"

Kyle crouched in the back of a long black cargo van as it bounced over the potholes and ruts of the city streets. He looked at his men—eight big guys, cramped together. Everybody in here was muscled up, a gym rat. There wasn't a man in here who couldn't bench press 225, or squat 300. Everybody was pounding at least creatine, and some of the boys were juicing steroids, human growth hormone, in a few cases more exotic stuff—these were serious dudes. Every one of them had a crew cut or a shaved head.

Kyle's body was like theirs, only bigger, if that was possible. His arms were like pythons, his legs like tree stumps. Veins popped out on his biceps, along his neck, his forehead, his chest, everywhere. Kyle was into veins.

Veins meant blood flow. Veins meant power.

There were five other vans just like this one in the convoy, and that told Kyle they were about to put forty or fifty hardcore, no-nonsense activists on the streets. Tight, long-sleeved T-shirts clung to muscular chests and torsos—each shirt black with the words GATHERING STORM in white. The letters looked vaguely like human bones, and had splatters of what looked like bright red blood along the bottom.

Hard eyes stared back at Kyle. These men were the sharpened point of the spear.

"I don't want to see any weapons out there," Kyle said. "No knives, no clubs, God help you if I see a gun. Brass knuckles. If you have anything on you, you are leaving it in the van. Got me?"

A few guys grumbled and muttered.

"What? I don't hear you."

The grumbles were louder this time.

"This is a rally and a march, boys. It's not a street fight. If the slopes make it a fight, okay. Defend yourselves and each other. Throw the little commies through a brick wall for all I care. Just know that when the cops come and they find you armed, that's a felony. We have lawyers on speed dial, ready to go, but if you get busted for possession of a weapon, you are not getting out tonight, and maybe not for a long time. I need to hear you on this. I don't want to see anybody put away. It's bad for you, and it's a bad look for the organization. Got it? Come on!"

"Got it!" someone shouted.

"Yo!"

"We got it, man."

Kyle smiled. "Good. Now let's go kick some ass."

The signs were piled in the back. Most of them said *America Is Ours!* One of them said *Chinks Go Home!* That was Kyle's sign. If his men were the sharpened point, he was the drop of poison at the very tip.

He was twenty-nine years old, and had been an organizer with Gathering Storm for just over two years. It was his dream job. Where did he find his recruits? Weight rooms, almost exclusively. Gold's Gym. Planet Fitness. YMCA. Places where big strong guys hung out, guys who'd had just about enough. Enough censorship. Enough of the thought police. Enough of the good jobs going overseas. Enough of the race mixing.

Enough of the religion of multiculturalism being rammed down their throats.

If someone had told Kyle five years ago that he was going to pull together groups of men—the best, the toughest, the most aggressive young white men he could find—and that they were going to put the fear of the Lord into the people dragging this country down… that they were going to restore America to greatness… and that he was going to *get paid* to do this? Well, Kyle would have said that person was an idiot.

Yet here he was.

And here were his boys.

And their man had just been elected President of the United States.

There was nothing but daylight up ahead, and they were going to run a long, long way. And anybody who got in front of them, who tried to stop them or even slow them down—anybody like that was going to get mowed under. That's just how it was.

The rear doors of the van opened, and the boys jumped out, grabbing their signs as they went. Kyle was the last one. He stepped onto the street, the night seeming to glow around him. It was cold out—even snowing a little—but Kyle was too ramped to feel it. The street was narrow, with four-story tenements crowding it on either side. All of the neon storefront signs were in Chinese, tangles of

31

meaningless gibberish—impossible to read, impossible to understand.

Was this still America? You bet it was. And people spoke English here.

The vans were parked in a line. Big damn white boys in black shirts were everywhere, a bouncing, writhing mass of them. They were an invasion force, like Vikings on a coastal raid. They wielded their signs like battle-axes. Their blood was up.

A crowd of tiny, startled Asians looked on in… what?

Shock? Horror? Fear?

Oh yes, all of these.

The first chant began, a little tame for Kyle's taste, but it would do for a start.

"America… is ours!"

The boys found their voices and the volume jumped a notch.

"AMERICA… IS OURS!"

Kyle flexed his arms. He flexed his upper back, and his round shoulders, and his legs. This was a rally, all right, and that's what he had told his men. But he hoped it became more than that. He'd been holding his anger back for what felt like a long time.

Rallies were good, but he really just wanted to crack some heads.

Within two minutes, he got his wish. As the line of marchers moved down the street, maybe fifty feet ahead of him, some shoving started.

A Stormer took a Chinese man by both shoulders and pushed him into a display of pocketbooks. The Chinese man fell across the display, which collapsed instantly. Two more Chinese men jumped on the Stormer. Suddenly Kyle was running. He dropped his sign and burst through the crowd.

He punched a Chinese to the ground, then waded into a group of them, swinging hard. His fists crunched bone.

And there was only more, he knew, to come.

CHAPTER NINE

9:15 p.m.
Ocean City, Maryland

"Not looking too good there," Luke said.

The elevator was all carpeting and glass walls. A long double line of buttons ran along a metal panel. He caught sight of his reflection in the concave security mirror in an upper corner. It was a strange, distorted, funhouse view of him, totally at odds with the reflection on the glass walls. The normal glass showed a tall man in early middle-age, very fit, deep crow's feet around the eyes and the beginnings of gray in his short blond hair. His eyes seemed ancient.

Staring into them, he could suddenly see himself as an old, old man, lonely and afraid. He was alone in this world—more alone than he had ever been. It had somehow taken him two full years to realize that. His wife was dead. His parents were long gone. His boy was hardened against him. There was no one in his life.

A little while ago, in the car, just before he stepped into this elevator, he had dug out Gunner's old cell phone number. He felt certain that Gunner still had that number. The boy would have kept the same number even after moving in with grandparents, even after getting the best new iPhone available. Luke felt sure of it—Gunner kept his old number because he wanted more than anything to hear from his father.

Luke had sent a simple text message to the old number.

Gunner, I love you.

Then he had waited. And waited. Nothing. The message had gone into the void, and nothing had returned. Luke didn't even know if it was the right number.

How had it come to this?

He didn't have time to ponder the answer. The elevator opened directly into the foyer of the apartment. There was no hallway. There were no other doors except the double doors in front of him.

The doors opened and Mark Swann stood there.

Luke soaked in the sight of him. Tall and thin, with long sandy hair and round John Lennon glasses. His hair was pulled into a ponytail. He had aged in two years. He was heavier than before, mostly around the midsection. His face and neck seemed thicker. His T-shirt had the words SEX PISTOLS across the front in letters

33

that could have been used to write a ransom note. He wore blue jeans, with yellow-and-black checkerboard Converse All-Star sneakers on his feet.

Swann smiled, but Luke could easily see the strain in it. Swann wasn't happy to see him. He looked like he had eaten a bad fish.

"Luke Stone," he said. "Come on in."

Luke remembered the apartment. It was big and hyper-modern. There were two floors, open concept, with a ceiling twenty feet above their heads. A steel and cable staircase went up to the second floor, where it connected with a catwalk. There was a living room here with a large white sectional couch. There had been an abstract painting behind the couch last time—crazy, angry red and black splotches five feet across—Luke couldn't quite remember what it looked like. In any event, it was gone now.

The two men shook hands, then hugged awkwardly.

"Albert Helu?" Luke said, using the name of the Swann alias who owned the apartment.

Swann shrugged. "If you like. You can call me Al. That's what everyone around here calls me. Can I get you a beer?"

"Sure. Thank you."

Swann disappeared through a swinging door into the kitchen.

To Luke's right, he could see Swann's command center. Very little had changed. A glass partition divided it from the rest of the apartment. A big leather chair sat at a desk with a bank of tower hard drives on the floor beneath it, and three flat-panel screens on top of it. Wires ran all over the floor like snakes.

On the far wall, across from the sofa, was a giant flat-panel TV set, maybe half the size of a movie theater screen. The sound was muted. On the screen, about a dozen police vans and cars were parked on a city street, lights flashing in the dark. Fifty cops stood in a line. Yellow police tape extended in several places. A large crowd of people stood behind the tape, stretching down the block and away from the scene.

LIVE the caption below the scene read. *CHINATOWN, NEW YORK CITY*

Swann came back with two bottles of beer. Instantly, Luke knew why Swann was getting heavier. He was spending a lot of time drinking beer.

Swann gestured at the TV. "Did you hear about that?" he said.

Luke shook his head. "No. What is it?"

"About forty-five minutes ago a bunch of neo-Nazis tried to do some kind of group march through the middle of Chinatown in New York. Gathering Storm, ever heard of them?"

"Swann, what if I told you I've spent the past two years living mostly in tents?"

"Then I'd say you've never heard of Gathering Storm. Anyway, they're actually a nonprofit organization, dedicated to preserving and promoting cultural... what? Whiteness, I suppose. American Europeanism? You know. They want to make America safe for white people. Jefferson Monroe is their major funder—they're basically his modern version of the brownshirts. There are probably half a dozen groups like this now, but I think they're the biggest one."

"What happened?"

Swann shrugged. "What else? They started up beating random people on the street. You've never seen these guys. They're a goon squad. Big guys. They were throwing people around. A couple of people in the neighborhood took offense. They lit the Nazis up with guns. A bunch of people were shot, five dead at last count. Shooters still on the loose. It's what they call a fluid situation."

"The people killed were all Nazis?" Luke said.

"Seems that way."

Luke shrugged. "Well..."

"Right. No big loss."

Luke looked away from the TV. He was having a hard time wrapping his head around what was going on. Susan Hopkins believed the election had been stolen. Her opponent, the incoming President, was funding a neo-Nazi group, which had just sparked a mini race war in New York City. Was this how things were done now? When had everything changed? Luke had been gone a long time, apparently.

"What have you been up to, Swann?"

Swann sat on the big white couch. He gestured at a seat across from him. Luke took it. It had the tangible benefit of facing away from the TV. From his spot, he could look out the darkened glass doors to Swann's roof deck. The hot tub gave off a pale blue neon light. Otherwise, it was mostly dark out there. Luke had slept on the deck once upon a time. He knew that in daylight hours, it gave a panoramic view of the Atlantic Ocean.

"Not much," Swann said. "Nothing, to be honest."

"Nothing?"

Swann seemed to think about it for a moment. "You're looking at it. I'm out on disability. When we got back from Syria, I just never could... go back to work. I tried a couple of times. But intelligence is a nasty business. I never minded it when it was other people getting hurt. But after Syria? I got panic attacks. The severed heads, you know? For a while, I was seeing them all the time. It was bad. It was too much."

"I'm sorry," Luke said.

"I am, too. Believe me. And it's not over. I'm a little bit of a recluse now. I keep my old apartment in DC, but I mostly live up here now. It's safe. Nobody can get in here if I don't want them to."

Stone thought about that for a second, but said nothing. It was true enough, as far as it went. The vast majority of people couldn't get in here. Honest, mainstream people. Nice people. But bad people? Killers? Black operatives? They'd get in here if they wanted to.

"I rarely go out," Swann said. "I order my groceries on the internet. I let the kid into the building from here, and monitor him coming up in the elevator. Watch him on the closed-circuit TV. I leave a tip for him in the hallway, he leaves the grocery bags at the door, and I watch him go back down. Then I go out in the hall and get my food. It's a little pathetic, I know that."

Luke said nothing. It was sad that Swann had been reduced to this, but Luke wouldn't call it pathetic. It happened. Maybe he could help Swann, get him back out into the world again, but maybe not. Either way, it would take a lot of work, and time, and Swann would have to want it. Sometimes psychological trauma like this never really healed. Swann was a prisoner of ISIS, about to be beheaded, when Luke and Ed Newsam barged in. He had been beaten and mock-executed before they got there.

A silence settled between them, not a comfortable one.

"There was a period of time when I blamed you for what happened to me."

"Okay," Luke said. That was Swann's truth, and Luke wasn't about to argue with him about it. But Swann had taken the mission on voluntarily, and Luke and Ed had risked their lives to save him.

"I realize it doesn't make much sense, and I don't believe it now, but it took me months of therapy to get to this place. You and Ed have this weird glow around you. It's like you're superhuman. Even when you get hurt, it seems like it doesn't really hurt. People get too close to you, and they begin to think this thing you have also applies to them. But it doesn't. Regular people get hurt, and they die."

"Are you in therapy now?"

Swann nodded. "Twice a week. I found a guy who will do it over a video feed. He's in his office, I'm here. It's pretty good."

"What does he tell you?"

Swann smiled. "He says whatever you do, don't buy a gun. I tell him I live on the twenty-eighth floor with an open balcony. I don't need a gun. I can die any time I want."

Luke decided to change the subject. Talking about ways that Swann could commit suicide... it wasn't cheerful.

"You see Ed much?"

Swann shrugged. "Not in a while. He's busy with work. He's a commander with the Hostage Rescue Team. He's out of the country a lot. We used to see each other more. He's pretty much the same, though."

"Do you feel up for doing some work?" Luke said.

"I don't know," Swann said. "I think that would depend on what it was. The demands, what I would have to do. I also don't want to jeopardize my disability. Are you paying under the table?"

"I'm working for the President," Luke said. "Susan Hopkins."

"That's cute. What does she need you for?"

"She thinks the election was stolen."

Swann nodded. "I heard that. The news cycles zip by at the speed of light these days, but that's a story with legs. She doesn't want to step down. So where do you fit in? And more importantly, where would I fit in?"

"Well, she's probably going to want some intel gathering from us. I imagine she wants to do some kind of takedown on these guys. I don't have any details right now."

"Can I work from here?" Swann said.

"I suppose. Why not?"

Luke paused. "But the truth is I'm a little concerned about this conversation. You're different from before. You know that. I would want to make sure you've still got your old chops."

Swann didn't seem bothered by that. "Test me any way you like. I'm in here day and night, Luke. What do you think I do with my time? I hack. I've got all my old chops, and some new ones. I might even be better than before. And as long as I don't have to go outside..."

Now Swann paused for a moment. He stared down at the beer in his hands, then looked up at Luke. His eyes were serious.

"I hate Nazis," he said.

CHAPTER TEN

November 12
8:53 a.m. Eastern Daylight Time
The West Wing
The White House, Washington DC

"There was violence all through the night," Kat Lopez said. "Kurt has the details, but the worst of it was in Boston, San Francisco, and Seattle."

"Why wasn't I told about this?" Susan said.

They walked along the halls of the West Wing toward the Oval Office. Their heels clacked on the marble floor. Susan felt better than she had in a while—well rested from a long night's sleep. She had eaten breakfast in the Family Kitchen without checking the news once. She was beginning to believe that events were taking a turn for the positive. Until a minute ago.

Kat shrugged. "I wanted you to get some sleep. There was nothing you could do about it in the middle of the night, and I figured today was going to be another hell of a day. Kurt agreed with me."

"Okay," Susan said. She supposed she meant it.

A Secret Service man opened the doors for them and they passed into the Oval Office. Kurt Kimball stood there, sleeves rolled up, ready to go. Luke Stone sat in one of the armchairs, in almost the same position he was in the night before.

Stone wore a plain black T-shirt with a leather jacket, jeans, and fancy leather boots. He looked fresher, less distant, more in the here and now than yesterday. His eyes were alive. Stone was a space cowboy, Susan decided. Sometimes he was just gone, out in the ether. That's where he went when he disappeared. But now he was back.

"Hi, Kurt," Susan said.

Kurt turned to her. "Susan. Good morning."

"Nice boots, Agent Stone."

Stone pulled his jeans leg up a couple of inches to reveal more of the boot for her. "Ferragamo," he said. "My wife gave them to me once upon a time. They have sentimental value."

"I'm sorry about your wife."

Stone nodded. "Thank you."

An awkward pause settled in. If she could, part of Susan—the emotional part, you might even call it the female part—would spend the next twenty minutes asking Stone about his wife, his relationship with her, how he had processed her death, and what he was doing to take care of himself. But Susan didn't have that kind of time right now. The hard-headed, practical part of her—would she call that her masculine part?—pushed on with today's agenda.

"Okay, Kurt, what do you have for me?"

Kurt indicated the TV screen. "Events have been moving fast. No surprise there. We had a mass shooting in New York City's Chinatown last night. A large group of operatives from Gathering Storm emerged out of a convoy of black vans at around eight thirty p.m., and went on a march south from Canal Street. It was a provocation, of course. Within minutes, they were engaged in fistfights with neighborhood residents."

"Gathering Storm, huh?" Gathering Storm was one of the Monroe-funded organizations that made Susan sick to her stomach. She often wondered exactly what it was these people thought they were doing. Of course, up until now the violence had been almost entirely threats made over the internet. Now it was real.

Kurt nodded. "Yes. They seem to recruit their activists based on size. The fist fights were completely one-sided for several minutes, until two contract killers from the Hong Kong Triads—apparently in New York on a murder assignment—opened up with Uzi submachine guns. The latest tally is thirty-six wounded, including a dozen Chinese, likely shot by accident, and seven dead, all of whom were members of Gathering Storm. Another three members are expected to die."

Susan wasn't sure what to say to all this. Good? That came to mind.

"The Triad members?"

"In NYPD custody, on multiple murder, attempted murder, and weapons charges. They have court-appointed translators, and last I heard a legal team is en route from Hong Kong. The Triads are well funded, to put it mildly, and the expectation is the lawyers will try to build a case for self-defense on the murders, and plead out the weapons."

"What do you think of that approach?" Susan said.

Kurt smiled and shook his head. "New York doesn't have the death penalty. That's about the only thing those guys have going for them right now."

"How about if I pardon them and send them home with medals?"

39

"I think we've got enough problems."

"Tell me more," she said.

"Well, once the news came out about New York, it seems the gloves came off. Groups of young men started entering Boston's Chinatown around ten p.m. and attacking people on the street. They seemed to be men who were drinking in nearby bars, as the four men arrested were all drunk."

"Four men were arrested? You said groups—"

"Yes. It appears the Boston police were somewhat more lenient than one might hope, and let the majority of the offenders go with a simple warning."

"What else?"

"A group from the Oakland branch of the motorcycle gang Nazi Lowriders entered the Chinatown in San Francisco and attacked people on the streets with sawed off pool cues and billy clubs. More than forty of them were arrested. Two of the victims in those attacks are in critical condition at area hospitals."

Susan sighed and shook her head. "Great. Anything else?"

"Yes. Probably the most exciting news. Jefferson Monroe is scheduled to speak at a rally of his followers this morning, perhaps to address the violence last night, perhaps to call for you to concede again. No one is quite sure what his script is going to be. The best part is where the rally is going to take place."

Susan didn't enjoy it when Kurt was being coy.

"Okay, Kurt. Out with it. Where is that?"

"Lafayette Park. Directly across the street from us."

CHAPTER ELEVEN

9:21 a.m. Eastern Daylight Time
Lafayette Park, Washington DC

It was a beautiful thing to witness.

They called it the People's Park, and today the people were all here.

Not the ordinary denizens of this park, where generation after generation of the rabble, the rabble-rousers, and the radicals—the unwashed, the losers of life—would camp out and protest the policies of one President after another.

No. Not those people.

These people were *his* people. A sea of people—thousands of them, tens of thousands—who last night had passed the word across social media that their man was speaking here today. It was a stealth move, a knife in the back, the kind of move Gerry O'Brien excelled at. He had obtained the permit for this gathering from the city just before close of business yesterday afternoon, and the news of it had spread like wildfire overnight, the flames fanned by hurricane-force winds.

Now the people were all here, wearing their giant Abe Lincoln hats and carrying their signs—handmade signs, official signs from the campaign, professionally made signs from the dozens of organizations that had supported the campaign. Most of the people were dressed warmly in heavy coats and hats against the unseasonable chill.

Jefferson Monroe gazed out from the makeshift stage at that teeming mass of humanity—it was like a rock and roll festival out there—and knew he was born for just this moment. Seventy-four years, and many, many victories: from his earliest days as a teenage moonshiner in the backwoods of Appalachia, through his time as an angry young strikebreaker, an ambitious company executive, and eventually a major shareholder and captain of the coal industry.

Later, he became a senator from West Virginia and conservative political kingmaker heavily funded by the same coal companies he once worked for. And now... President-elect of the United States. A lifetime of striving, long decades of climbing up from the bottom, clawing his way, and suddenly, quite by surprise (an outcome no one expected, not even him), he was the most powerful man on Earth.

He was here to force the sitting President to leave the White House early, and allow him to enter. It was as audacious as anything he had ever attempted. Past the crowds and across the wide thoroughfare, he could see the White House in the distance, rising on a green knoll. Could she see him from there? Was she watching?

God, he hoped so.

He turned away from the crowd, just for a moment. Behind him on the stage was a crowd of people. O'Brien was there, the mastermind of this campaign, the dark lord of the white supremacists, a man at least as driven as Monroe was himself. Even now, he was barking something into a cell phone.

"I want that bird," Gerry the Shark seemed to be saying. But how could that be right? *I want that bird?* What a strange thing to say! At a moment like this?

"I want it, okay? I want it to land just like we talked about. Tell me you can do that. Okay? Good. When?"

Monroe shrugged it off. Dealing with Gerry was more than just a wild ride—it was a lesson in surrealism. The President-elect decided to ignore his closest advisor for the time being. Instead, he spoke to the other people on stage.

"Are you seeing this?" he said, as he covered the microphone with his hand and indicated the massive crowd. "Are you *seeing* this?"

"It is the best thing I've ever seen," a young aide said.

Behind him, clapping began in the crowd—not random, but rhythmic, thousands of hands clapping at once—CLAP, CLAP, CLAP, CLAP...

A chant was about to go up. This is how it started, with clapping, and in some cases stomping. And here it came, the voices rising.

"U-S-A! U-S-A! U-S-A!"

It was a good one, a good one to start on.

Monroe took his hand from the microphone and gripped the stand instead. He raised a hand, quieting the chant within seconds. It was like he simply turned down the sound on a machine—a TV, or a radio. But it wasn't a machine, it was thousands and thousands of people, and he controlled them, effortlessly, with a gesture. Not for the first time, he marveled at that power, a power that he had. Like a superhero.

Or a god.

"How's that global warming treating you?" he said, his voice echoing over the multitudes. Laughter and cheers rippled through the crowd. Personally, Monroe knew from climate scientists employed by his companies that global warming was a fact of life, and would be a serious issue a century from now, or sooner, perhaps even a threat to civilization itself. As President, he might quietly look for ways to implement policies that lessened the threat somewhat, without harming industry profits. In the meantime, his companies were gradually increasing investment in the renewable energy fields—the solar, wind, and geothermal technologies that were the future.

But his people didn't want to hear any of that. They wanted to hear that global warming was a hoax, perpetrated in large part by the Chinese. So that's what Monroe would tell them. Give the people what they want. And anyway, it was cold out today, an unseasonably cold day in early November, and that was evidence enough—there couldn't be any such thing as global warming.

"Today is our day, did you know that?"

The crowd greeted that idea with a roar of approval.

"We came from nothing, you and I did. Okay? And we came from nowhere. We didn't grow up in fancy upscale Manhattan or San Francisco or Boston penthouses. We didn't go to special private schools for special people. We don't sip lattes and read the *New York Times*. We don't know that world. We don't want to know that world. You and I, we've worked hard all our lives, and we've earned everything we have, and everything we will ever have. And today is our day."

Their cheering was an eruption—an earthquake—of sound. It seemed like some great beast was beneath the surface of the Earth, sleeping dormant for centuries, and now it would rend the ground and burst forth in a frenzy of violence.

"Today is the day we are going to remove one of the most corrupt administrations in American history. Yes, I know, I know. She said she's not leaving, but I tell you what. It's not going to last. She's leaving, all right, and a lot sooner than anyone thinks. It's going to happen a lot sooner than *she* thinks, that's for sure."

The cheering went on and on. He waited for the crowd to die down. Monroe's people hated Susan Hopkins. They hated her, and everything she stood for. She was rich, she was beautiful, she was spoiled—she had never lacked for anything in her life. She was a woman in a job always done by men.

She was a friend to immigrants, and to the Chinese, whose cheap labor practices had destroyed the American way of life. She was a hedonist, a former jet-setter, and she seemed to confirm everything heartland people suspected about the celebrity class. Her husband was gay, for the love of God! He had been born in France. Could there be anything more un-American than a gay Frenchman?

Susan Hopkins was a monster to these people. In the far reaches of internet conspiracy websites, there were even those who claimed that she and her husband were murderers, and worse than murderers. They were devil worshippers. They belonged to a Satanic cult of the mega-wealthy who stole and sacrificed children.

Well, today Monroe would give his people the murderer part. He wished he could be there inside the Oval Office and see her face when this news broke.

The crowd had quieted again. They were waiting for him now.

"I want you to listen to me for a minute," he said. "Because what I'm about to tell you is a little bit complicated, and it's not easy on the ears. But I'm going to tell it because you have to know it. You, the American people, the true patriots, deserve to know. It's very important. Our future is at stake."

He had them. They were ready now. Here it came. The Hail Mary pass. The bomb. Jefferson Monroe geared himself up and launched it.

"Five days before election day, a man turned up dead near the Tidal Basin right here in Washington, DC."

His people had gone silent. A dead man? This was something new. It was not the typical Jefferson Monroe rally topic. It seemed that thousands of pairs of eyes were riveted to him. In fact, that was indeed the case. *Give us something*, those big hollow eyes seemed to say. *Give us the meat.*

"At first glance, it seemed like the man had committed suicide. He was shot in the head, the gun was found near his body, and his fingerprints were on the gun. It didn't make much impact in the news at the time—people die every day, and often enough, they take their own lives. But I knew, okay, folks? I knew that this man didn't kill himself."

The eyes watched him. Thousands and thousands of eyes.

"How did I know that?"

No one said a word. Jefferson Monroe had never seen such a large group of people so quiet in his entire life. They sensed something big was coming, and that he was the one bringing it.

"I knew he didn't commit suicide because I knew this man personally. I'd almost say he was a friend of mine. His name was Patrick Norman."

Jefferson was no stranger to telling big lies. Even so, and unlike many politicians, he felt a certain twinge when he did it. It wasn't guilt. It was the sense that somewhere out there, someone knew the truth, and that person would work tirelessly to bring the truth to light. In fact, it wasn't even somewhere out there—at least three people standing behind him on the stage knew the facts. There were probably a dozen others in the organization. They knew that Jeff Monroe had never once spoken to Patrick Norman.

He pressed on.

"Patrick Norman was not suicidal—far from it. On the contrary, he was one of the best and most successful private investigators in the United States, and he made a lot of money. I know what he made because I was paying him. He was working for my campaign at the time of his death.

"Campaigning is a dirty business, folks. I'll be the first to tell you that. Sometimes you do things you're not proud of to get a leg up on your opponent. And I hired Patrick to look into corruption in the Hopkins administration, and in the business dealings of the soon-to-be *former* President's husband, Pierre Michaud. Okay? Do you see where this is going?"

A ripple of assent, a loud murmur, went through the crowd like a rolling wave.

"Patrick called me on the phone a couple of days before he died, and he said, 'Jeff, I've got the dirt you're looking for. I just need to follow up on a couple of last leads. But this thing I have—the bad things she's done—is going to blow this election wide open.'"

This was a lie stacked on top of a lie. Norman never called him. He never called him Jeff—he never called him at all. He had no dirt on Susan Hopkins, even after nearly a year of looking. He had determined that she was probably squeaky clean, or if not, the dirt was buried so deep that no one would ever find it.

"What Patrick suggested to me was that Hopkins and her husband accepted bribes from foreign leaders, including Third World dictators, in exchange for favorable treatment from the United States government. He also suggested that there was a quid pro quo going on in support of Pierre Michaud's sham charities. If the dictators would make Michaud look good by letting him build his fake water systems—water systems that help no one, folks!—the USA would sell them weapon systems. This is shocking stuff. And folks, that was the last I ever heard from Patrick Norman. He had the dirt on Susan Hopkins. Then he died, apparently by his own hand."

Now a ripple of boos went through the crowd.

"But it wasn't by his own hand, right? Yesterday afternoon, the Washington, DC, medical examiner's office released their

45

findings. Patrick Norman did not fire the gun that killed him. And he had marks on his body consistent with a struggle. All indications are that someone killed him and made it look like a suicide."

He paused and let the moment draw its breath. These were the true parts, and the parts that were especially damning.

"Five days before the election, Patrick Norman, the man with the dirt on Susan Hopkins, was murdered."

The crowd exploded into a fit of ecstasy. This was what they wanted, all they had ever wanted—something that seemed to confirm everything that they just knew about Susan Hopkins. She was corrupt to her core, and she would have someone killed to cover her trail of deception.

As the crowd cheered, the cheer began to morph into something, the chant that had emerged late in the campaign. It was the most dangerous chant of all, one that Gerry the Shark had released into the public sphere through his Gathering Storm goon squad.

"KICK...HER...OUT!... KICK...HER...OUT!"

Then a strange and wonderful thing happened.

Even as his people chanted violence, a white dove flew down from the sky, hovered about Jefferson Monroe for a moment, then alighted onto the right shoulder of his wool coat. It flapped its wings a couple of times, then settled down and relaxed. Now he had a dove on his shoulder. The crowd erupted.

It was magic. More than that, it was a sign. A sign from God.

He moved carefully, trying not to alarm the bird.

I want that bird, Gerry the Shark had shouted into the telephone.

Monroe raised his left arm, trying to quiet the crowd. It worked, sort of.

"This is a dove of peace," he said. "And this is how we're going to do it, folks. Peacefully, through the rule of law. Through the enforcement of the laws of the United States. Through the peaceful transfer of power which has been one of our great traditions since the earliest days of the Republic.

"Because we are a nation of laws, Susan Hopkins must vacate the office of President this very day, and leave the White House. The Washington, DC, metro police and the medical examiner have done their jobs—they have determined that Patrick Norman did not kill himself. And now I call on the Justice Department and the FBI to do their jobs—and investigate President Hopkins for murder."

CHAPTER TWELVE

11:45 a.m. Eastern Daylight Time
The Situation Room
The White House, Washington DC

"Is it a warrant for my arrest?" Susan Hopkins said. "Is that what they've issued?"

Kurt Kimball turned the sound down on the video monitor. They had just watched Jefferson Monroe's speech again—Luke had seen it three times now.

Although there were other festivities at Monroe's rally earlier this morning, it didn't matter what else came after that. A minor country music star had taken the stage and tried to entertain the crowd with a song about America, but within seconds people were already drifting away.

They hadn't come for music—they had come for a public lynching, which was pretty close to what they had gotten.

Now Luke glanced around the Situation Room, watching the reactions. It was a packed house, a gathering of the tribes. People from the election campaign, Secret Service, Susan's people, the Vice President's people, some people from the Democratic Party. Luke didn't see a lot of fight in the eyes of these people. Some of them were obviously monitoring the proceedings in search of a good time to jump ship before it sank to the bottom of the ocean.

Scenes like this were not Luke's normal environment. He felt out of place, and even more than that. He recognized that a group of people were trying to make difficult decisions, but he didn't have a lot of patience for the process. His typical response to a problem had always been to think of something, then act on it. Meanwhile, Kurt Kimball seemed confused. Kat Lopez seemed stricken. Only Susan seemed calm.

Luke watched Susan closely, looking for signs of collapse. It was a habit he had picked up in war zones, especially during downtime between battles—he would become acutely aware of how much the people around him had left in the tank. Stress took its toll, and people were worn down by it. Sometimes it happened gradually, and sometimes it happened instantly. But either way, there came a time when all but the most hardcore fighters would fold under pressure. Then they would cease to function.

47

But Susan didn't seem to have reached that place yet. Her voice was steady. Her eyes were hard and unflinching. She was in a bad place, but she was still fighting. Luke was glad about that. It would make it easier to fight alongside her.

Kurt, at the front of the room near the big projection screen, shook his perfectly bald head. "No. You are a person of interest in the case, but not a suspect. The Washington, DC, Metro Police, specifically the Homicide Division, have simply made a request for an interview. They would like you to come in to their headquarters. You would have your legal counsel with you, and available at all times. That said, if you grant them the interview, you could become a suspect during the course of it. At which point, you could be arrested."

Kurt glanced at the White House legal counsel, a straight-laced man in a three-piece suit, and a mop of sandy hair on top of his head. He had two aides with him.

"Would you say that's right, Howard?" Kurt said.

Howard nodded. "I would not grant them an interview at this time, and certainly not an in-person interview. Not here, and under no circumstances at one of their facilities. You could go in and have a hard time getting out again, especially in the current climate. If they want to do an interview, it should be over the telephone or maybe a video conference. You're busy, Susan. You're President of the United States. You want to meet your responsibilities in this case, but you also have a lot of other things to do."

"Doesn't that make Susan look guilty?" a young guy in a blue suit and a crew cut said. He sat directly across the conference table from Luke. He looked like he was nineteen years old—in the sense that a lot of nineteen-year-olds still look like they are twelve. "I mean, we have nothing to hide here. I'm very confident of that."

"Agent Stone," Susan said. "Do you know my campaign manager, Tim Rutledge?"

Luke shook his head. "Haven't had the pleasure."

They reached across the table and shook hands. Rutledge had a firm grip, overly firm, like he had read in a book somewhere that a firm grip was important.

Rutledge looked at Luke. "And what is your role here, Agent Stone?"

Luke stared at him. He figured the best way to answer was honestly.

"I don't know."

"Agent Stone is a special operative. He has saved my life on more than one occasion, as well as my daughter's life. He's probably saved everyone in this room's life at one point or another."

"Who do you work for?" Rutledge said.

Luke shrugged. "I work for the President." He didn't see any need to go into his past, the Special Response Team, Delta Force, any of it. If this guy wanted to know that stuff, he could find it all out. The truth was, Luke felt strangely disconnected from that person, the person he had once been. He wasn't sure what good he could do here.

"Well, I work for the President, too," Rutledge said. "And I can tell you that these allegations, or whatever they are, are not true. Not one word of it. Susan had nothing to do with this man's murder, nor did the campaign, nor did Pierre. There's been no corruption. There's been no pay to play with Pierre's charities. I know this because we dug deep at the start of the campaign to see where the vulnerabilities were, to find any skeletons. Financially, there were basically none. I know there have been some personal issues, and it's possible they played a role in the outcome of the election, but Pierre is about the squeakiest clean businessman I've ever run across."

"Did you know the dead man at all?" Kurt said.

Rutledge shrugged. "Know him? No. I knew of him. I never met him or spoke to him. Pierre's security director alerted the campaign to the guy's existence probably nine months ago. There had been a number of attempted hacks into company databases, all leading back to Norman's investigation agency. Pretty amateurish stuff. From there, Pierre's people determined that Norman was working for Monroe, but no one worried about it too much. And we certainly weren't going to murder him. As I indicated, there was nothing for him to find. You have to remember that all of this was in the context of last summer, when we all knew the people were never going to vote in a crazy person like Jefferson Monroe as President of the United States."

Three people over from Rutledge, a man raised his hand. He was a weak-looking middle-aged man with thinning hair. He had a long nose and no chin to speak of. His body was thin and utterly without muscle tone. He wore an ill-fitting gray suit that he seemed to swim inside of. But he had hard, hard eyes. Here was one person in the room who was definitely not afraid.

Oddly, he wore a *Hello, my name is* sticker on the front of his suit. It said, in thick scribbled black magic marker, *Brent Staples.*

Luke knew the name. He was an old-school campaign strategist and public relations man. Luke thought he and Susan had

had a falling out at one point, but they must have patched things up for the campaign. A lot of good that had done Susan.

"I hate to say this," he said, and Luke could tell he actually relished saying it, whatever came next. "But Jefferson Monroe is looking less and less crazy, while the people in this room are looking more and more so."

"What are you trying to say, Brent?" Susan said.

"I'm saying that you're out on a limb again, Susan. You are all by yourself in a very awkward place. I'm telling you that you are becoming isolated from the American people. From a regular person's perspective, you lost the election, and that hurts. There might have even been some malfeasance on your opponent's part. But nobody knows if that's really true, and if it is true, nobody knows what kind of impact it had on the outcome. Meanwhile, you're saying you won't step down. Also, a man has been murdered who was investigating you. And it seems you're leaning toward saying you won't give the police an interview. My question to you is: who's starting to look like the criminal here? Who is starting to look like the crazy person?"

Kat Lopez stood in the corner of the room. She shook her head and glared at Brent Staples. "Brent, that's out of line. You know Susan didn't murder anyone. You know that this is a dog-and-pony show dreamed up by Monroe and his hitman Gerry O'Brien."

"I'm telling you what it looks like," Staples said. "Not what it is. I don't know what it is, and that doesn't really matter anyway. What it looks like is everything."

He gazed around the room, hard eyes taking everyone in, daring them to tell him otherwise.

Young Tim Rutledge took up the challenge. "It looks to me like they murdered the investigator so they could pin it on Susan," he said. "It looks to me like they stole the election through voter fraud and by tampering with the machinery. That's what it looks like to me."

Luke finally decided to chime in with something. Now he realized what was wrong with this entire meeting, and since he did, he might as well point it out. Maybe it could help them.

"It seems to me," he said slowly, "that you need to take back the initiative."

Throughout the room, all eyes slowly turned to him.

"Think of this as combat, a battle. They have you on the run. They have you in disarray. They do something, and you react. By the time you react, they're already doing something else. They are on the attack, and you are in a disorganized retreat. You have to come up with some way to attack them, set them on their back foot, and retake the initiative."

"Like what?" Brent Staples said.

Luke shrugged. "I don't know. Isn't that your job?"

For several minutes, Kurt Kimball had been huddled in a corner with two of his aides. Something had clearly distracted him. Now he turned back to the room.

"I like your idea, Stone. But it's going to be hard to retake the initiative at this moment."

Stone raised an eyebrow. "Oh? Why's that?"

"We just learned that at least a hundred West Virginia state troopers, and Wheeling metropolitan police, are en route to Washington in a long convoy. They intend to come directly here to the White House, take Susan into custody, and bring her to the DC Metropolitan police headquarters themselves."

"They have no jurisdiction," the White House counsel, Howard, said. "Have they lost their minds?"

"It seems that everyone has lost their minds today," Kurt said. "And they have a claim to jurisdiction, however slight."

"What is it?"

"Both police forces, along with a dozen others from nearby states, are routinely deputized as auxiliary Washington, DC, cops to provide overflow security for the Presidential inauguration events every four years. They claim that renders them permanent deputies."

Howard shook his head. "It won't hold up in court. It's silly."

Kurt put his hands in the air, as if Howard had pulled a gun on him. "Whether it will hold up or not, they're on their way here. Apparently, they think they're going to walk in here, take Susan, and walk back out of here with her."

There was a long pause. No one in the room spoke. The silence spun out as each face looked from one to the other.

"They'll be here in thirty minutes," Kurt said.

CHAPTER THIRTEEN

12:14 p.m. Eastern Daylight Time
Outside the White House
Washington DC

"No one gets inside," the tall man said into his walkie-talkie. "Are we clear? I want personnel centered at the gatehouse, but I also want eyes in the sky watching every possible point of entry. Shooters on the roof."

"Roger that," a voice squawked from the handset.

"Tell those shooters use of deadly force is green light. Repeat, green light on deadly force, but only if necessary."

"On whose authority?"

"Mine," the man said. "My authority."

"Copy," the voice said.

The tall man's name was Charles "Chuck" Berg.

He was forty years old, and had been in the Secret Service for nearly fifteen years. He had been the head of the President's home security detail for more than two years. It had come about by accident, the result of a disaster. He had been on her personal security detail the evening of the Mount Weather attack, when she was the Vice President. He had almost certainly saved her life. Everyone else on the team had been killed.

He had changed that night. He only saw it in retrospect. He had already been thirty-seven years old, in a job with a high level of responsibility, and married with two children—but in a sense, that was the night he became a man. He became who he was supposed to be. Before then? He was just a big kid with a job that let him carry a gun.

Susan trusted him after that night. And he trusted her. More than that—he felt protective of her—and not just because it was his job to feel that way. He was younger than her by a decade, and yet he felt almost like he was her big brother.

Survival—saving someone's life—is an intimate thing.

He knew there was nothing to these corruption charges, or this murder charge. And he'd be dipped if he was going to allow anyone in to take the President of the United States into custody—especially not a bunch of yahoos wielding a fake bench warrant from far outside any reasonable claim to jurisdiction.

He had just done a perimeter check on foot. He was moving up the driveway, back toward the White House. Just ahead of him, a dozen heavily armed men in business suits moved briskly along the road. It was a sunny day, and cold. The shadows of the men on the ground showed sharp, high-powered rifles and shotguns poking from their sides.

The guardhouse was just up ahead. It was protected by concrete barriers. There was both a STOP sign and a DO NOT ENTER sign on the fence. More men in suits stood by the entrance. The body language of the men was alert, tense. They had the overstuffed look of men wearing bullet-proof vests or armor under their clothes.

Construction vehicles were setting down taller, thicker, and heavier barriers in front of the existing ones. They were just putting the finishing touches on the barriers now. The new barriers created a narrow chute, which was also a Byzantine maze of sharp right and left turns. It would force any vehicle to slow to a crawl. Wider vehicles, like trucks or Humvees, wouldn't be able to pass through it at all.

NOTICE, a sign read. RESTRICTED AREA. 100% ID CHECK.

There weren't going to be any ID checks today. No one was going in or out.

In the near distance, perhaps two hundred yards away, men in black uniforms moved into position on the roof of the White House. Those guys were the real deal, Berg knew. The shooters. Secret Service snipers, any one of whom could easily put a bullet through his heart from this distance.

A Black Hawk helicopter took off from a helipad behind a copse of trees on the White House grounds. It headed east, then banked lazily to the north. Snipers lounged in the open bay doors.

This was just the visible defense. There were more than a hundred men and women guarding the perimeter of the White House grounds, including military units. No inch of the fencing or the walls around the property was not under surveillance at this moment. In addition to the circling Black Hawks, there were three Apache helicopter gunships hovering out over the Potomac River. Those Apaches could take out the entire approaching line of police vehicles in seconds.

It was the mismatch of all mismatches. The NBA champions versus the local junior high school B team.

Chuck pulled out his cell phone. He had this crazy sheriff from Wheeling, West Virginia, on speed dial. Was the man on a suicide mission? Chuck was about to find out.

The phone rang three times.

"Paxton," the man said. His deep, gravelly voice had a slight drawl to it. You wouldn't necessarily call it Southern. You might say it was Appalachian hillbilly.

Chuck pictured him in his mind. He had requested a research brief on the sheriff when he first heard they were coming. Bobby Paxton was a broad man in his fifties, an ex-Marine who still sported a flattop haircut. He was known as a no-nonsense, law and order type. More than that—for years, his department had been dogged by police brutality complaints, especially against young black males in custody.

Paxton himself was also on the record as flirting with any number of cockamamie conspiracy theories, up to and including the idea that elements of the federal government were cooperating with a race of seven-foot-tall aliens from outer space, who had given the American military advanced technologies like particle beam weaponry and anti-gravity flying machines.

It was possible that Paxton was insane. And if so, this could turn into a long day.

"Sheriff," Chuck said. "Where are you now?"

"We are two minutes from your location. You should get a visual on us shortly."

"Sir, I've said this to you before, and I'm going to say it one last time. Any message you have for the President is one I will accept from you at the front gate. Neither you, nor any of your personnel, will enter the White House grounds. There is no way—a zero percent chance—that you will take the President into custody today. You have no jurisdiction on federal property, nor within the city of Washington—"

"We do have jurisdiction," Paxton said. "My entire force has been—"

Chuck continued without missing a beat. "And the department with jurisdiction, the Washington, DC, Metro Police, has declined to enforce the warrant that you carry."

But Paxton didn't stop either. "...deputized as auxiliary police officers of the city of Washington, DC."

"Sir, you are on a fool's errand, and a dangerous one at that. I'm concerned that someone is going to get hurt out here today. And I can tell you that it won't be any of my people."

"Son," Paxton said, "you are on the wrong side of history. If you have any sense, you will step aside and let me do my job. We are coming in, regardless of what you decide."

Chuck Berg's shoulders slumped. He sighed heavily. This was how the man was going to ride this? Straight into a brick wall? So be it.

"Sheriff, we have helicopters in the air. We have marksmen on the roof. You are already in our crosshairs. You must know that. Please also know that five minutes ago, I authorized the use of deadly force to maintain the integrity of the security zone around the White House and its grounds. I urge you to leave your paperwork with me at the guardhouse. If you, or any of your men, attempt to go any further than that, you will be responsible for the consequences. If you, or any of your men, draw a weapon, you will also—"

"And you will be a murderer shoring up the dying rule of a despot," Paxton said. "Is that the legacy you want? Is that how your children and grandchildren will remember you?"

"Sheriff—"

"The Nazis were just doing their jobs, son."

"Please don't get anyone killed out here, okay?" Chuck said. "It's not worth it."

"Good day, Mr. Berg."

Chuck was about to say something more, but the line had already gone dead. He shook his head and switched back to his walkie-talkie.

"Is everything ready?"

"All units are in position. Choppers are following the motorcade, which is about seventy vehicles long, a line of motorcycles in front. It's going to be a traffic jam when they reach those barriers."

Chuck nodded. "Good. I want your men prepared to fire. We aren't playing games. I'm going to be standing out front, and I don't want to take a bullet over this nonsense."

"Copy."

"Do you have a visual on Sheriff Paxton?"

"We do. He's leading the pack. The very first motorcycle."

"When he dismounts, give me a laser sight in the middle of his chest. A big red dot right on his heart. I want him to know we mean business."

"Will do."

"And you know what? Also give me a slow flyover by one of the Apaches. But no matter what happens, I want no engagement from them. Be very clear: no engagement. It's just for show. I don't want a bloodbath on my hands."

"Roger that."

Chuck handed the walkie-talkie to the agent nearest him. He slid his phone in his pocket. Then he walked up to the barrier. It was higher than his navel, and he stood nearly six feet, five inches tall. He took a deep breath. He should see them any second, and sure enough, he did.

The first bike appeared over a low rise—it was a big police highway cruiser, with a large rounded windshield. It slowed as it reached the barriers, executed a turn, then continued, going slower and slower as it navigated the switchbacks. The bikes behind it did the same. A couple of cars followed. Within seconds, the whole thing was moving at a crawl—half the speed of a funeral procession.

What did they think was going to happen? They were going to storm the place? Not likely. Two choppers flanked the procession, guns in the doorways trained on the motorcycle cops.

The first bike stopped about twenty yards away. The man on it removed his helmet and stepped off the bike. He bent and removed something from one of his saddlebags.

"Watch him!" someone said. "Eyes sharp."

Chuck glanced to his left and right. Along the barrier was a line of men, guns mounted on tripods and trained on the newcomers.

Berg recognized the man from his photo. It was Bobby Paxton, and what he had removed from his bag was some kind of ledger or booklet. More motorcycles pulled up and he waited for his officers to dismount. Once half a dozen had gathered, Paxton and his men approached the barrier.

Paxton had a big chest and shoulders. He was good-looking in the sense of a model from an old cigarette advertisement. He was broader than Chuck by a lot, but several inches shorter. The concrete barrier came nearly to chest height on him. He glared at Chuck. His eyes were narrow and hard. Crow's feet made deep lines at the edges. His men spread out behind him in a wedge shape.

Chuck noticed that Paxton was wearing medals on his chest. Combat ribbons. A purple heart.

Suddenly a red dot appeared among the medals—the laser sight he had asked for. Another one appeared right at the man's hairline. Chuck nearly laughed at that one—clearly it was meant as a gift for him, an inside joke.

"Sheriff," Chuck said across the barrier, "I'm Agent Chuck Berg of the Secret Service. I'm head of security for the White House."

Paxton simply stared at Chuck for another moment.

Chuck indicated Paxton's chest, as if he had soiled his shirt with a spot of spaghetti sauce from lunch. "You've got a little something there."

Paxton glanced down and saw the laser sight.

"You won't be able to see this, but there's another one on your forehead. You are one second away from seeing the man upstairs."

In person, the sheriff was a man of few words. Either that, or the situation had rendered him tongue-tied.

Chuck suddenly felt light, and loose. This crazy motorcade, more than 100 cops from West Virginia riding two hours to the White House, only to be stopped dead in their tracks at the entrance. It was a farce. It was a bad comedy skit.

"Agent Berg," Paxton said, "I have here a warrant for the arrest of Susan Hopkins." He indicated the bound document in his hands. The paperwork itself was hidden inside some kind of thick cover. "I demand that you allow me to pass and take Ms. Hopkins into custody."

Chuck shook his head. "I'm afraid I can't do that, as we've already discussed. But if you'd like to give that paperwork to me, I will make certain that it finds its way to the appropriate place."

Paxton seemed to consider what to do. Chuck wondered if the man was so slow he simply couldn't come up with an adequate response. Chuck could almost smell the wires burning inside the sheriff's brain.

As they stared across the barrier at each other, the ground began to rumble beneath their feet. A shadow passed across the sun. Berg, the sheriff, and all the sheriff's men glanced up as a US Army Apache helicopter flew slowly above their heads. The chopper was bristling with weaponry. Paxton would know, as well as or better than anyone here, that his people had no way to respond against that thing. Never mind a response—if it attacked them, they would have precious little hope of survival.

Gradually, the rumble subsided as the chopper dwindled into the distance.

Chuck looked at Paxton. "Still think you're coming inside?"

Paxton's eyes were hard. "Is that an attempt to intimidate me?"

Chuck shrugged. "It's a clear communication, showing everyone where they stand. We don't want any casualties today, do we, Sheriff?"

There were no choices here. There was no way inside. There was no way to continue. One suspicious move and the shooting would start. Paxton himself, laser sights on his head and chest, would be the first one to die.

Finally, the sheriff seemed to grasp this. He stepped to the barrier.

"Inside this cover is the complaint against Hopkins filed by my office, and the warrant, signed this morning by Judge Phillip Broley."

Chuck took the booklet the man handed him. His hands ran over the soft, rich cover.

"Is this real leather?"

Paxton nodded. He gestured at the booklet with his chin. "Those are historical documents, and they need to be protected. They have original signatures. One day, they will be displayed in museums, as much as the Declaration of Independence or the Gettysburg Address."

Chuck held the booklet in his hands for a moment. "Oh my," he said. "Historical documents. I promise we will safeguard them. I even promise you this—President Hopkins herself will review them."

Then he handed the booklet to the agent next to him.

He extended a hand across the barrier. "Sheriff Paxton, it was a pleasure to meet you today, sir."

Paxton reached across and also shook. It seemed a reluctant gesture on his part.

"Agent Berg, this isn't the last you'll be hearing from me."

"I'm certain of that," Berg said.

The handshake ended. Paxton, with nothing left to do, turned as if to go. To Paxton's right, in the phalanx of cops spread out behind him, was a young state trooper. Suddenly, the kid was in motion.

"Is that it?" the young trooper said. His face was angry, incredulous.

"That's it," Chuck said.

"You son of a bitch," the kid said. He stepped toward Chuck, pulling his gun as he did so. He was a fast draw. He had the gun out lightning quick.

"Don't—" was all Chuck managed to say.

A single gunshot rang out. The effect of it was odd—the bullet found its mark before Chuck heard the shot. It had come from somewhere behind him, a sniper's supersonic round. The sound of it echoed across the White House grounds and the city streets.

The kid didn't dance. He didn't jitter. The shot entered through his left temple and blew out the back of his head. He was dead before he hit the ground, less than a second later. He dropped bonelessly, like a rag doll.

All around Chuck, guns were trained on the cops across the barrier. Chuck himself hadn't moved. Nor had Paxton.

"DOWN!" Secret Service agents screamed. "GET DOWN!"

Behind Paxton, the rest of the cops were dropping to the tarmac. Paxton alone did not move. He looked to his right and behind at the dead cop. The kid's body was oddly askew on the ground—its legs jutting out at odd angles that never would have been possible during life.

Chuck couldn't take his eyes off of it.

"That's the legacy of tyranny, and of treason," Paxton said.

He paused for full effect.

"That's your legacy, son."

CHAPTER FOURTEEN

1:30 p.m. Eastern Standard Time
The Oval Office
The White House, Washington DC

"Madam President, this is my resignation letter."

Susan sat in a high-backed chair, staring up at Chuck Berg, who stood near the double doors. He was big, and there had always been something boyish and awkward about him. It wasn't his physicality—like most Secret Service agents, he had been a standout athlete as a young person. It was just that, despite everything, he had always seemed somewhat apologetic, as if he never really felt he deserved his role.

Theoretically, they were having a working lunch in the Oval Office. It felt more like a bunker at the end of a world war. And they were on the losing side.

Forty-five minutes ago, just after the shooting outside the White House gates, Haley Lawrence, the Secretary of Defense, had resigned. He was a Republican and a good conservative. He was a thoughtful man and had been a tremendous asset to this administration. But he was getting too much pressure from within his party to continue. The death of a police officer, no matter how insane the assignment he was on, had been the last straw.

Susan glanced around the room at who was left. Luke Stone. Kurt Kimball. Kat Lopez. Tim Rutledge. Marybeth Horning was on the other end of the video monitor. It was good. These were loyal people. She could trust them. Things were spiraling out of control, and she needed her people with her.

She looked back at Chuck and shook her head. "I won't accept it, Chuck."

"Have you seen the TV?" he said. "They're calling for my head on a plate."

Susan shrugged. "You followed protocols to the letter. You warned the sheriff that the use of deadly force was authorized. That was up to him to communicate that to his people. His officer drew a weapon. You didn't ask him to do that."

Susan was feeling especially callous today. She knew all about the young man who had died. Kat had given her the facts and figures. Twenty-seven years old, former Marine with a tour of duty in Afghanistan. Three years on the police force. A wife pregnant with their first child. All very sad.

Okay, then keep your hot gun in your pants and don't get killed over nothing. That's what she would tell the kid if he were standing in front of her now.

"Anyway," she said, "if I listened to everything they said on TV, I'd be in pretty bad shape, wouldn't I?"

Chuck hesitated before speaking again. He seemed to be choking back some emotion or other. He felt guilty about the dead cop. Of course he did. But Susan wasn't buying it. If she did, then that meant... what?

"Kat? What are your thoughts?"

"I think Chuck stays on," she said. "Our point of view is that the West Virginia police coming here was a completely extra-legal—"

"Illegal, if you prefer," Kurt said.

Kat shrugged. "Okay, illegal. An illegal attempt to circumvent the laws of the United States, and protocols for Presidential succession that have been in place a long time. The Secret Service did the right thing, protecting the President and the sanctity of the office. The man drew a firearm. His commanding officer had been warned that any aggressive move would be countered with deadly force. Not much else to say, is there?"

Susan glanced at Luke Stone. He was sitting sprawled in his chair like a teenager. If he had any thoughts, he hadn't shared them so far.

"Luke, do you want to weigh in on this?"

He barely shrugged. It was as if he was bored. "People do silly things in serious situations. Then they die. I lost count long ago of how many times I've seen that happen. What surprises me more than anything is a guy like that survived thirteen months in Afghanistan. He must have manned a supply depot at the air base."

Chuck was shaking his head. "I'm sorry, Susan. I really am. I'm not doing this as a gesture. I really am resigning. It's been a great run here, but I think it's over. What happened today has suggested to me that my priorities are out of whack. I've been working twelve-hour days for way too long. I authorized the use of deadly force—in retrospect it was a very bad decision. I really need to take some time, reflect, and be with my family."

"Chuck," Susan said, "you can't do this. I am emphatically, passionately, not accepting your resignation, Chuck. You are one of the most valuable members of my team. I'd sooner have this place hit by a meteor than see you walk out of here."

He stood, uncertain. He placed the sheet of paper in his hand on the table.

Susan looked at it. "Either pick that thing back up or watch me crumple it into a ball and slam dunk it into the wastebasket."

"I'll hit a three-pointer from here," Kurt Kimball said.

The air went out of Chuck like he'd been punched in the stomach. He picked up the piece of paper. "I'll stay through Monroe's inaugural," he said.

"If he makes it that far," Marybeth Horning said through the video monitor.

After Chuck left, Susan slid deeper into her chair. She looked around the room at what remained of her team. "That's one disaster averted," she said.

* * *

"You don't owe anyone anything," Pierre said over the phone, his voice soothing, relaxed. He wasn't angry, she realized. He might even be relieved.

"With all the sacrifices you've made, people need to stand up for you. That's my opinion. I watch the news shows, Susan. There are protests and riots going on all over the country. There's a lot of vindictive rhetoric coming from the right side of the aisle, and a lot of collective hand-wringing coming from the left. If your own people can't defend you in this moment, against trumped up charges..."

His voice trailed off. She could picture the noncommittal hand gesture he made.

She sat in the living room of the White House Residence, alone as always, listening to his voice. He and the girls were too far away. She had drifted from them, become unavailable, and abdicated her responsibility. Pierre was basically raising them as a single father. That couldn't stand.

Yes, she and Pierre were no longer together in any realistic sense, but he had made it clear to her again and again that she was always welcome. His homes were so big, and there were so many of them, that they could lead separate lives under the same roofs, if they wanted. They would barely have to run into each other. Heck, the Malibu beachfront place was in her name. She could kick him out, if she wanted.

She smiled at that idea. She would never kick him out of anywhere.

"Why don't you come home for a while?" he said.

She nearly laughed. "For a while? You know as well as I do that my term is over. If I walk out of here now, and don't fight this stolen election, I'm not coming back. Everything will move on without me."

He did laugh. "I'm okay with that. We want you here. The girls want you more than anything. They're teenagers now, Susan. They need their mother. There's a lot for them to navigate. The world is more complicated than it used to be."

Susan closed her eyes. She could picture it. A beautiful life with her daughters. Pierre in the background, doing his thing. There would be some growing pains, certainly, some adjustments to make. But she could re-enter private life. Then, maybe when the girls were a bit older, she could look at...

It was as if he read her mind. Once upon a time, he would do that every day.

"Politics isn't going anywhere," he said. "You probably won't be President again. But you're still young. There's the Congress, the Senate. You could be Governor of California one day. It's just like running a country, only better because everyone here agrees with you."

It was a beautiful fantasy, and in Susan's life, fantasy had always had a funny habit of becoming reality. But a dark thought occurred to her.

"What about the charges against me?" she said.

"Susan, you must be tired. There are no charges. It's smoke and mirrors. The DC Metro police want to interview you, okay? They can easily do that via satellite uplink while we spend December in Austria. Salzburg, the Alps, a little skiing, fires and hot drinks at night. Sounds good, doesn't it?"

It sounded a lot better than good. It sounded like old times.

"Susan, you didn't murder Patrick Norman, nor did your campaign. No one on my end did it. Meanwhile, there's no evidence of corruption because there is no corruption. Monroe was doing what he does best—lying. Patrick Norman got nowhere. We know this because while he was trying and failing to infiltrate our computer systems, we did infiltrate his. I have all of his agency's files on a server up in San Jose. He had nothing. There was nothing to have."

A long pause passed between them.

"Listen," Pierre said. "How can you tell when Jefferson Monroe is lying?"

She shook her head. She was tired. She had gone straight from campaigning hard, sixteen-hour days, to this... nightmare.

"I don't know, babe."

"It's easy," he said. "Just look to see if his mouth is moving."

It was the oldest joke in the book, but it brought a smile to her face. Monroe stole the election—she was almost certain of it. He and his people were textbook dirty tricksters. And they were much too forgiving of, and cozy with, the extreme right. But they were no real threat to democracy. The United States was strong enough to weather four years of their shenanigans.

Still, one last thought occurred to her, the last lonely sentinel guarding a wall that until today had seemed unassailable.

"But if there are no real charges, then why am I leaving?"

His answer was blunt and simple, but also kind, in its own way. "Because you lost the election, honey. Maybe they stole it, maybe they didn't. It would be hard to prove that either way. Elections get stolen sometimes. And afterwards, the people who lost go home.

"You can walk away, and there will be no shame in it. Call it a leave of absence. Call it anything you want. Let Marybeth Horning become Acting President, ramp the administration down, and turn off the lights when it's over. I have a hunch she's going to make her own run for that office soon enough. Give her a little taste of it, just enough to whet her appetite.

"You did everything you needed to do. You led the country out of dark times. Chaos. You pulled us through. And you lit a lamp for women like Marybeth, or even your own daughters. Anything is possible now."

His voice became softer. "Anything."

There was another pause.

"You did that. You. The country owes you a debt of gratitude. And if it means anything, I am very, very proud of you."

Susan's throat was tight. Tears began to stream down her face. She could barely speak now.

"You know it means the world to me," she said.

* * *

"Marybeth, how is my house?"

Marybeth came on the video screen, eyes elfish behind her round-rimmed glasses. She wore a blue wool sweater—it could get chilly in the Vice President's residence. Susan pictured the house: a beautiful, turreted and gabled Queen Anne–style 1850s mansion on the grounds of the Naval Observatory in Washington, DC.

Susan had lived there for five years as Vice President, and for about six months after she became President, while they were rebuilding this place. She often thought of that house—it was one of her most favorite places she had ever lived.

Throughout her time there, she had often retreated upstairs by herself to the study. It was a comfortable old room, with a sitting area, and stocked with hundreds of books. She would stand at the big bay window, staring out at the beautiful rolling lawns of the Naval Observatory campus. The afternoon sun moving west would cast perfect light, like the light playing on windows in the paintings of a master artist.

In the old days, during her time as Vice President, when Thomas Hayes wanted nothing to do with her, she was free to make what she would out of the position. Those years were a time of optimism for her, a time when she met and spoke to thousands of Americans—some on top of the world, some hopeful for the future, some without hope. She felt privileged and honored, on a daily basis, to be in that position. It seemed like a lifetime ago now, but in her mind, that house would always be indelibly linked to those great days.

"Your house is doing fine," Marybeth said. "As beautiful as ever. One night, when I'm out of town, you should come for a sleepover. Have a little reunion here."

Susan smiled at the thought of it. As a result of the Mount Weather disaster, security protocols had changed. The President and Vice President were never to be in the same place at the same time. Since Susan had picked Marybeth as Vice President, the two women hadn't seen each other, except across video screens.

"I would like that."

"So do it, baby. You're the boss."

Not for long.

Susan took a deep breath. "Marybeth, I'm not going to mince words with you here. I'm calling to tell you something. You have been an inspiration to me throughout my entire adult life. I've always looked up to you and respected you."

"Don't date me, little girl," Marybeth said. "I'm only a couple of… well… years, depending on what you mean by the word year. You get the idea. I'm not that much older than you."

Susan ignored the jokes. "You're more or less the whole reason I ran for the Senate that first time. I did it because my hero Marybeth Horning had done it, and if she did it, maybe I could do it."

Marybeth looked serious. "Susan, is that what you called to tell me? If so, you can save it for later. You are everyone's hero, including mine. You shattered the glass ceiling and made anything possible, not just for future generations of girls, but also for women now, in the present tense.

"You're a decade younger than me, but I can consider you a mentor. Watching you work these past two years has been a lesson I'll never forget. I thought I had to shout and scream and be strident to play with the big boys, and what I learned is it's not true—all I have to be is tough, and firm, and honest with myself. I have to be true to the best that's within me, and within all of us. I learned that from you."

Susan let the words flow out, the words that she almost couldn't bear to hear, especially coming from her own mouth: "Marybeth, I'm stepping down."

Marybeth's owl eyes stared through the screen at her. She sighed heavily. "Are you sure?"

Susan nodded. "Yes."

"When is it happening?"

"Today. We're scheduling a press briefing for six p.m."

"Can I talk you out of it?"

"No. I'm afraid not."

Marybeth nodded. "Okay. You don't make decisions lightly. I know that."

"I'm sorry to leave you in the lurch."

"Baby girl, you are not leaving me in the lurch. Far from it. You made me more prepared for something like this than I ever could have been on my own. I'll take it from here. I'm ready to do it. And I promise you this—I'm going to get to the bottom of the election irregularities. I'm going to fight these bastards tooth and claw, and if it's possible to do, I'm going to get these results overturned. And when that happens, I want you to come back and take your rightful place again. In fact, you should just announce me as a placeholder. Tell them you're taking a little holiday."

"Will you stand with me up there today?" Susan said. "Will you come up and be with me at the podium when I pass the torch to you?"

Marybeth smiled. "It will be my honor to stand with you. We're like two long-lost sisters who have been separated for far too long."

CHAPTER FIFTEEN

"Mr. O'Brien?" a voice said.

It was a young female voice, just outside his door. Gerry the Shark sat behind his vast desk. He could picture the face, and the body, without having to see them. Her name was Katie, and she was a campaign aide, actually an intern. Good-looking, fresh-faced.

Fresh meat.

She had joined this movement, and gotten this close to the action, because her father was a rich, hardcore true believer in business-friendly conservative dogma—trickle down economics, tax breaks, union busting, rollbacks of environmental and workplace regulations. Gerry was fine with all that stuff, to the extent he thought about it, which wasn't much.

It was all beside the point, and the girl's father was a loud, ignorant blowhard. But he was also an early supporter and a major financial contributor to the campaign. So it probably wouldn't do to eat his precious daughter as a late afternoon snack, would it?

Gerry smiled to himself. He was sitting in here with the lights off. It was late afternoon, and the day outside had turned bleak and overcast. So it was getting a little bit dark in here, dim was probably a more accurate word, and the girl was afraid to come in. In truth, Gerry sat in the dark a lot. He did his best thinking in the dark. His mind could clear. There were fewer distractions. Nothing to look at. Everything fell away, leaving pure concentration.

Gerry knew what the kids in the organization thought of him. He was some kind of dark lord from a fantasy story, or the Star Wars movies. He could read people's minds. He was an evil genius. He could kill people just by thinking about it.

Funny. This was also exactly how he saw himself.

They probably drew straws to see who had to enter here and report to him.

"Come in," he said.

She slipped through the crack in the door without opening it. She stood on the far side of the room from him. He looked her up and down, taking his time. She had long straight hair. He could tell that she was self-conscious about her body. Her sweater was rather tight. Her skirt was a little short. Of course. There were young men on the campaign as well. She was advertising for them, but not for him.

"What can I do for you..." He snapped his fingers, as if he had forgotten her name. She was so far below him, you see, just one more young face among many. It was hard to keep track of them all.

"Katie, sir."

"Yes, Katie. What can I do for you?"

Sharing the information put her back in her element—this was what she was here to do. "We just got word from one of our leakers inside the White House. He confirmed the rumors you had already heard. Susan Hopkins is going to make an announcement this evening. They are starting to alert the media. It looks like it will be set for six o'clock."

"What is the announcement?" Gerry said.

She shook her head. "He isn't sure. They're keeping it tight-lipped. But he thinks she is planning to step down and hand over the presidency to Marybeth Horning."

Gerry didn't answer. He just stared at the girl, letting his eyes roam all over her body. A moment passed. The light in here was growing fainter all the time.

"Mr. O'Brien?"

"Yes."

"Is that all?"

"Yes, Katie. Thank you."

She slipped out, much the way she had come in. Gerry barely moved. Little Katie left his thoughts almost as quickly as she had entered them. He made a tent on his desk with his fingers. Marybeth Horning, the ultra-liberal. It would almost seem like a step backward, having her take charge of the dying administration. But it was actually a step in the right direction.

He pictured her, a caricature of the mousy college professor, who was anything but. She was tough, she was a passionate speaker, she was a leader not just of women, but also of men. She would press on with the election machine fraud and voter suppression investigations—he knew she would. She would resist any calls to step down. She might even try to turn the Patrick Norman murder investigation back on them.

She would make a formidable opponent.

Without warning the door to the office burst open and the lights came on. Gerry blinked against the sudden stark brilliance of the lighting. He fought the urge to cover his eyes with his hand.

Jefferson Monroe stood, ramrod straight and tall near the doorway. He had excellent posture for a man his age. His steely eyes looked at Gerry.

"I never understand why you sit in the dark all the time," he said.

"Helps me think."

"Okay, thinker, have you heard the latest?"

"Of course."

"And? I'm not sure how trading one fire-breathing liberal for another helps us."

Gerry took a deep breath. Jefferson Monroe was a great American, but not always the brightest bulb in the package. Sometimes he needed other people to do his thinking for him. "Jeff, today was the best day yet. Obviously, it was tragic that the Secret Service elected to kill a police officer, but it plays right into our hands again. They are in full retreat. They lost their Secretary of Defense today, and also their head of security, so I hear. Meanwhile, Marybeth Horning is not Susan Hopkins. She's not the chess player Hopkins is. She could be one day, I suppose, but that's a worry for another time. I predict that she's not ready for the big stage. The Hopkins administration is falling apart, and Horning won't have time to put her own team together. We will roll right over her."

He paused and stared up at the President-elect.

"The brass ring is almost within our grasp," he said.

"I hope you're right about that."

Gerry shrugged. "I know I'm right. Once Horning is done, that leaves the third in line of succession, the Speaker of the House. That's Karen White, she of the funny hats and inappropriate clothing choices. She's one of ours. She's also a lightweight, as you well know. She will invite us inside with her, and soon after, she will hand us the reins."

Monroe raised his index finger, a very common gesture for him. Sometimes during interviews, he wagged that finger in admonishment. Gerry loved it when he did that on TV. In person, not so much.

"That's if Marybeth steps down, and only if she does so abruptly, without choosing a new Vice President before she goes. We could end up playing a game of Russian dolls with these people, a new one popping up as each one leaves."

Gerry shook his head.

"Leave Marybeth Horning to me. If I were you, I'd stop worrying and start getting ready."

He looked right at Monroe.

"Within forty-eight hours, we're going to be inside the White House."

CHAPTER SIXTEEN

6:07 p.m. Eastern Standard Time
The Press Briefing Room
The White House, Washington DC

The suit didn't agree with him.

Luke stood near the front of the packed media room. He wore a dark blue suit. A small man with a bald head, thick glasses, and a measuring tape had come and fitted him for the suit this afternoon. Within an hour, a courier had brought Luke the suit, a new pair of shoes, and a selection of five ties to choose from.

He wore his own leather shoulder holster, outfitted snugly with his own Glock nine-millimeter, under the open suit jacket. He imagined that the suit fit him perfectly. It was just that clothes like this had always made him feel constrained.

Total freedom of movement was important to Luke. It had saved his life many times. A suit did not provide this.

To Luke, a suit might as well be a straitjacket.

It occurred to him how much he would like to tell Gunner about it. Gunner's younger self would have found it funny. On a whim, Luke pulled out his cell phone, snapped a quick photo of himself, and sent it in a text to the number that was once Gunner's. He typed a quick caption for it.

Your dad in his clown costume.

He sent it into the void without hope of hearing back, then focused in on his environment again.

He scanned the crowd. He would guess that the room had about a hundred seats. It had a gradual slope, upward from the front, as though it doubled as a movie theater. Every seat was taken. Every space along the back wall was taken. Dense throngs of people stood in the wings on both sides of the stage.

The people—the Washington press corps—looked hungry. Their eyes were on fire with anticipation. It was as if they were sharks and there was blood in the water. Ever since the shooting earlier today, there had been a Susan Hopkins Deathwatch on.

How much longer would she be President? Las Vegas bookmakers were giving odds and taking wagers. Even money said she would be out by nine a.m. tomorrow. Luke had considered trying to place a bet himself—he happened to know that she would be gone half an hour from now. Her husband had already sent a private airplane to take her home to California. The Marine One helicopter was waiting on the White House pad to take her to Joint Base Andrews, where her plane awaited.

It was time for Luke to begin thinking about what he was going to do. He was back among the living for the first time in a long time. It had been very brief episode, and it was a little sad to watch Susan's time as President come to an end like this. But she was moving on with her life, and he should do the same. It was a big world, and it was an open book to him. Africa, Europe, Asia... he could go almost anywhere, and do almost anything. He could survive—and thrive—in any environment.

There was a sudden flurry of activity, almost a commotion. It was Susan. She came out from the side entrance, flanked by big Secret Service men.

As Luke watched, she went to the podium: Susan Hopkins, the former supermodel, the former Vice President, who had taken the Oath of Office after the President had been murdered, and who had once spent a long night escaping one assassination attempt after another. She had shown courage that night, and had governed with intelligence, toughness, and flexibility. She had turned out to be a lot more than anyone first thought.

This would be her last address to the American people as President. She wore a pale blue suit for the occasion, her blonde hair in a bob. The suit seemed bulky, a telltale sign she was wearing bulletproof material beneath it. Of course she was—half the country was howling for her blood right now.

On the podium, she was nearly surrounded by bulletproof glass panels. Secret Service agents flanked her on the stage. Marybeth Horning, who had been standing at the front edge of the crowd, made her way up to the podium as well. Luke knew that this was the first time since Marybeth had become Vice President that the two women were in the same room together.

The crowd of the reporters barked like dogs, their raised voices a mad Babel.

"Madam President!"

"Ms. Hopkins!"

"Susan, over here!"

"Did you murder Patrick Norman?"

"What did you know and when did you know it?"

Susan held her hands up, like twin STOP signs, asking for quiet. Her face was serious, stern. The Susan Hopkins that people once knew was nowhere to be seen—the enthusiastic, gung-ho queen of daytime talk shows, of community 5K fun runs and political rallies? That woman was gone.

She looked tired, drawn, diminished. She had always been short—now she looked small. They had finally sucked the essence out of her. Even so, she stood as tall as she could muster. She looked like someone ready to go out with dignity.

A crackpot scheme to deliver a fake arrest warrant had led to the death of a young hothead who pulled his gun while covered in the laser sights of world-class marksmen. That was the final straw, the thing that brought the grand Susan Hopkins experimental flying machine crashing back to Earth.

Luke shook his head. He wasn't political, and never had been. He had worked for conservative and liberal administrations. His job was keeping Americans safe. Everybody else could argue over what that meant.

But this? This was a shame.

"I wonder if you would let me speak a moment?" Susan said. She stood at the podium, studiously ignoring their questions.

Gradually, the room started to quiet down. There was no sense continuing to yell at her if she wasn't going to respond. It got quieter and quieter. She was ready to speak. She stepped to the microphone again.

Then everything changed.

"Susan, look at me!" someone shouted.

The sound was shrill, almost a scream.

All eyes turned to the source, including Luke's. Before he could quite focus, a collective gasp went around the room. A reporter stood there, in the midst of a group of reporters just like him. He was an overweight man in a dress shirt, a red tie hanging askew, and a windbreaker jacket. He was pointing something at Susan.

Suddenly, people were ducking, moving away from the man. He pointed his arm directly at Susan, not more than twenty yards from her.

The Secret Service dashed toward him.

Instinctively, Luke stepped between the man and Susan. He stood directly in the man's line of sight. For a split second, he was sure the man had a gun. What else could it be? Then it resolved into something else. It became...

"BANG!" the man screamed. "BANG, BANG, BANG!"

...a smartphone.

An instant later, Secret Service agents tackled the man, big heavy bodies driving him to the ground.

Luke looked at his own chest. If it had been a gun, there would now be blood appearing there, but there was nothing.

BOOM!

Luke turned just in time to watch Marybeth Horning's skull come apart, brains and blood and bone exploding out the back as a high-caliber round hit her head.

People screamed and ducked. People crawled on the ground. A logjam of bodies piled up at the exit doors.

There was another shooter. *Another shooter?* How could two shooters get in here? This was the White House! How could one get in?

But the first one… was not a shooter.

Luke turned, scanning the room. The shooter was tall, well-dressed in a three-piece suit. Luke darted back the way he had come, stepping in front of Susan from the new angle. He drew his gun, crowd be damned.

BOOM! BOOM! BOOM!

Luke fancied that he could feel the breeze from the first two shots. The third one went through his upper arm. The pain there was searing.

Just behind him, Susan Hopkins stumbled backward, her body shuddering as the third round hit her. Why was she still standing? The Secret Service should have had her on the floor by now. One agent seemed to step away from her just before she was hit.

Luke was distracted by the activity behind him.

"Get her on the floor!" he screamed.

BOOM! Another shot hit him, this time in his midsection. He looked down. It was real. There was blood on his white shirt.

Right behind him, Susan was still standing—he felt her there. He had eaten that one for her.

He looked back at the shooter. Another one like that and Luke was going to have real problems. He aimed his own gun.

BANG! He hit the guy chest high, right side.

The man spun around sideways, almost fell, but didn't. He grabbed a young woman standing there in shock, pulled her closer, and used her as a shield.

Luke tried to get another shot at him. He sighted, but he didn't have a shot. The woman's head, her body mass, was in his way.

Suddenly the man's head exploded, spraying blood upward in a fountain. The man dropped straight down, like a trapdoor had opened beneath him, and the woman ran screaming. Luke looked to his left and saw that Chuck Berg had worked his way to the guy's blind side and taken him out.

Adrenaline surging, Chuck was inside the fog of battle—Luke could see it in his eyes. Chuck was a good agent, but he was making split-second decisions, and at this moment he couldn't tell friend from foe. Now he aimed at Luke.

Luke dropped his gun and raised both his hands.

"Chuck," he croaked. "It's Stone. Good guys. I'm one of them."

Suddenly his tongue was thick in his mouth.

His arm and shoulder ached dully, but that wasn't the issue. He glanced down at his chest. The blood was a pool of red on the white background of his dress shirt, and spreading fast. In a few seconds it was a lake. Soon it would be an ocean.

He sank to his knees.

Man, this was dumb.

He had come in to help Susan out, a favor for old times' sake. Now he was hit, a worse injury than any he had sustained in years of combat.

People were still screaming. Their wailing sounded like sirens. Other people were crying. People crawled like worms, and like dogs. They squirmed over each other like a new birth of tadpoles—an explosion of writhing bodies.

Chairs had collapsed. There was blood all over the floor. Luke stared at the scene around him, but couldn't make sense of it.

His hands were numb. Suddenly he felt cold. That was not a good sign.

He was no longer on his knees. Now he was on his back, staring up at the ornate ceiling. There were words carved into the molding. He tried to read them.

Congress shall make no law respecting an establishment of religion, or prohibiting the free exercise thereof; or abridging the freedom of speech, or of the press; or the right of the people…

He began to fade, darkness coming in from the edges. The President was shot, maybe dying. The Vice President was definitely dead.

Was he dying? He thought maybe he was. There was no fear in that thought, but also no comfort.

The darkness spread around him. It seemed to reach for him, envelop and encase him. The scene faded.

Then it turned completely black.

CHAPTER SEVENTEEN

Timeless
Between Alive and Dead

He drifted, listening to sounds that were just beyond his hearing. There seemed to be voices murmuring somewhere nearby.

Then it seemed to him that he was sitting in a bright room, almost like the waiting room at a doctor's office, or an emergency department at a hospital. The room was cold and sterile, antiseptic. He was still wearing his tailor-made blue suit and bloodstained dress shirt. He noticed he was in a lot of pain.

There were a lot of other people in the room, sitting in chairs and facing him—row upon row of people. He was at the front, facing back toward them. The eyes watched him impassively, not angry, but not kind either. Every single person in the room was looking at him—many, many people, almost all men, but also a handful of women and children.

A woman walked by dressed in the uniform of a nurse from a bygone era—white sneakers, white skirt and blouse, white hat on top of her head.

"Excuse me," he said. "Excuse me?"

"Yes?"

He gestured around the room with his chin. "Who are all these people?"

The woman looked at him closely, her eyes narrowed. "You don't know?"

He shook his head. "No."

"These are the people you've killed. This is the waiting room, and they're waiting to see what happens to you."

He looked around the room again, all the eyes watching him, emotionless. There must be a hundred people—even more than that.

It gave him a creepy feeling, all those eyes. He wanted to get away from them.

Luke blinked, and suddenly he was in a dark place. There was a loud sound, a roaring sound, all around him. The people were gone, just like that, in an instant. He welcomed their disappearance. But there was a lot more pain here. Searing pain, tearing through his body, through his mind. He didn't welcome that.

He was on his back. He tried to get up. The pain cut through him like a knife. He was impaled on a great spike of pain. He grunted in agony.

"He's awake!" a woman shouted.

Suddenly, men with masks were around him. They tried to hold him down. He fought them, all hands. Even through the pain, his hands were much faster than theirs. He grabbed a man by the face, ripped his mask off. The man backed away before Luke could reach his throat.

Two big guys, both masked, held Luke down by the shoulders. The pain in Luke's right arm was so intense, he started to shriek. Two nearby people stepped away at the sound of it.

"We need an injection here!" a man said.

"It's coming. It's coming."

Luke felt the needle go in. Within seconds, everything changed. He took a deep breath. He relaxed. The two men holding him down slumped, but didn't get off him.

"I thought you said he was sedated."

"He was."

A man stood over him, staring down. It was the man whose mask he had ripped off. He had put on a new one. His eyes showed Luke nothing—compassion, anger, threat, nada. They were intelligent eyes, but empty. They could be looking down at an interesting science experiment.

"Where am I now?" Luke said, his voice thick and sluggish.

"You're alive, and lucky to be. I think that's probably good enough."

The darkness flowed in again, a black flood coming from all sides.

"Sleep," the man's voice said. "You're going to need it."

CHAPTER EIGHTEEN

7:14 p.m. Eastern Standard Time
The Oval Office
The White House, Washington DC

He was in, and it was easy.

Gerry the Shark stood at the edge of the crowd, watching the proceedings. Beneath the scuffed leather of his shoes was the Seal of the President of the United States. He dug his right foot into the carpet a little deeper, and slid it forward and backward.

Yes. Rub their faces in it.

Just being in here had a strange effect on him. There was something surreal, dizzying, even intoxicating about it. It was the power. It made his head feel like it was spinning on his shoulders. He could be floating up near the ceiling, like a kid on laughing gas at the dentist's office.

No, he would never be President of the United States. But it didn't matter. He was the power behind the power. He was the kingmaker. He was the architect who had made this happen. All of it—the campaign, the victory, the destruction of Susan Hopkins and her time here. He was Jefferson Monroe's brain.

He glanced around the room. Three tall windows, drapes closed, but which he knew looked out upon the Rose Garden. Near the center of the office, where he stood now, a comfortable sitting area was situated on top of the lush carpet. Ahead of him and to the left, the Resolute Desk—that long-ago gift from the British people—was near the far wall.

That's where the small throng stood, near the Resolute Desk, ready to carry out the ceremony that for two centuries had indicated the bestowing of that monstrous power that Gerry now felt surging through his body and leaking from his pores.

What was the power?

It was power over the lives of 300 million people.

Power to punish enemies and reward friends.

Power over the vast economic activity of the richest country that had ever existed.

Power over the greatest military force the world had ever seen.

Power, if he so chose, to launch a firestorm of destruction that would bring that very world to its end.

And right now that power was being handed to a dupe, a fool, the second woman President in United States history, a person so unfit for the job that if the circumstances of her elevation weren't so tragic, she would be the butt of late-night jokes for the next two months. She still might anyway.

At the desk, two men and the woman stood. Photographers snapped pictures of them, flashbulbs popping. Two video cameras were set at different angles.

One of the men at the desk was short and bald. He wore a long robe. He was Clarence Warren, Chief Justice of the United States. This was the third time he had sworn a President in during a time of crisis and emergency succession. First, he had sworn in Bill Ryan, Speaker of the House of Representatives, when Thomas Hayes had perished at Mount Weather and it was thought that Vice President Susan Hopkins was also dead. Then, the next day, he had sworn in Susan Hopkins when it turned out that Bill Ryan was one of the plotters in the coup.

Now, he would do it again, swearing in Karen White, Speaker of the House, when it was thought that Susan Hopkins was dead, and her Vice President, Marybeth Horning, was clearly dead. That last part gnawed at Gerry the Shark.

Hopkins had been shot at least three times, and had gone down. White House security had announced that she died, but where was the body? En route to the hospital, but what hospital? There had been no cooperation on this. The shooting had happened an hour ago, and Marybeth Horning's body was still in the press briefing room, surrounded by yellow tape. If Hopkins had really died, then her body should be somewhere they could see it.

Habeas corpus, wasn't that a big issue that the liberals so often wrung their hands over? This was *habeas corpus* with a whole different meaning, but even so:

Produce the body!

Another lingering question was that of Hopkins's pet black ops expert, Luke Stone. He had reappeared suddenly after an extended time... where? None of Gerry's people knew the answer to that. All they had was that he was gone, and after the election, he popped up again. People thought he had burned out and drifted away, but no one could say that for sure.

Luke Stone was a dangerous person. A man who did not take no for an answer. He didn't know how. He was a man you didn't want as your enemy. A man who Gerry would love to see lowered into the ground with full military honors. And very soon.

Stone had also been shot, but no one was saying where he was. No one had even acknowledged that he was present in the briefing room. Why was that? Was he dead, dying? Another secret. Gerry shook his head without realizing he was doing it.

Luke Stone was no one to have floating around out there, with no leash on him. There were secrets here, of course, ones that couldn't see the light of day. The Luke Stones of this world were very good at digging up things that should remain buried.

Gerry took a breath. His heart galloped along in his chest. Once they seized the reins here, he was going to find out exactly what happened to Susan Hopkins and Luke Stone. Elements of the Secret Service loyal to the previous administration were hiding that information, but very soon those people were going to find themselves under some intense questioning, more intense than they had ever considered possible.

Habeas corpus, indeed.

In Gerry's book, that was one little rule already on the chopping block, one among many. It was quite possible that a handful of White House security team members were about to become an early test case for how long people could be held without charges being filed, without access to a lawyer, and without anyone even knowing where they were. In the old days, in other kinds of countries, they used to call it "being disappeared."

Fine. He would do it—he would find Hopkins, and he would find Stone. In the meantime, he tried to focus on the ceremony. American history was being written right in front of his eyes.

He soaked in Karen White, the subject of today's festivities.

She was slightly overweight. Her cheeks were puffy. Her eyes were red from crying. She wore a garish electric blue suit with some sort of large purple gemstone tied at her throat. She wore a red hat that Gerry could only describe as a cross between a bowler and a Shriner's fez. Her clash of colors made him want to stare at the floor, but at the same time drew his eyes again and again, like a car crash unfolding in slow motion. He could not look away.

She was being sworn in as President of the United States! What in the name of God's green Earth was she wearing?

Directly across from Karen White, towering over her and holding a Bible open in his hands, was Jefferson Monroe. He wore a black suit, with a dark tie. He looked dignified and serious, his white hair swept back over the top of his head.

Just a tall, good-looking older man—a statesman, the President-elect—called to carry out a solemn duty. No, he wouldn't be sworn in today. In two months from now, on Inauguration Day, on a proper stage on the Washington Mall, in front of the Capitol Building, he would be sworn in before a crowd of hundreds of thousands, and millions more on TV and the internet.

But until that time, a caretaker would be sworn in. To Gerry, it was as good as the real thing.

Karen White's right hand was raised. Her left hand was on the Bible that Monroe held out to her. Until this moment, she had been the Representative from North Dakota, and the Speaker of the House. How had she even become Speaker? Simple. After the debacle that was Bill Ryan, the powers that be wanted someone in that position who was no threat to anyone. Someone with no ideas of her own, no urge to seize power, and no ability to wield it should events ever shove her into its path.

That was Karen White in a nutshell. She was a weak-minded fool who wore funny clothes, and even funnier hats.

"I, Karen Melinda White," she said, "do solemnly swear that I will faithfully execute the Office of President of the United States."

"And will to the best of my ability," Judge Warren prompted.

"And will to the best of my ability," White said.

"Preserve, protect, and defend the Constitution of the United States."

White repeated the words, and in the eyes of many, many people, suddenly became the most powerful person on Earth.

Gerry the Shark knew better.

CHAPTER NINETEEN

Time Unknown
Deep Underground

He was alive.

He woke with a start. Normally, he would sit straight up in bed, but the pain in his midsection and in his left upper arm were too much. Also, he didn't know where he was, or who was here, so it was better not to move just yet. Instead, he lay quietly, staring up at the rounded white ceiling.

The light was dim in this room. All of it came from recessed bulbs in the ceiling—there were no windows, and so, no natural light. He sensed someone sitting in a chair, across the room and to his left. He sensed someone else to his right.

He shifted his head to the right just a touch. A person was lying there on a cot. He turned his head fully. It was Susan. She lay on her back, head propped on a pillow, eyes closed, face serene, her body draped in a sheet. Her breathing was slow, measured. She did not seem injured in any way.

He let his mind drift back to those last moments in the press briefing room. Susan was shot, maybe three times. But he remembered how bulky she looked when she first appeared at the podium. She'd been wearing ballistic material under her clothing, and from the looks of it, something heavy.

"Are you awake?" a male voice said.

Luke didn't bother to pretend. Wherever he was, they had him. He was shot, in some pain, and on his back. He wasn't going to retake the initiative by playing dead. And anyway, they had patched him up. His entire midsection was encased in thick, hard bandages, as were his upper arm and shoulder. If they wanted to kill him, they probably wouldn't have saved him first.

"Agent Stone?"

"Yes."

"How are you feeling?"

"I've felt better."

Luke looked to his left now. Chuck Berg sat nearby in a folding chair. He still wore the standard Secret Service attire—blue suit, badge. The room they were in was stark and empty. There were these two cots side by side, Luke and Susan laid out like corpses in the morgue. Luke had an IV drip. There was some machinery on wheels, rolled up against the far wall.

"Hi, Chuck. You must be glad you didn't resign. You would have missed all the fun."

Berg shrugged. "That was fun I could have lived without. But I guess I'm on the job a little while longer."

"Where are we now?"

"We're in a private bunker in the Blue Ridge Mountains, south of Shenandoah National Park. After the Mount Weather disaster, Susan's husband had this place built as a refuge of last resort. It's small compared to a government facility, but it's modern and comfortable. We are keeping Susan's whereabouts a secret for the time being. Most people seem to think she's dead. We're trying to encourage them to think that."

"How is she?"

"Susan? She's fine. The bullet that went through your arm and hit her was a high-powered round. It lost most of its momentum, and didn't penetrate the armor she was wearing, but her upper body is plenty bruised up. Other than that? Nothing really. She's under sedation because the doctors thought it best. I imagine you know that Marybeth Horning was killed. Susan saw it happen. Marybeth was a mentor and an inspiration to Susan. She's... having a hard time absorbing it."

Luke nodded. It hurt to do even that much. He knew Horning was dead. He watched her head come apart.

"How am I?"

Berg shook his head. "Not as good as Susan, I'm afraid. They stabilized you on the helicopter, then did surgery as soon as we got here. We're in the medical facility now—the operating theatre is just a few doors down. It's okay here, not as advanced as a person with gunshot wounds might like. You lost blood, most of which has been replaced. The drip you're on now is just saline to keep you hydrated. Your arm lost a bit of bone—if you're in pain, I imagine that's most of it. You're not going to have much range of motion for a while—you might never get it all back. But you were also hit in the lower chest, and that's worse.

"It took them a couple of hours to fish all the fragments out. One of your lungs collapsed and had to be reinflated. You're on antibiotics for possible infections. They tell me you're stitched up like Frankenstein. You were running a high fever for about eighteen hours, but seem to have gotten better. You're pretty much indestructible, you know that? You're on tranquilizers yourself right now, but for some reason, you're already awake."

Luke wasn't interested in his amazing powers of recovery. People had remarked on it his entire life. He wasn't sure it even existed. Usually, he was just clever enough to avoid taking a serious hit. Also, he had swallowed Dexedrines like candy in combat zones for the past twenty years—it took a lot of drugs to have much effect on him.

"Eighteen hours?" he said, addressing the topic that did interest him. "When is it now?"

Chuck glanced at his watch. "It's a quarter to nine at night, November thirteenth. The shootings happened a little after six yesterday afternoon."

Luke thought about that. He had lost a full day.

In the past, losing time and disappearing like this might have alarmed him. He would be concerned that he should somehow contact Becca and Gunner. But Becca was dead now, and Gunner didn't want to hear from him. Amazingly, there was no one to contact. There was no one to tell that he was okay.

Luke was completely alone in the world.

"Do we know what happened?" he said.

"At the briefing room? We have pieces. Keep in mind that we're operating under the radar, so we don't have access to the normal channels. But we know the story they're putting on TV, and we know that it most likely isn't true. That story claims it was all a complete coincidence."

"A coincidence? What does that even mean?"

"There seemed to be two men working together," Chuck said. "A decoy to attract attention and draw the Secret Service away from the President, and a shooter. But they're saying it isn't true.

"The decoy, who was on the left, the heavyset one, was Paul Dobson. Thirty-seven years old, he's a stringer for several wire services. He's had a White House press pass for five years, since the Hayes administration. The story goes that he's been covering up some severe mental illness—delusions, depression, possibly a psychotic break. He pointed his cell phone at Susan, which is a very good way to get killed."

Luke remembered standing directly in front of the man, trying to block his shots at Susan. If he had been holding a real gun, Luke would be dead now.

"Dobson was captured, and what we hear is that he has harbored an obsession with Susan for years. He seems to think he was in a relationship with her. Now that she was stepping down, and that information had been leaked so thoroughly that apparently everyone in the room knew it, he was afraid he was never going to see her again. He was just trying to get her attention."

"Do you believe that?" Luke said. "He was trying to get her attention by pretending to fire a gun at her, in a room full of heavily armed Secret Service agents, one second before a real shooter started firing? That would be quite a coincidence."

Berg shook his head. "I don't believe it, but that's what they're putting out to the public. I think they were working together. Unfortunately, we have no way to prove that at this moment. What seems to back up this story is that he has no record of gun ownership, no military training, and there's no evidence out there that he knew the other shooter at all. He's just a guy who has written for newspapers since he was in college. And he's crazy."

"Who was the real shooter?" Luke said.

"Michael Benn," Chuck said. "Twenty-nine years old, former Army, discharged early for reasons that are unclear. Honorable, though."

"What division?" Luke said.

"Tenth Mountain."

"Deployments?"

"Iraq, but in a support capacity based inside the giant embassy compound we have there. He never saw combat."

"What else?"

"He'd been writing for a small, liberal-leaning news website for the past few years. The White House press people liked him, liked what he was writing. So he got into the briefing room with the big players from the *New York Times*, CNN, FOX, and the *Washington Post*. They do that—they sprinkle some friendlies in, no matter how small-time. It guarantees decent coverage and at least a couple of softball questions. We vetted him. I don't remember anything in the file to suggest a threat. Just a young guy, a veteran, with a decent record and ambitions to become a newspaper reporter. Now this. A bloodbath. It doesn't make sense."

"How did he get the gun inside the White House?" Luke said.

Berg stared at Luke a long minute. He shook his head. "He didn't. There's no way he could have. You can't walk into the White House briefing room with a gun. You'd never even come close."

"Do you know what you're saying?"

Berg nodded. "It was an inside job. Someone brought the gun in for him. One of our people. One of *my* people."

Luke thought back to the Secret Service agent who seemed to step out of the way when the shooting started. Would he recognize that guy if he saw him again? You bet he would. And the guy would wish he hadn't.

"What happens next?"

"Do you feel like walking?" Berg said.

"If I can manage it."

"Then come take a look."

CHAPTER TWENTY

9:45 p.m. Eastern Standard Time
South of Canal Street
Chinatown, New York City

"They've started."

His name was Weng Kaibo. Here in the United States, he went by the name Michael. Michael Wing. It was easier for the Americans to deal with this. Many Chinese living in the West did it—reverse the order of the names, and change them to something more familiar. He had stuck with his real name for a while, but he grew tired of people calling him "Mr. Kaibo."

He gazed out his fourth-story window at the activity going on down in the street. He and his family lived just a few blocks south of Canal Street, the historic northern border of Chinatown.

One block away from here a fence was going up. There was a construction crew out there, protected by the police. Of course the police. The Chinese were dangerous now. Two Chinese gangsters had killed the Gathering Storm protestors two nights ago. Of course, dozens of Gathering Storm thugs had attacked helpless people in the street. They had demolished storefront windows. And one night later, a white man had killed the President and the Vice President. But it was the Chinese who must be fenced in.

The lights at the construction site were very bright, and the sounds were very loud. The heavy trucks rumbled, shaking the ground the smallest amount. Wing could feel his building trembling beneath his feet. When the trucks went backward, they emitted a high-pitched beeping noise that cut through all other sounds. BEEP... BEEP... BEEP...

Wing was glad that he lived a block away. People living at the end of the street must feel they were inside a nightmare right now.

Wing was inside the nightmare, too. He knew that.

The men had dug a narrow trench over there. And slowly they were erecting a fence. The bottom of the fence fit into the trench. As he watched, a group of men tilted the high fence up, guided it into the trench, then stood it up tall. As the men held it up, other men came and filled in the trench again, pouring wet concrete to stabilize it.

Wing found that he was fascinated by the work being conducted. He could stare at it all night and never look away. He was watching himself become a prisoner, and it was happening in slow motion. Not just himself—his wife, his two children, all his neighbors, his extended family and his friends. Everyone. Everyone was being imprisoned.

The fence was a see-through metal hurricane fence, maybe two stories high. It would not be hard for a young man to climb up and over. This suggested to Wing that the fence was only temporary, a fast and imperfect solution that would nevertheless be an effective cage for most of the people. And something more permanent would be along soon enough.

As he watched, another length of the tall fence tilted upward. The work seemed to happen slowly, but in fact the fence was going up rapidly. Ten crews as diligent as this one could probably encircle the entire neighborhood by dawn.

He turned back inside the apartment.

His wife sat on the sofa with their youngest child—the girl, Kira—on her lap. They both stared absently at flickering images on the TV.

"Everyone must report to the public school to get electronic bracelets fastened to their ankles," his wife said. "Starting tomorrow. We are to be monitored, even the children. We will be charged a small tax for each bracelet. It is not very much—ten dollars per week, a total of forty dollars each week for our family."

Wing shook his head. "Rumors. I don't believe it."

She shrugged. "You thought the fence was a rumor."

He said nothing. It was true. Until just a few hours ago, he had dismissed the idea of a fence. All day, he had dismissed it to anyone who would listen. "They will never build a fence," he said. "This is America. It's impossible."

His wife went on mechanically, not even looking up. The colors from the television lit upon her face. "If you do not arrive to receive the bracelet within two days, it will be assumed that you are a criminal, and you will be subject to arrest. Perhaps you are in the country illegally, or are wanted by the police. Only a criminal would not want his location known."

"We will not wear bracelets," Wing said. "I will go back to China before I see anyone in my family wear a bracelet."

She looked at him now, her eyes cold and dead. She was so beautiful, and the look in her eyes shattered his heart. He did not know if he would ever be able to pick up all the pieces. How would he protect her? How would he protect their children?

"What makes you think they will let you leave?" she said.

CHAPTER TWENTY ONE

10:15 p.m. Eastern Standard Time
Deep Underground
Blue Ridge Mountains, Virginia

"Tim Rutledge has been arrested."

Luke limped into a small, ultra-modern command center, walking with an aluminum cane. He wore surgical scrubs and a pair of cheap flip-flops on his feet. He also wore an orange fuzzy sweater—it was cold down here. His taped-up midsection was impossibly sore—it felt like he would never bend at the waist again. His left arm throbbed, even through the painkillers. Next to him, Chuck Berg seemed like the picture of health and vitality.

Kurt Kimball looked up as they entered. He seemed very much himself—tall, bald, strong, in dress pants and dress shirt and a blue windbreaker jacket. The only thing about him that belied the circumstances was the dark rings under his eyes.

"Here comes the hero team," he said. "The two men who once again saved the President's life."

"We call it winning ugly," Chuck said.

Luke didn't say a word. Any uglier a victory and he'd be dead.

"Hello, Agent Stone," Kurt said. "I didn't realize you were even awake. Up and about already?"

Luke shrugged stiffly. "I thought I'd check the place out. You know, take the grand tour. Then Chuck and I are going to do some wrestling. After that, maybe some wind sprints in the corridors."

The room was white, oval-shaped, with an oval conference table. Kat Lopez was here, and some young staffers. It was a small group, half a dozen people. There was a large flat video monitor at the head of the table, with smaller ones embedded in the table at each seat placement.

"What's the situation?" Luke said.

"The world has been turned on its head," Kurt said. "Care to sit down? I'll give you the rundown."

Luke settled gingerly into one of the conference chairs. "You guys have anything to eat?" he said. "Seems like a while since I've been fed."

"We have premade sandwiches," an aide said. "Chicken salad. Tuna salad. They're not bad. Small bags of chips. Cans of soda or bottles of water. Coffee."

89

Luke made his order. Basically, all of it. He looked at Kurt.

"I'm ready."

Behind Kurt, his screen came alive. "We are in hiding down here," he began. "We are going on the assumption, unproven thus far, that the shootings in the press briefing room were a decapitation strike carried out by Jefferson Monroe's organization. The intent was to eliminate Susan and Marybeth Horning, and thus install the third in line of Presidential succession, the Speaker of the House, as the new Acting President."

"The Speaker is…" Luke said.

"Karen White of North Dakota. Fifty-four years old, unmarried, from a safe Republican district, and with a wholly unremarkable career as a Representative. She has mostly been known for her eccentric fashion sense. She took the Oath of Office sometime last night. Since then, Monroe and his minions moved into the White House and have the run of the place. We assume that she is little more than their puppet."

"Your assumptions seem to have some basis in reality."

"Yes."

"What have they been doing since they took over?" Luke said.

"More than you might imagine anyone could do in less than thirty hours. They have quietly pulled the plug on the White House investigation into election fraud and voter suppression. They have declared Susan dead, and claimed that they are keeping her body in an undisclosed location in preparation for a state funeral."

Luke thought about it for a few seconds. He found that he was easing into this. Until the shooting, he had been skeptical of Susan's claims of a stolen election. And it hadn't mattered that much to him—politics were politics. They didn't interest him. Conservative President, liberal President. Ebb and flow. Things changed, the people got fed up, and things changed back. Meanwhile the republic lumbered along, most of it on a sort of autopilot run by the vast federal bureaucracy and state-level politicians.

But this? This was different.

"They have to do that," he said. "Susan being dead legitimizes their early takeover."

Kurt nodded. "Yes."

"Which suggests that they know she's alive, but just don't know where."

"Bingo."

"Which also suggests they're looking for us."

Kurt nodded again. "Naturally."

Luke looked around the room. "We should get out of here."

Kat Lopez was standing now. She shook her head. "Logistically, it would be very hard. We can't even use our cell phones for fear of being detected by ECHELON, the NSA's data-mining operation. The way this bunker is set up is essentially as a satellite location of Pierre Michaud's company. The phones are rerouted extensions of his office in suburban DC. The emails are internal communications. Everything is firewalled from outside penetration. If we try to move, we will call attention to ourselves. Anyway, there's nowhere else to go, certainly nowhere near as secure as this. Security is such a major concern that although Pierre knows we're here, he hasn't made any move to come here yet. In fact, he's still in California, in an undisclosed location. His representatives are making official inquiries about Susan's body."

"What happens when they find us?" Luke said. "When someone in the know leaks the information?"

Kat just shrugged. "We haven't gotten that far yet."

"There is reason to believe they're working on exactly that," Kurt said. "Several members of Chuck's White House security team have been arrested, all on suspicion of helping the shooter get his gun inside the White House. Haley Lawrence, Susan's former Secretary of Defense, has also been arrested, but we know he didn't help the shooter. And so has Tim Rutledge, Susan's campaign manager."

"They're going to try to work them over until they give up our location," Kat said.

Luke nodded. "Do any of them have this location?"

"A couple of my people do," Berg said. "But they'll hold out a long time before they divulge it."

Luke let that one go. He imagined Chuck had never seen anyone waterboarded before. Anyway, they probably hadn't gotten to that point yet—waterboarding Secret Service agents was a big step to take. If they had taken it, this place would already be crawling with Jefferson Monroe's goon squad.

"What else is happening?" he said.

Video footage appeared on the monitor. The screen was split into four quadrants, each one showing a construction scene.

"Immediately upon assuming office, they started erecting barriers around Chinatowns in four major cities—New York, Boston, San Francisco, and Los Angeles. It was one of Monroe's major campaign promises, and he's making good on it right away. Earlier today, they began implementing a surveillance protocol—residents of the Chinatowns will have to wear digital monitoring devices on their ankles, much like those worn by individuals remanded by the courts to house arrest.

"Residents of the Chinatowns will have to apply for permits to leave the neighborhood, and their whereabouts will always be known. The precedent for these moves, obviously, are the Jewish ghettos imposed by the Nazis during World War II, and the yellow stars the Jews were forced to wear to identify them. All of it updated for the modern era, of course. They've also declared that they're going to issue a ruling on the Chinese island-building in the South China Sea, sometime in the next twenty-four hours."

"A ruling?" Luke said.

"That's what they're calling it."

"That's what they do in Iran and Saudi Arabia," Luke said. "They issue rulings."

It was shocking to imagine these things happening in the United States. To the extent he thought about issues of this nature, what he'd been fighting for all these years was to protect an open and free society. Not autocrats who holed up inside the White House and issued *fatwas* against their many enemies.

He shrugged to himself. The changes wouldn't stand. He wouldn't allow them to. He would die fighting them, if need be.

"What else?" he said.

A video image appeared of Don Morris leaving the federal supermax facility in Colorado. The Rocky Mountains loomed in the background as Don, dressed in a blue suit, stepped into a waiting black limousine.

"Karen White pardoned several of the Mount Weather conspirators today, including your old boss Don Morris. There is even talk of releasing Bill Ryan, though they haven't done that yet. The public outcry would be too large."

"Do they have ties to that conspiracy?" Luke said.

Kurt shook his head. "We don't think so. We think instead that they are simply seeking to undermine the legitimacy of Susan's rule. If the conspirators are no longer guilty, then Susan never should have become President."

For a moment, Luke had the sense of staring across the Grand Canyon. The scope of their audacity was breathtaking.

"What ties do they have to the shooter?" he said.

"None that we know of. The shooter himself is a bit of a mystery. We know he was in the military starting at eighteen, but his early life is murky, to say the least. It seems he was taken from his mother by Child Protective Services when he was a boy, and that he bounced around in foster homes and child welfare facilities.

Most of those records have either been lost because they were from before computerization, or they've been expunged. But there are large time gaps in his childhood, his military service, and his adulthood that need to be filled in. If we had that information, we believe we'd have a clearer picture of what the relationship is."

"What are they saying about him?" Luke said.

"That he was a fan of Susan's," Kat Lopez said.

"That's great," Luke said. "Another number one fan, pointing a gun at her."

"The story goes that when he found out how corrupt she was, and how she had murdered Patrick Norman, he was so bitterly disappointed in her that he decided to kill her. Apparently, he had been viciously criticizing her around his office the past twenty-four hours. It was quite a turn-around for a man who had spent the past two years singing her praises in print."

Luke began to see what his role here might be. Perhaps Kurt was leading him to the realization. If they could tie the shooter to Jefferson Monroe, they could take down his Presidency. If they couldn't, there wasn't much hope of doing anything. Certainly not while hiding underground.

"You think Michael Benn was a plant of some kind. A mole, sitting and waiting for the order to kill Susan. And the other guy was sent to run interference for him."

Kurt nodded. "We think it's possible."

"Why would Benn sacrifice himself?" Luke said. "Really, why would either of them do it? It's one thing to be a mole, but it's quite another to go on a suicide mission. You don't waltz into a room, shoot at the President and Vice President, and expect to waltz back out again. Whether you get killed or not, your life is over either way."

Kurt shrugged now, but said nothing. Luke looked around the room. Susan's people were all staring at him.

"You want me to go out there and find out," Luke said.

"If you're up for it," Kat Lopez said. "You look pretty banged up, but if you think you still have it in you, you're obviously the best chance we've got."

Luke saw the truth in that. He had been out of the game for two years, but the bench was not very deep right now. He wasn't going to win a track meet any time soon, but he still had resources available to him, people he could call on. And the other side had no reason to suspect he was coming.

Even so, there might be an easier way.

"Why not just produce Susan?' he said. "Go to the media first, tell them Susan is still alive, and simply reverse the decision putting Karen White in charge?"

Kurt shook his head. "We wish it was that simple. One of the first things they did was fire the Attorney General and most of the upper tier of the Justice Department. Earlier today, the new Acting Deputy Attorney General issued a posthumous indictment of Susan on conspiracy and murder charges in the death of Patrick Norman. Even in death, they plan to investigate her role in the murder. If Susan resurfaces, she's going to be arrested."

"Now who would want to arrest me?" a voice said.

They all turned. Susan Hopkins, dressed very similarly to Luke, except with a wool coat over her surgical scrubs instead of an orange sweater, stood in the open doorway.

"Susan, you shouldn't be up yet," Kat Lopez said.

Susan sighed heavily. "But I am. I'm up."

"How are you feeling?"

She ran a hand through her hair. "Like I got hit by a Mack truck."

* * *

"Susan, I think you need to get out of here."

She stared at him, her big doe eyes haunted and afraid. It was the most vulnerable he had ever seen her look.

They were inside a bedroom in the living area of the bunker. The room was impersonal, even cold, with a full-size bed on a metal frame, a couple of accent chairs, a table, and a square rug on the floor. There was no lamp—all the lights in this entire facility were recessed in the ceiling. It seemed like a place a person might live in for an eternity—more like a space age prison cell than a room.

Susan sat on the edge of the bed. "Why would I do that?"

Luke shrugged, standing just across from her. "Too many people know about this place. Some of Chuck's people know about it, and they've been arrested. They are in what amounts to Jefferson Monroe's custody at this moment. They're not going to hold out forever. The doctors and nurses that treated both of us—they're not here. They left. I'm not blaming anyone, but that was foolish to let them go. People talk."

Luke was making one last try to talk some sense into her. This argument had gone nowhere with her people an hour ago. He was convinced they had to leave, and yet they all wanted to stay put. They felt safe here. But they weren't safe.

"Will you at least think about it?" he said. "If you decide it's time to leave, they will listen to you."

She nodded, but it was half-hearted. "I will think about it."

Luke himself was leaving in a few minutes.

They had gotten him some clothes from somewhere. A pair of jeans, a shirt and hunting jacket, a pair of boots that fit. Kurt Kimball or Kat Lopez had obviously been thinking ahead. Pierre's people had dropped him a car for when he went topside, the keys on top of the tire on the front passenger side. He even had the name of a doctor he could visit to get his wounds cared for and his dressings changed.

All he had to go on was the name of the shooter—Michael Benn—and the story of his recent past. It was enough. It was a start, anyway. He could build from here.

He was in a lot of pain, despite having taken more painkillers. The pain was okay, he decided. It would slow him down physically, but it would keep his mind sharp and alert. It would be hard to sleep through this kind of pain.

Susan shivered. She was still wearing the surgical scrubs, and it was cold down here. The chill never seemed to leave.

"Do you think they're trying to kill me?"

"You don't need me to tell you the answer to that," Luke said.

She shook her head. "No, I don't."

Her breath hitched, and she started to tremble. "I don't think I can take it anymore, Luke. You know, the first time, when you and I met, it almost broke me. The thought that someone was trying to kill me... I nearly shattered into pieces. But this time, it feels so much closer. And Marybeth..."

"It's okay," Luke said.

"No, it isn't. We were never supposed to be in the same place together, and I invited her to that stupid press conference. I got her killed, do you realize that? I didn't mean to, but I did. You can never let your guard down, Luke. Not even for one minute. You can never..." Her voice trailed off.

Her face broke up now, and she hugged herself, but she didn't cry.

Luke didn't think—he acted. He went to her, sat on the bed next to her, and put his arms around her shoulders. She was much shorter than he was, maybe by half a foot. She stiffened at his embrace, but then slowly relaxed into it. She let out a forceful exhalation, as if she'd been holding her breath for a very long time.

"You saved my life again," she said. "And this time you got shot because of it. I don't know how I'm ever going to thank you."

"It's okay," he said. "People always tell me I'm bulletproof."

Susan was shaking all over now. She turned to him, reached her arms around his back, and pulled herself even closer. They squeezed together, body to body.

That was the moment Luke felt everything change.

No longer was their relationship professional.

Now, it was something else. Something personal—more personal than he'd ever imagined. It was surreal. He, and the President of the United States.

"I've wanted this," she said. "For a long time, I've wanted this."

"I have, too," he said, and he realized the truth of it. The words amazed him.

"I don't know if it's a good idea," she said.

Luke didn't know either. But his hands did. They moved along her back and found the gaps in her hospital clothes—they found her bare skin. They went slow. She pushed herself even closer to him, and now she cried quietly against his chest. She started to move her body against him.

He didn't know if he was ready for this, and he didn't know if the timing was right. He'd better know soon, because in a moment it would be too late to stop.

An intercom buzzer sounded.

"Susan?" a woman's voice said.

Susan breathed deeply and stopped what she was doing. She pulled gently away from Luke and flipped a black switch in the wall near the bed. Just above the switch was a red button—an alarm, in all likelihood.

"Yes, Kat?"

"We need you to come back to the conference room, if you can."

"What is it?"

"The White House has just issued their ruling on the South China Sea islands."

Luke thought about that—why would they issue it in the middle of the night? Because it was daytime in China? Because people in the United States were already asleep or on their way to bed?

"Is it bad?" Susan said.

There was a long pause over the intercom line.

"Kat?"

"It's the start of the apocalypse," Kat said.

* * *

The car was a disgrace.

It was a late-model, dark-blue four-door sedan, totally forgettable—not the kind of car Luke ever got the urge to drive. It probably topped out around eighty miles per hour.

It was parked at the end of a dirt track, surrounded by a copse of dense woods, about a quarter-mile walk from the entrance to the bunker. In the dark of night, he could barely see it until he was almost on top of it. The keys were resting on top of the tire on the front passenger side, just where they were supposed to be.

No one would ever look twice at this car. Pierre's people had dropped it here sometime in the past couple of hours. Inside the glove box, Luke knew he would find a blank white key card, which would open the door to room 528 at the high-rise Sheraton Hotel in Arlington—not quite DC, but close enough. He had the room as long as he needed, and the key would also get him the garage entrance—he would never have to speak to the people at the front desk.

In the glove box, there would also be a permit to use the hotel garage, and half a dozen throwaway cell phones with prepaid minutes.

Beneath the front passenger seat, there was going to be a loaded Glock nine-millimeter handgun, with two more fully loaded magazines lying next to it. In the trunk, under the carpet, in what should be the wheel well for the spare tire, there was going to be a Remington 870 pump shotgun, with a couple of boxes of ammo and three flash bang grenades.

These things were a start. He could pick up more as he went along. He glanced around at the woods. The air was crisp. It was a cool night in the mountains, bordering on cold. But things were about to get a whole lot hotter.

He slid gingerly into the driver's seat. He opened the utility box on the dashboard that once upon a time would have been called an "ashtray." Inside was a prescription for morphine-based painkillers. It was on the stationery of a doctor in Alexandria who would see him at a moment's notice, night or day, to change his dressings or deal with any other medical issues. The man's cell phone number was written in careful block handwriting on the back of the prescription.

Luke reached slowly between his legs to the floor mat. He pulled up the edge—here was a thick envelope. He opened it and found what was promised—$10,000 in cash, mostly tens, twenties, and fifties, but also plenty of ones and fives. No hundreds. He had requested that specifically. A hundred-dollar bill, even in this day and age, called attention to itself.

"Okay," he said. "This is good."

He was on his own. Once he left here, he had no plans to come back, and no way of contacting them directly.

He eased the car back along the track until it became a narrow paved road. He followed that to the tall iron gate. It opened for him automatically, sliding sideways, then closing behind him. The lock mechanism came together with an audible CLANG.

He glanced back at the property. There were high concrete walls all around it, topped by fencing, itself topped by looping razor wire. DANGER, said signs placed on the wall every twenty or thirty yards. HIGH VOLTAGE.

It was impossible to tell from the outside what the place was. A person who found their way here might think it was an electricity-generating plant, or some kind of chemical storage facility.

What would a spook think, though, watching this place from the sky?

He followed the winding road down the mountain, then drove side roads for an hour, heading gradually to the north and east. He felt calm, and it was a pleasant enough drive, hill country giving way to small farms.

He turned on the radio, dialed it in to a news station. A woman's voice gave him the bad news, news he already knew from Kurt Kimball.

"President Karen White tonight issued a ruling that declared China must immediately abandon its artificial islands in the South China Sea, or face attack from the United States. Evacuation of the islands must begin in the next forty-eight hours. If American planes don't detect large-scale evacuations underway by that time, then the United States is prepared to destroy the islands using tactical nuclear weapons launched from American warships in the area. The Chinese government responded, calling the American demands a dangerous provocation, and further asserting that the islands are Chinese territory. Here is Chinese Foreign Minister, Li Tse Tung, speaking at a hastily organized news conference in London this morning."

The voice changed to that of a man. "China is a sovereign nation, and had interests and territories in the South China Sea many centuries before the United States came into being. We will not abandon those territories, or forsake those interests, at the command of the United States, or anyone. President White is flirting with a confrontation that can only end in disaster for all involved."

The woman announcer came back on. "In Tokyo, the Nikkei Index plunged on the news of the American announcement. And in London, the FTSE Index was poised to begin the day dramatically lower than yesterday's close. Meanwhile, overnight the Canadian immigration website was overwhelmed with traffic and crashed for the second time in as many days. A Canadian immigration official, speaking on condition of anonymity, suggested that the country intended to freeze its immigration procedures, accepting no new applications for a period of up to six months."

Luke turned it off. If the US launched tactical nuclear strikes against China, no one was going to escape the aftermath by moving to Canada.

He drove on in silence.

After a while, he began to sense civilization growing closer. He parked in a paved lot above a small river. A hundred yards upriver from him, there was an old covered bridge—this would be a scenic spot in the daytime.

He took one of the cell phones from the glove box. Might as well take a chance now and burn one. It was time to get started. He pulled himself out of the car and stepped to the river's edge. Just sitting in the car for an hour had stiffened up his body dramatically.

Even so, he felt good.

The phone rang three times.

"Hello?" Mark Swann said. His voice sounded uncertain, even paranoid. He was awake at three a.m., the world was ending, and someone was calling him on the telephone.

"Mr. Helu?" Luke said. "Albert Helu?"

"Yes."

"Do you know who this is?"

"Yes," Swann said. "I do."

"Have you been following the news since last we spoke?"

"Of course."

"Are you ready to work?"

There was a pause over the line. For a second, Luke thought Swann might have hung up on him.

"Albert?"

"Is there something I don't know? About what happened? Something they aren't showing?"

99

Luke nodded, but of course Swann couldn't see a nod. "Yes."

"In that case, I'm ready."

"Good. I need you. You're the best there is. Okay?"

"Okay."

Luke had to be careful here. ECHELON was listening. It was sifting through millions of phone calls, texts, direct messages, and emails. It would trip over certain words and phrases, then focus in like a shark. In short order, it could trigger satellite and drone cameras. Once they picked him, up they were not going to put him down. Luke did not want that.

"The man. You know the one. He has a name. My hunch is more than one. Answer yes or no. Do you know that name?"

"Yes."

"I need everything. Where has it been? Who does it know? Who knows it? More than anything, I need to know why."

"Okay. I think I can get you that."

"Good man," Luke said. "But don't think you can. Know it."

"Naturally."

"Next order of business," Luke said. The phone call was already running long for his tastes.

"Yes."

"Our old friend. The big man. Where is he?"

There was another hesitation over the line.

"He's ah, on the campus. Between jobs overseas. Teaching a couple of classes in the meantime."

Luke nodded. The big man, of course, was Ed Newsam. The campus was the FBI training facility and headquarters at Quantico.

Good enough.

"You think he'll be surprised to see me?" Luke said.

"I was," Swann said.

"Thanks, Albert."

"Please," Swann said. "Call me Al."

Luke smiled and hung up the phone. He glanced around the parking lot. Still no one here but himself. He opened the back of the phone and pulled the battery out. Then he dropped the phone on the ground and stepped on it. He stomped it, shattering the glass and crushing the components. He stomped it again, the black plastic casing cracking into fragments. After another minute of this, he scooped up the whole mess and threw it all into the river. He pocketed the battery—he would toss it out the window on the highway.

One cell phone was cooked.

Five more to go.

CHAPTER TWENTY TWO

November 13
7:05 a.m. Eastern Standard Time
Quantico, Virginia

Luke was tired.

He leaned against a gleaming black Hummer H3 parked at a McDonald's two miles from the gate of the Quantico training grounds. He had gotten a few hours' sleep in his hotel room, but not nearly enough. Coffee wasn't going to cut it today.

The parking lot was nearly empty. The restaurant had just opened five minutes before. Luke had arrived here one minute ago. He had looked over the other available cars—a tiny, beat-up Toyota Tercel, and an even smaller Mazda—and he guessed that this giant Hummer was the right one.

Ed Newsam walked out of the McDonald's wearing a brown leather jacket, carrying two large white paper bags in one hand and a cup of coffee in the other.

Ed was big—that was the first thing the eye took in. Watching him cross the parking lot was like watching a storm move in. He was a black man, mid-thirties, hair shorn very close to the scalp, close-cropped beard, stacked and chiseled, with a chest that seemed four feet wide, arms at least twenty inches around, legs even more. He looked like he'd be hell in a gunfight, and even worse in a street fight. Luke happened to know it was true—every word of it.

Ed moved fluidly, even with a little spring in his step—he wasn't tired at all.

As he approached the car, he spotted Luke leaning there. He did a double-take, like he was seeing a mirage, or a ghost. Luke watched as Ed's eyes fixated on the aluminum cane in Luke's hand.

Luke indicated the bags in Ed's left hand. "They make you pick up breakfast for the whole office?"

Ed smiled. "This is my breakfast."

Now Luke smiled. "I know."

Ed nodded at the cane. "That's some accessory."

Luke shrugged. "I got shot."

Ed nodded. "I watch TV, brother. I know you got shot. I mean the cane itself. Not exactly stylish, you feel me? Looks like something my grandma used to gimp along on. She also wore a certain type of hosiery for her varicose veins."

"Well, I'm not wearing those," Luke said.

Ed stopped a few feet short of Luke. He stared at him a moment, more fully taking him in. Then he glanced around the parking lot, as if trying to spot something he had missed before.

"How did you find me?"

"I guessed."

"You guessed?"

Luke shrugged. "Sure. You're at Quantico. Knowing you, you probably come into work early." He gestured at the McDonald's with his chin. "I've seen you inhale two thousand calories' worth of this stuff in one sitting. So I figure that's where you catch breakfast. Once I got here, picking the car was easy."

Ed's eyes narrowed. Luke could tell he didn't completely believe it, not all of it. "I might have used the drive-through."

Luke shook his head. "And miss a chance to flirt with the girls behind the counter? I doubt it."

Ed smiled again. "You know me a little too well." He gestured at the Hummer. "You want to take a ride?"

Luke nodded. "Yeah."

They drove away from the gates at Quantico. Five minutes later, Ed pulled into the parking lot of a little league baseball park. Three baseball diamonds stretched away into the distance, small rings of bleachers surrounding them. Ed was parked near the backstop of the first ball field.

He opened his bag of food, pulled out a stack of white Styrofoam containers, and opened one of them. It was a hotcake and sausage breakfast, the triple stack. Ed poured a container of light brown syrup on top of the mountain of pancakes and the dark brown sausage, which was cut into a circular shape. Slowly, methodically, he began to demolish the food using white plastic utensils that looked so fragile, they might disintegrate in his hands. He didn't offer anything to Luke.

He finished the first stack in a few moments, then opened the next one.

"How's your cholesterol?" Luke said. "Ever get it checked?"

Ed shook his head. "Why don't you start?" he said.

Luke shrugged. "Okay." He wasn't quite sure how to do that, so he decided to dive right in. "I'm working for the President."

"Karen White?" Ed said. "Jefferson Monroe?"

Luke shook his head. "Susan Hopkins."

Ed turned to look at Luke. He stopped chewing.

Luke nodded. "Yes. She's alive. The last time I saw her was about six hours ago. She's not even injured. Not really."

102

Ed stared straight ahead now, his eyes scanning the empty fields. "She's not the President anymore."

"Not at the moment, no."

"So what are you doing for her?"

Luke took a deep breath. "I'm investigating the attempt on her life, and the assassination of Marybeth Horning."

"Aren't people already doing that?"

Luke felt the friction here, the resistance. Ed knew what Luke was doing, but he was going to make him say it out loud. And once it was out there, where they both could see it, what was Ed going to say?

"No one is looking at it from the angle I'm taking," Luke said.

"Which is?"

"The shooter was working for Jefferson Monroe and his organization. They knew that Susan was about to step down, so they killed her replacement, and they tried to kill Susan herself."

"Why would they do that?" Ed said. "She's stepping down and leaving a newbie in her place—and in a couple of months they'll have the White House anyway."

"The reason they did it was to stop the federal investigation into the election fraud and voter suppression that tilted the results in Monroe's favor. Marybeth Horning was going to continue it. As of yesterday, they've halted it."

Ed smiled and shook his head. He seemed to look far away now, past the ball fields, to a place that once existed, but no longer did. His eyes almost seemed to rim with water. Almost, but not quite.

"My man," he said. "Where you been, Luke? I missed you."

"I went away for a while," Luke said. "I had some things to figure out."

"Did you figure them?"

Luke shook his head. "I don't really know."

Ed sighed heavily. "I wish I could help you, I really do. We did some great things together. But I'll tell you, I've been on nine missions abroad since the last time I even saw you. A couple of those jobs were months long, with deep cover. I've moved on, and the SRT seems like a lifetime ago now. I'm a commander with the Hostage Rescue Team, and I'm mentoring young hotshots just breaking in with us. I'm seeing my little girls regularly for the first time in too long—and they're not as little as they used to be. I know what you're asking… and you're asking me to risk a lot. Everything, basically."

"Ed—"

103

"It doesn't even make sense, you know that? The things you're saying? They don't make sense. I mean okay, you suddenly reappear after two years, just in time to get shot on national television. Then you turn up and ruin my breakfast because you want me to drop everything and come on a mission—seems like old times, right, Ed? Except it doesn't seem like old times at all. You flaked hard, you know that? You left people—me—in the lurch."

Luke nodded. "I know I did. I'm sorry."

"The SRT would have been something else with you in command, it would have been hot as hell, but you decided to let it die so you could wander off into the desert for forty years. The rest of us stayed behind and continued to build our lives. No. We *rebuilt* our lives, Luke. I could almost forgive that part, the fact that you flaked, that you let something important drop. You had your reasons."

He paused for a moment.

"But what you're saying now doesn't add up. It makes no sense. You want to tell me that the shooter, who was a Susan Hopkins supporter for years, walked into the White House and opened fire because Jefferson Monroe, or his people, paid him to do it? He went on a suicide mission, no chance of escape—death or life in prison were his only options—for money?"

Luke shook his head. "I'm not saying he did it for money. I don't know why he did it. But he didn't act alone, I know that. There was another shooter one second ahead of him."

"A crazy person," Ed said. "Who didn't even have a real gun, and there's no evidence they knew each other."

"How did the real shooter get the gun in?" Luke said.

Ed shrugged. "I don't know the answer to that. But the Bureau proper and the DC Metro cops are investigating it. I'm sure they'll come up with something. And when they do, it'll turn out to be something people have been overlooking for years. A head-smacker—I can't believe we didn't think of that."

"Is this what you want?" Luke said. "The things that are going on right now? Cages being built around Chinatowns? Jefferson Monroe to become President?"

Ed raised an index finger. "Now that's a different story. But I don't go on an operation to topple the man just because I don't like him. You know the game. He got voted in, one day he'll get voted out. Or he won't. But life will go on just the same. He'll be gone sooner or later, no matter what he does. And all the stupid things he did will start to get undone the minute the next President is sworn in."

"They're planning tactical nuke strikes in less than two days from now."

"Saber-rattling," Ed said. "That's all it is. They think Susan looked weak on China. They want to look strong."

"Ed…" Luke said, but he didn't know what the next words should be. *When did you become so cautious? When did you decide your career was more important than your country?*

When did you become such a grown-up?

"Say, man," Ed said. "Let me drop you back. I got to be at work in a little while. I like to get in early, get my head together before the day starts."

"Okay," Luke said.

Ed looked at him for a long minute. "It's been good seeing you, Luke. It really has. Whatever you decide to do, I wish you the best with it."

* * *

"Did you talk to the big man?" Mark Swann said into Luke's ear.

"Yes. I just left there."

"What did he say?"

"He said no."

"No?"

"He's not interested."

Luke was driving north on Interstate 95 back toward DC. Traffic was beginning to slow down and back up as he approached the city. The people ahead of him kept tapping their brakes. Brake lights came on, brake lights went off.

He was trying to make this call at high speed, and in an area crowded with cell phone calls, on the off chance someone tried to intercept it. If things slowed down enough, he would get off at the next exit, turn around, and head south again. Traffic was barreling along at a good clip over in the southbound lanes.

"Wow. That kind of surprises me."

Luke nodded. "Me too. But let's get past that. What do you have for me?"

"What I've got is a man of mystery."

"Do tell."

"The person who interests us…" Swann began.

The words *Michael Benn* floated across Luke's mind, but he didn't say a word.

105

"Had a funny habit of disappearing, then turning up somewhere else, sometimes with a different name. He was taken from his mother at the age of six, because of unspecified abuse or neglect happening in the home. I won't say where. He had a sister who was three years older, and who I've been unable to locate. She was also taken from the home. She also had a name, and that name dropped off the map years ago.

"But back to our boy. He was placed in foster care right away, and there was a record of a foster family having him for six months. Then he was taken from that family for unspecified reasons, was placed in a child welfare facility, and disappeared."

"Disappeared?" Luke said. "In what sense?"

"In the sense that he was gone, and there is no record of where he went. That could be because of poor record-keeping at the time, but we're talking about the 1980s here. Things were already going digital. When he reappears, it is three years later, and he's at a home for mentally ill children. In Canada."

Luke didn't like the sound of that. The call was already getting too specific. Much more of this kind of talk, and they were going to start tripping some keywords. Still, he needed to know.

"What was its name?"

Swann didn't say a word.

"Albert? Just do it."

"Allen Memorial Institute. It's a hospital affiliated with McGill University in Montreal."

Alarms went off in Luke's head. It sounded too much like something—something very dark, something from the distant past, something that was supposed to have gone away, and something that Luke knew almost nothing about. But ECHELON would know, and ECHELON would be listening for any reference to it.

Luke dared not speak its name. Not now, and not over the phone. But it was a lead, and he had an idea how to find out more.

"Albert?" he said again.

"Yes."

"It's getting kind of hot in here. I think I need to cool off a bit."

"In that case," Swann said, "I'll hang up and chat with you another time."

"Keep digging," Luke said.

"I will."

The line went dead. The cars up ahead had come to a complete standstill. Washington, DC, traffic—it was one thing Luke sure hadn't missed. He glided to a stop and looked at the phone in his hand.

He had to get rid of this thing.

CHAPTER TWENTY THREE

8:29 a.m. Eastern Daylight Time
The West Wing
The White House, Washington DC

It was all wonderful fun for Gerry the Shark.

His heart was beating faster than it had in a long, long time. It was amazing what a little brinksmanship could do to ramp up the excitement.

The generals were nervous about bombing the Chinese. The President-elect was uncertain that they had the legal right to detain and imprison Chinese people in the United States—he felt maybe it was a step too far. And the Acting President appeared to be having a nervous breakdown.

Gerry the Shark alone felt completely on top of things. Oh, he was stressed out, all right. And his mind was racing. After all, he was human, just like anyone else. But it was good stress.

When he was a kid, things would sometimes go to the edge. Breaking and entering, gang fights, beat-downs. There were people in those days who could hang with it, and there were people who couldn't. Gerry could always hang.

A head peeked in the door.

"Mr. O'Brien?"

Gerry was sitting with his feet up on the polished oak desk inside his new office at the White House. Officially, he was a White House policy advisor, and his bright, spacious office was at the far end of the hall from the Oval Office. That was fine with him—if it wasn't for the street cred of having his office in the West Wing, he'd just as soon have it another building. He had meetings to take, and at times it was going to be better if the names of the attendees remained his little secret.

"Yes. Come in."

The person stepped inside. It was a kid Gerry liked, more of a man than a child—probably in his early thirties. Malcolm, his name was, and he was someone Gerry could assign responsibility, and have hope that the job would get done within a reasonable amount of time, and with a fair amount of competence. He was also a man who could keep secrets.

"Yes, Malcolm?"

"Sir, that special agent you've been looking for, the one who got shot by Michael Benn during the Marybeth Horning assassination?"

"Yes. Luke Stone."

"Well, he turned up about an hour ago in a McDonald's parking lot in Quantico. One of our men was surveilling an FBI agent who worked with Stone at the FBI Special Response Team. His name is Edward Newsam, and he's a commander with the FBI Hostage Rescue Team now. And sure enough, Stone turned up in a McDonald's parking lot right outside Quantico, where Newsam apparently buys breakfast nearly every day. The two men drove to a different parking lot and talked for about half an hour."

"Do we know anything about Newsam?"

Malcolm looked down at a computer tablet he was carrying. "Newsam, Edward J. Thirty-five-year-old African-American male, former Delta Force operator. Divorced with two young children. He's seen a lot of combat and has received numerous medals, commendations, and citations, both when he was in the military and while working for the FBI. Much of his career history is classified, but I do know that he's been awarded at least two Purple Hearts and a Bronze Star."

"Do we know what was said between them?"

Malcolm shook his head. "No. But our man ditched Newsam and is now following Stone. Newsam passed through the Quantico main gate at seven fifty-two and logged into his computer several minutes later. Whatever was said, it didn't seem to change Newsam's plans for the day."

Gerry nodded. "Good. Continue to monitor Newsam's logins and his other work activities. If nothing out of the ordinary pops up, then leave him alone. We don't want to tip him off that we're watching him, and if he doesn't get involved, then we have no reason to tangle with him. Meanwhile, where is Stone?"

"He's stuck in traffic on his way into the city."

Gerry the Shark smiled. Traffic jams were for the little people—people like Luke Stone. Gerry had erased traffic jams from his life. Suddenly, it was almost as if he had never sat in one before. Either the road was cleared by the Secret Service before he ever got there, or he puddle-jumped it in a helicopter.

"Okay. Keep tabs on him, and close a noose around him. When the opportunity presents itself, I want him taken into custody. Alive if at all possible, but dead if necessary. He may have information that's valuable to us, but I'd prefer to see him dead than have him escape. Do it in an isolated location, where no one will witness it, and no civilians are likely to get in the way. Stone is a very dangerous man, he's a rancid leftover from the Hopkins administration, and the sooner we get him off the street, the better off everyone will be."

"Will do, sir."

Good boy, Gerry almost said, but didn't.

"And Malcolm?"

"Yes?"

"When I say close a noose around him, I mean very gradually. The men who track him need to keep their distance. Stone is an experienced black operator. If he so much as smells us, he will disappear."

"Of course," Malcolm said. "Our men are the best."

Gerry nodded at the truth of this. They'd been building a small private army of special operators for close to a year—ever since the campaign kicked off in earnest. Blackstone Recruiters, High Adventure, Triple X Outcomes—Gerry had worked with all of them. These were the consulting firms that specialized in hiring men coming out of the most elite special forces—American, English, Israeli—anywhere that trained the best of the best.

"Sir?" Malcolm said before disappearing.

"What else?"

"The President-elect would like to see you when you have a moment."

* * *

"Gerry, I've got problems."

It was a sunny day, and light streamed in through the tall windows that ringed the Oval Office. Jefferson Monroe stood at one of the windows, turned away from Gerry the Shark and gazing out at Rose Garden, mostly fallow this time of year. For an instant, Gerry imagined throwing a sharp dagger at Monroe's back, like a magician wowing the crowd by seeming to put his assistant's life at risk.

The President-elect was wearing a pale blue dress shirt. Gerry pictured a knife appearing in the middle of it, bright red blood flowing from the wound, staining Monroe's expensive designer shirt.

"Why don't you tell me what they are, Jeff, and we'll see if we can work them out."

"You don't know?" Monroe said.

Gerry shook his head. "Not offhand. Things seem to be going well. We zoomed in here pretty much like I said we would, more than two months before your actual inauguration. The election fraud investigation is basically dead. There's nothing but daylight ahead of us. We are no longer fighting the power. We are the power."

Monroe turned around. He looked tired—more tired than Gerry had probably ever seen him, and Gerry had campaigned with him sixteen hours a day for months on end. Gerry imagined that the old boy wasn't sleeping much. Gerry wasn't sleeping either, but he was twenty years younger than his boss and built for lack of sleep.

"That's one way to look at it," Monroe said.

Gerry smiled.

They were alone in the Oval Office, two men at the very top of the power structure that ran the entire world. In Gerry's mind's eye, he saw Washington, DC, and its environs—the Capitol Building, the Supreme Court, the monuments to history, the many federal agencies and lobbying firms, the Beltway, all of it, extending out into the suburbs, and then the far exurbs. The whole thing existed as a life support system for this very room. Gerry O'Brien and Jefferson Monroe were standing inside the womb of creation. If only he could make Monroe understand this.

"Show me a different way to look at it," Gerry said.

The old man began to tick items off his fingers.

"The Acting President spent the night crying in her room, so I'm told. She is horrified that we have threatened nuclear war against the Chinese, and has yet to emerge from the White House Residence. I've been informed that she told her own staff she would like to walk the threats back, and perhaps host a meeting with the Chinese President to clear up any misunderstanding."

Gerry shook his head. Karen White couldn't hang. That much was clear. "Let me speak with Karen," he said. "I'll go upstairs and see her right after I leave this room."

Monroe nodded. "I wish you would."

"I will. Next?"

"The Joint Chiefs are in open revolt at the prospect of attacking China. Not necessarily the fact of it, but the timing. Everything I'm hearing is that we are not ready to hit them within two days. Such an operation would normally take months of preparation and coordination. As I understand it, we have to be ready for the Chinese counter-strike. Since we told them what we're going to do, when, and where, their counter-strike will likely come immediately after our attack, and possibly even before it. The generals are very disturbed by this possibility, and are telling me the situation could quickly spiral out of control."

Gerry took a deep breath. "The Chinese are going to back down and evacuate those islands. I know they are. I know it because we're strong and they're weak. But that's beside the point. The generals need to get on our page in the playbook, or we need to bring in better generals. These people have to recognize that civilians control the military, and not the other way around. They do what we tell them to do. What about the guy who was Chairman of the Joint Chiefs until Hopkins had him arrested a couple of years ago? The one who wanted to launch a massive first strike against Russia?"

Monroe nodded. "Robert Coates."

"Right," Gerry said. "He's out of jail, isn't he?"

"He's been out for a year. They went easy on him, considering that what he did amounted to an impromptu coup attempt. He was stripped of rank and discharged from the military."

One thing Gerry loved about Jefferson Monroe was his easy knowledge of who people were and what they were doing. He was the ultimate gossip columnist. He was more than just a people person—he was an encyclopedia of people. He was a politician to his core, a man who never forgot a face, or a name.

"You know him?"

Monroe nodded. "I've known him for thirty years. He's okay. He's also about as hawkish as they come."

"Let's bring him on board."

Now the President-elect shrugged. "Susan's National Security Advisor, Kurt Kimball, is missing in action. Whatever he thinks he's doing by not showing up here, it's a dereliction of duty at best, and treason at worst. We can replace him with Coates and we don't need to ask anyone's permission—no Senate hearings, nothing of the sort."

"Done," Gerry said. "I'll have my staff track him down and get him in here this afternoon. He's probably still got people inside the Pentagon. He can get the ball rolling in the right direction."

Gerry paused, but only for a second. It was exhilarating moving pieces around the board like this. Jefferson Monroe needed someone to do his thinking for him, and The Shark was just the man for it. It was a delicious irony that Monroe was keeping track of events, and reporting them to Gerry. It was clear who made the decisions around here.

"Next?"

"The security fences that we're building around Chinatowns. The press is killing us on this. I'm afraid we're starting to look really, really bad. The ACLU is filing motions to put a stop to construction in all four cities where it's happening. Protests are popping up everywhere, especially at the construction sites. Police are holding back the demonstrators for now, but it's early. Soon we might have to send in the National Guard to keep the workers safe. And even that night not matter. In New York City, the labor unions told their members to walk off the job sites. As of early this morning, they've done exactly that. Work on the barriers there has ground to a halt."

That kind of thing made Gerry want to scream. Who were these people to undermine the safety and security of the United States? Who were they to go against the wishes of the White House?

"So we bring in scabs if we have to," he said. "And we water cannon the demonstrators."

Monroe shook his head. "Gerry, you're a smart man. You know that's not how things happen. We're moving very fast here, maybe too fast. There's pushback, and you can't always steamroll your way over it. It's much too soon for water cannons and replacement workers. And I don't think I have to tell you that the side with the water cannons is the side that eventually loses."

"Spoken like a true politician," Gerry said.

"I was in the Senate for twenty-four years."

"We ran as outsiders, Jeff. And the people who voted for you want things done. They don't want to wait."

They stared at each other for a long moment. Gerry could already see this bogging down into a quagmire of court cases and public relations battles. That was bad. But the whole thing could be cured if war with China broke out. What public figure wanted to be seen as in bed with the enemy?

"Listen, here's how I see it," Gerry said. "There is long precedent for detaining possible enemies of the state, especially during wartime. We put more than a hundred thousand Japanese in internment camps during World War Two.

"Much more recently, there was REX 84 and REX 97, Readiness Exercises 1984 and 1997, respectively. In the event of a national emergency, both plans called for the suspension of the Constitution, the declaration of martial law, the replacement of elected officials with military personnel, and the detainment of large numbers of American citizens deemed as security threats.

"And they were both based on Operation Garden Plot, the plan written in 1970 during the Nixon administration, which called for widespread detentions of up to twenty-one million people. Elements of Operation Garden Plot are still in place. We're not doing anything out of the ordinary. We're not outliers here."

"Most people aren't aware of those plans," Monroe said. "And the internment of the Japanese in camps is now considered a disgraceful and embarrassing episode."

Gerry pointed at him. "Exactly. The Japanese were taken from their homes and put in camps, often without warning. They lost everything they owned, and their lives came to a sudden halt. What we're doing is a lot more humane. The Chinese can stay in their homes and they can keep all their stuff. They can go on about their business. And we know where they are at all times. It's the best of both worlds."

Jefferson Monroe stared at him another long while, then suddenly broke into a smile. "We did it, son. Didn't we?"

Now Gerry smiled as well. "We sure did."

"I was skeptical of you at first," Monroe said. "But you know that already. I didn't like people from New York City—so brash, so pushy, and so obnoxious. It's too much! The world revolves around them, or least they think it does."

"Thanks," Gerry said.

"Well, that's my point, isn't it? I won't say I was wrong all those years. I still think many people from New York are the worst of the worst. I hate them. But that doesn't include you. You're brash, you're pushy, but you back it up with real knowledge and real ability and a work ethic as strong as any down-home country person I've ever known. I am proud to know you. I think we make an incredible team."

Monroe paused and looked around the room as if he'd never seen it before. It was quite a place. "This is the Oval Office, and we own it for the next four years."

Gerry nodded. "You bet."

And inside he thought:

What do you mean "we"?

* * *

"How are you feeling, Karen?" Gerry said.

Karen White, the Acting President of the United States, was sitting at the breakfast nook in the upstairs Family Kitchen of the White House Residence. On the white Formica table in front of her was a half-eaten banana, still inside its peel, and a bowl of oatmeal she appeared not to have touched. A dark circle of brown sugar had solidified on top of the cold gruel.

She was, however, sipping slowly from a coffee mug.

"I'm feeling fine," she said, a hint of defensiveness in her voice. Why wouldn't there be? It was after nine o'clock, and she was still in here. Workdays at the White House started early and ran late. The day had raced out ahead of her, and she showed very little interest in catching up.

She was wearing some kind of light purple pantsuit, with a matching beret or tam-o'-shanter on her head. The suit had very subtle moons and stars etched on it. You had to look twice to really see them. The suit, combined with the hat, made her look like some kind of teacher at a school for wizards—a wizard professor.

Her eyes were puffy and red, probably from crying. That ruined the effect somewhat. As far as Gerry knew, wizards didn't cry.

Gerry stood in the doorway. He glanced around. The nearest Secret Service agent stood about fifteen feet away, a little bit down the hall. The man was giving them room to talk. Good.

"A bit of a roller coaster ride we're on," Gerry said, offering up the understatement of the morning.

"If you want to call it that."

Gerry smirked. "What would you like to call it?"

Karen shook her head. She didn't look at him at all. Instead, she gazed down at her oatmeal and began to stir it slowly, making a spiral out of the brown sugar.

"Don't pretend events are outside your control, Gerry. I'm not an idiot. I know what you're doing. You're manipulating everything from behind the scenes. And don't think for a minute that I'm the only one who sees it. I wouldn't be surprised to see your skinny ass in front of a firing squad before too much longer."

Gerry's smile faded. Now he just stared. He felt cold toward her, empty, like she was a bug, something to be stepped on. President? President of what? She didn't even command this room.

"Karen, I have no idea what you're talking about."

Something in his tone made her look up. Their eyes met.

"No?" she said. "Let me ask you a question. Did you murder Susan Hopkins and Marybeth Horning? I tend to think that you did."

"Karen…" What did you say to an accusation like that? His first thought was: *Susan Hopkins isn't dead. She's still out there somewhere, and we're going to find her.*

"It was all a little convenient, wouldn't you say? Susan is about to step down, Marybeth dies, and suddenly I'm President."

"Would you prefer if you weren't? That would be easy enough to arrange."

Her eyes hardened. "Your lizard brain probably won't understand this, but I *liked* Susan and Marybeth. They were rivals of mine, and good strong women. We agreed on almost nothing, but I respected them, and they respected me. I would rather see the worst tax-and-spend liberal instincts realized as policy in this country than to see either one of those women die by violence."

Gerry shook his head. He'd had enough. It was time to pull the plug on Karen. And the solution to the Karen problem was as simple and as elegant as a lightning strike. He hadn't been planning to enact it this early, but why not? In for a penny, in for a pound, as Gerry's old grandmother used to say.

"They didn't respect you, Karen. Please put that idea out of your mind."

She dismissed him with a sudden wave of her hand. "They did respect me. That's something you'll never—"

"Karen, how could they possibly respect you? You're a basket case. You're a national laughingstock. Look at your career in the House. What measures have you ever put forward that showed any discernible results? Wait… never mind that. Forget it. Look at what you're wearing. You're the President of the United States, Karen! This isn't the fourth grade play."

Her eyes were on fire now. She glared at him in something like rage. But whatever she was thinking or feeling, her mouth couldn't find a way to express it. And that was because her synapses were gummed up with drugs.

Gerry pushed on, lining up the kill shot.

"Here's what I know about you, Karen. Please don't try to deny it, because I have copies of all the paperwork, I know the aliases you use, and I've traced everything back to you. I have the doctors who write your scripts, and I have the hammer poised above their heads. Think they won't give you up to save their medical licenses? Think again.

"You're mentally ill, Karen, and you've been hiding it for years. You're on serotonin re-uptake inhibitors for major depression, at least three different prescriptions. You're on both Xanax and Ativan for anxiety, and you're probably addicted to them. You take Ambien to fall asleep at night, and you take Adderall to wake up in the morning. You're on an anti-psychotic medication, usually given to schizophrenics, to help you manage your obsessive-compulsive disorder."

He paused. The Family Kitchen had suddenly become very quiet. She had turned away from him and was now staring at the wall. It was an odd thing for an adult to do, but Karen really was an overgrown child, wasn't she?

"You're a pill popper, Karen, and you're an absolute mess. And don't think for a minute that I'm the only one who knows this."

She just kept staring at the wall, saying nothing. Something about that bothered him, and in an instant, he knew what it was. She was trying to escape from him. She was trying to maintain some small semblance of freedom from the power of his will.

Well, he wouldn't stand for it.

"Look at me, Karen."

She shook her head the slightest amount. "I can't."

"You will look at me right this minute. Either that, or I will walk back downstairs to my office and anonymously leak your medical records to the *Washington Post*, the *New York Times*, and CNN, all at once. I will connect the dots for them. An hour from now, your political career will be over. Is that what you want?"

Her voice was small. "No."

"Then turn around and look at me."

She did as she was told. She moved slowly, creakily, like some ancient wind-up toy. It took a long moment before she could raise her eyes to meet his. The fire was long gone. She was his prisoner now, and she knew it. He could do whatever he wished with her. She knew that, too.

"Here's how we're going to play this," he said. "You're going to go back to your quarters, clean yourself up, and change your clothes. You're going to dress like a big girl today. If you don't know how to do that, I will send one of my staffers to help you find something to wear. We'll order something in if we need to. Still with me?"

"Yes."

"Okay, once you are dressed like an adult, you are going to make two moves in very quick succession. They will both happen this very afternoon. The first is you are going to appoint Jefferson Monroe as your Vice President. The second is you are going to resign, and Jeff is going to take over as President. He's going to become President in two months anyway, so we might as well get started now."

She shook her head. "But what will people—"

"Karen, you're not in a position to ask any questions. Your only job now is to do exactly what I tell you to do. Is that understood?"

She went right back to being the abject child. "Yes."

Gerry nodded. He enjoyed his power over her. If only she were young and beautiful, this little meeting could get a lot more interesting.

"Good. If you choose, you can go right back to being Speaker of the House. I don't care. If I were you, I think I would check into a nice, quiet rehab for a few months and start to wean myself off all these drugs, but that's up to you. Once you step down, I'm going to leave you alone and let you do whatever you want."

He started to leave, but then stopped again. He raised his index finger.

"Keep this in mind, though. I'm not going anywhere. If you ever mess with me or Jefferson, if you try to block a vote from going our way in the House, if you say one disparaging word in public about either of us, I will drop the bomb on you. I will ruin you. Do you understand?"

She nodded. "Yes."

"Good. We all need allies here in Washington, and I bet that one day soon, Jeff and I are going to need you."

He clapped his hands, very loud. Twice.

"Now let's roll."

CHAPTER TWENTY FOUR

9:45 a.m. Eastern Daylight Time
The Vietnam Veterans Memorial
The National Mall, Washington DC

"Not everything is what it appears to be," the tall elderly man said. "Many things are, but many others are not."

The man wore a long leather coat, a duster, a style for a much younger man. The man's hair was so white it almost seemed to reflect the rays of the sun back into deep space. He didn't face Luke directly.

Instead, he faced away from him, one person among many looking at the glassy black stone of the memorial wall—seeing the names, yes, but also seeing their own reflection. The man held a sheet of heavy sketch paper in one hand, and a thick graphite pencil in the other.

The wall stretched far to their left and their right, etched with the names of more than 58,000 Americans, almost all of them men, who had died or gone missing in the Vietnam War.

"For example," he said, "I have no doubt that the vast majority of these men you see here were exactly who they claimed to be." He shook his head. "But not all of them. No sir, not all."

He spotted what he was looking for and moved to the wall slowly and with apparent difficulty. As Luke watched, the old man pressed the paper against the wall and ran the pencil across a name several times, and with wide, jerking movements, like someone in the grip of palsy. He was one of at least twenty people doing exactly the same thing. They were all making "rubbings," usually of the name of a loved one, a popular thing to do here. Far to the old man's right, the sharp spire of the Washington Monument towered like a god, gazing down on the activities of its children.

After a moment, the old man creaked back to where Luke stood. He held up the paper for Luke's inspection.

"Staff Sergeant Joshua L. McKenney, United States Marine Corps. Died tragically in the Battle of Hue during the 1968 Tet Offensive."

The old man's hand shook the smallest amount. "The only problem is that the man's real name was Peter Rickman, and he was an Agency operative. The Marines were his cover story. He was no more in Hue during the Tet Offensive than I was. He was deep in the jungles of Laos and Cambodia, gathering intelligence on the whereabouts of a man named Pol Pot, who would become such a problem for people a few years later."

"Why the cover-up?" Luke said.

The old man smiled. "Simple enough. We were never supposed to be in Laos or Cambodia." He gestured at the pathway. "Shall we walk?"

They moved along the stone walkway that followed the bend of the wall. It was a cool day, and people wore heavy jackets and hats. Up ahead, the memorial wall ended and the walkway curved to the left and into a stand of trees.

A short distance away from the wall was another memorial, a tall bronze statue. Luke knew it as *The Three Soldiers*. It depicted three men in combat dress, unhurt but perhaps physically exhausted, and easily identifiable as a white man, a black man, and a Hispanic man. They stared across empty space at the wall, appearing to take in the names of their fallen brothers.

Luke flashed back to the first time he had visited this place, as a small child thirty years before. He knew that the words engraved on the wall were the names of men who had died, and he knew what dying was. At some point, the sheer number of names had overwhelmed him, and he had burst into tears.

Too many. Too many.

He had been unable to stop crying until he arrived home.

"What can I call you?" he said to the older man.

"Call me Ishmael."

Luke nearly laughed out loud. Usually, the man went by some nondescript name—Paul or Hank or Steve. Ishmael? It suited him—the main character from *Moby Dick*, a young man who went on an adventure, and survived a disaster that killed everyone around him.

Ishmael had lived in the dark nether reaches of the spy world for long decades, and had carried out more betrayals than Luke liked to think about. He had caused a lot of headaches for people who tended to cure their aches and pains with razor blades and rat poison.

Yet here he was, living in Washington, DC, right under the very noses of the people who should be happy to put him in the ground once and for all. But perhaps revenge had an expiration date. After a certain amount of time had passed, maybe no one cared anymore. And maybe this man was so ancient that all the people who had once wanted to kill him were dead.

"I've got problems," Luke said.

Ishmael nodded. "I'd say you do, yes. A man disappears into the wilderness, materializes suddenly, and then right away gets shot on national television. I'd say that's a man with problems. You know Crazy Horse used to do the same thing? He'd go away by himself on extended vision quests. His braves would wonder if he was ever coming back."

Luke ignored all of that. "Michael Benn," he said.

The old man shrugged. "Careful."

"He was a man with a complicated past."

"I've rarely seen an assassin with a simple and straightforward one."

"He was in foster care as a child, then he disappeared for three years. When he turned up again, he was in Montreal, housed at a mental hospital called Allen—"

Ishmael nodded and finished Luke's sentence. "Memorial Institute."

He looked straight at Luke for the first time. His face was like wrinkled parchment. His eyes were deep set and pale blue. They were old eyes, eyes that knew secrets. They were eyes without pity, without remorse, without... judgment. Judgment was a luxury men like Ishmael couldn't afford.

"I can't say that I'm surprised. Although I suppose I'd have preferred if you said something else."

"What is it?" Luke said.

"You know what it is. Or at least, what it was."

To their left, a different, narrower path split off from the main one. Ishmael indicated that direction. They took several steps, but the path dead-ended at a stone bench with green wooden slats going across—an old park bench.

Ishmael smiled. "Almost no one seems to know this bench is here. It's my private bench." He settled into it slowly, gingerly, like a man long accustomed to pain.

Luke remained standing.

"Tell me," he said.

A long sigh came from the old man. "It's MK-ULTRA, of course."

"The old CIA mind control program," Luke said.

The man nodded. "Who but one of its graduates—or perhaps a true believer of a righteous cause—would sacrifice himself for a mission with no hope of escape? I was a young man when I saw the original memo from 1952, which created the program. I committed the relevant passage to memory. It said: *Can we get control of an individual to the point where he will do our bidding against his will and even against fundamental laws of nature such as self-preservation?"*

He gave Luke a long look. "The short answer is yes, we can."

Luke waited. Sometimes with Ishmael, you had to take the long way around. Sometimes you had to begin at the beginning.

"It started in 1945," the old man said, "near the end of World War Two. The Office of Strategic Services, which soon became the Central Intelligence Agency, began to track down and capture German scientists, then bring them to the United States in secret. Many of the scientists were experts in medicine, rocketry, aeronautics, and electronics, as you might imagine. But some had been involved in brainwashing and torture, especially on concentration camp prisoners.

"They had already done the work, you see? It was work that ethical considerations wouldn't allow us to do. Why lose that knowledge? Why let those men die in the final agonies of the war? Why let the Russians capture them instead?"

"Why not hang them at Nuremburg?" Luke said. "If they committed crimes against humanity?"

Ishmael smiled. "Luke Stone, always a difficult student. You don't hang them because you aspire to commit similar crimes, and these people can teach you how. The lessons got underway immediately. The program was first called Project Artichoke, then Project Bluebird, and finally MK-ULTRA.

"The experiments took place at more than eighty institutions, including at least forty-four colleges, as well as hospitals, prisons, and pharmaceutical companies. Thousands of American and Canadian citizens were its unwitting playthings—including some fun and rather well-known names. Theodore Kaczynski, the Unabomber, was experimented on while he was a student at Harvard. Whitey Bulger, the murderous Boston gangster, was a subject during a stretch he served in federal prison."

"But how does this relate to a child in foster care?" Luke said.

Ishmael shrugged. "In the way that seems most obvious. Children were often taken from orphanages and group homes for the purpose of experimentation. These were unwanted children, throwaways, whom no one would really miss.

"In the case of your friend Michael, if he hadn't done something that made him a household name, who would ever have known where he spent his time as a child? Who knows now? If you believe the TV, he started his life as an ambitious teenager from a hardscrabble background who joined the military, and ended it in the White House briefing room as a disillusioned former supporter of the President."

"Allen Memorial Institute," Luke said.

Ishmael nodded. "It was a psychiatric hospital on the grounds of McGill University in Montreal. The program there was called Subproject 68, and it was run by a Scottish psychiatrist named Ewan Cameron. I never met him, but by all accounts, Cameron was a madman. His experiments were designed to *de-pattern* his victims, erasing their minds and their memories, then rebuilding their personality in a manner of his choosing. To achieve this result, Cameron went to extremes.

"He used drug-induced comas, at one point putting a victim in a coma for nearly three months. He used high-voltage electric shocks, often administering up to three hundred sixty shocks per person. He used isolation and sensory deprivation, locking his patients in specially designed sensory deprivation chambers for weeks at a time. They were basically morgue drawers that he slid them into.

"He also used rape and sexual abuse. In particular, he believed that mind control slaves could be created through repeated sexual, verbal, and psychological trauma when the subject was most vulnerable—during childhood. He thought he could induce multiple personality disorder through deliberate abuse, with the goal of tailoring personalities for specific purposes. When successful, the victim could be triggered to become these separate personalities at will, and in many cases, have no memory of it afterwards."

"And he was right," Luke said. It wasn't a question.

Ishmael nodded. "He was right. He found that you can create willing sex slaves through these techniques—very valuable things to have, sell, and trade among friends. And you can also create sleeper assassins, individuals who lie in wait, going about their normal lives, until you give them the signal to act. If you do your programming correctly, they act in such a way that they die during the operation. I believe your friend Michael fits this bill."

Luke shook his head. "Didn't the CIA pull the plug on those experiments in the 1970s? Benn wasn't even born until the 1980s."

"Theoretically, they pulled the plug in 1973," Ishmael said. "But not everyone got that memo. And people like Ewan Cameron had students and assistants who never even worked for the Agency in the first place. A man in your line of work might appreciate how someone conducting these types of experiments might be reluctant to give them up just because someone in a faraway office said to stop.

"Some of the people who were involved are still around, freelancing. Find out who performed the mind control training on Michael, and who was handling him in the recent past, and you will have your guilty parties. If it turns out they are closely aligned with your new President, that wouldn't surprise me in the least."

"I need a name," Luke said.

"Of course you do," Ishmael said. "We all need something. But asking me for a name is like asking me to leap from a cliff and then flutter harmlessly to the bottom."

"I can protect you."

The old man gazed at Luke now. For a moment, he seemed to be looking through him, in fact, at some other scene in the vague distance. But then he focused on Luke's midsection, where he probably knew the worst of Luke's injuries were hidden.

"You can barely protect yourself, never mind me."

"Even so."

The old man sighed, and this time it was like the air hissing out of a tire, long and slow, until the tire went completely flat. "If you get me killed, I'm going to be very annoyed. I'm old, that's true, but I still rather enjoy my life, and I'd like to keep it a while longer."

"Tell me," Luke said.

"Sydney Franz Gottlieb. His friends call him Sid. He's a psychiatrist with a practice catering to wealthy neurotics down in the Old Town in Alexandria. He went to med school at McGill, and interned at Allen Memorial. He's old now, but perhaps not as old as me. He's a rather accomplished man, with numerous books and articles published on childhood psychological and psychiatric disorders, and how to treat them. And he's an exceptional networker with many friends. Some of those friends are dangerous."

Ishmael looked at Luke with baleful eyes.

"When you go to see him, don't tell him I sent you."

CHAPTER TWENTY FIVE

10:45 a.m. Eastern Daylight Time
Washington DC

Ishmael arrived home on his tree-lined street with a bag of autumn produce from the local farmer's market. He was in no hurry, and it was a nice day—sunny despite the cold. He moved slowly out of habit—he liked to give the impression that he was infirm, an old man who was no threat to anyone. Sometimes he even put on a slight limp.

"How's the leg?" his neighbors would often ask him, especially when bad weather was in the forecast.

"Oh, you know," he'd say. "Feels like we're in for some rain."

He went up the narrow stairs and into his apartment, still with lingering thoughts of the conversation he'd had with Luke. It was dangerous talk, of course. He wouldn't consider sharing that type of information with anyone but Luke.

Luke was hard to catch, that much was clear. And even if one day the bad guys did capture him, he would probably take most of his secrets to the grave with him. In spycraft, the rule of thumb was that any man could be broken eventually if the right type of pressure were applied. But if there was one who couldn't, Ishmael would put his money on Luke Stone.

Ishmael opened the refrigerator to deposit his goodies. A large pile of fur was heaped on the white tile floor of his kitchen. At first, he thought one of the cats was merely sprawled out there. It was Fidel, a big lazy yellow tabby. Sprawling out on the floor was nothing new for Fidel. In fact, Ishmael barely looked at him.

Then he did.

There was something abnormal about the way Fidel lay there. Ishmael's heart raced off in a wild tattoo. Rat-a-tat-tat. The cat looked almost like it had been broken, or even smashed. Ishmael approached Fidel cautiously.

His heart pounded in his chest.

Run, you idiot.

The cat was demolished. It was humped and bloodied, like it had been tortured and killed by a cruel and sinister child. A streak of blood stained the tiles beneath its carcass. Where were the other cats? Where was *the dog*?

My God.

RUN. *RUN.*

He turned and a man stood behind him. The man had just emerged from the bathroom hallway. The man was tall with an almost nondescript face, wearing a shirt and tie covered by a light autumn jacket. He looked to Ishmael like a man in his mid-fifties, maybe a little older.

Behind him stood a taller, much broader and younger man. The man wore a bushy mustache like he was on an African safari in some past era. In fact, he was dressed like a man on safari—in utility pants and a vest, both lined with numerous pockets.

The faces of the men were blank. They were all business. It was the look of men who were hired as private contractors to protect truck convoys in war zones, then suddenly started spraying groups of civilians with automatic fire. It was a bad, bad look. It was the look of men trained in military techniques, but who operated without military discipline. It was the look of murder for hire.

Ishmael turned to bolt for the door, but another young man stood there. This one was also young—much younger than the other two—black, broad and strong-looking. His thick hair was styled in an eccentric fashion, sticking up in tufts and curls as though he had just rolled out of bed. His eyes were hard, but not blank. The eyes said he had seen a few jobs, and made it through by doing exactly what the bosses told him.

The doorway was blocked. The path to the windows was blocked. Ishmael couldn't outrun these men, and he couldn't outfight them. Suddenly, he felt old—old and stupid for playing spy games well past the time for it. Up until a moment ago, he'd been convinced of his own superiority—he still had the nerve, he still had the cat's eyes, he could still do the mental and psychological gymnastics to stay one step ahead.

Now he was badly exposed for everyone in this room to see.

"Can I help you fellows?" he said.

The tall man lit a cigarette.

"That's fine, go ahead and smoke in my home. I don't mind."

The man shrugged. "Kent Philby, right? That was your name once upon a time, wasn't it?"

"Who wants to know?"

The man with the mustache ambled out from behind the small man. He was big, even bigger than at first glance. Ishmael watched him approach. It was like watching a storm blow in from the sea. He angled toward Ishmael across the sparkling tiles, taking his time, not hurrying at all.

126

"The gentleman asked you a question. It isn't polite to answer him with a question."

"You men are in my home. Did you ever consider that? Uninvited, I might add. I think that puts me in charge of asking questions."

The man feinted with his left hand, then delivered a hard right across Ishmael's jaw. Ishmael stumbled backward, crashed into the kitchen table, and landed on top of it. He rolled over and fell to the floor.

The mustachioed man came and, smiling, stood over him. His thick workman's hands, like the mechanical claws that sift through scrap metal at the junkyard, reached down and picked Ishmael up by the shirt. The man backed up and swung him around in a large circle, then let him go.

Ishmael felt himself crossing the room as if he were flying, his feet barely scraping the ground. He hit the far wall, plowed into it, then bounced off and stumbled backward. He turned, pinwheeling for balance. He spilled and slid across the floor.

Then the tall man was standing over him. Ishmael looked up at that hard face. The man took a drag on his cigarette.

"Kent," the man said. His voice was matter-of-fact, calm, there may even have been a hint of humor in it. "I want to talk to you. I know who you are. You're Kent Philby, former rogue CIA agent and paid informant for the KGB and Mossad. God knows what else you've done—the dossier was too long to bother reading through. I gather, from the bit I skimmed, that you had a fun time during the Cold War. Those days are over. You imagined that everyone forgot about you, but you were wrong. They left you alone and in place, in case one day your country might need you. Today is that day."

The man's eyes held his. "Do we understand each other?"

Ishmael looked at him quizzically. "I'm sorry, I think you must have the wrong man. This… Philby you speak of…"

The tall man glanced at his henchman, the man with the mustache. The man with the mustache kicked Ishmael in the side of his neck. It wasn't a hard kick, but the tip of his shoe was sharp, and the flesh and bone of Ishmael's neck were weak and tender.

More words from the tall man. "All right. Here are the rules. I'm going to ask you some questions, and you're going to answer them. You're not in a position to pretend you don't know what I'm talking about. You're not in a position to ask me any questions. Do we understand each other?"

Ishmael nodded this time.

127

"What? I didn't hear you."

"I understand."

The man smiled. "Good. Kent Philby?"

"I don't want to seem rude," Ishmael said, "but I don't think we've been properly introduced. For example, I haven't gotten any of your names."

"Last chance. Is your name Kent Philby?"

Ishmael shrugged. "I suppose that all depends on what the word *is* means."

The mustache man kicked him again, this time in the midsection, and much harder than before. The pain was like an explosion, radiating outward through his body. Ishmael rolled over and gasped, holding his side. He had never felt so old.

He lay on his back again, his teeth gritted.

The tall man's face loomed over him.

"Kent? Kent Philby, American traitor and triple agent?"

Ishmael looked away. "Go to hell."

* * *

Under duress, an hour can seem like a long time.

Kent Philby opened his eyes and was surprised to find himself on the floor again. For a while, they had put him in the chair. He looked at the floor around his head. The tiles were tacky with blood.

He nodded to himself. He was Kent now. He thought of himself as Kent. He hadn't used that name in a long time, but they had... reminded him... of how appropriate a name it really was.

The black man, really just a kid, the one with the crazy hair, stood over him. He was English, and spoke with a West London accent.

"Well, well, well. Look who's awake."

The tall man came out of the bathroom. He was not smiling. Another lit cigarette dangled from his mouth.

"Kent, I see you're up. How nice. Anything you'd like to tell us about your conversation with Luke Stone this morning? Like, for instance, what his plans are for the immediate future, or maybe where Susan Hopkins is hiding."

Kent lay back on the tiles and sighed. "I told you. I don't know what Stone plans to do. He's an old friend of mine, that's all. Susan Hopkins is dead, for all I know, and for all Stone knows as well."

The tall man nodded at the black kid.

"Roland?"

The black kid cracked his knuckles. He smiled. *Roland.* The fact that the tall man had called him by a name—any name at all—was a very bad sign. It meant they didn't care what Ishmael knew about them. They didn't expect that Ishmael was going to be around to give someone his report.

"Mate, I'm starting to grow bored with you," the kid said. "Do you see what I mean?"

Then the pain came again. And when the pain came, it became easy to drift and remember pleasant things.

In his mind, he pictured Havana, Cuba. He had lived there for a time as a young man. Hot sun, narrow, crowded streets, old Spanish architecture, and palm trees lining the grand boulevard. He saw the oceanfront drive, great old tail-finned American cars cruising its length, young boys diving into the water from its walls. He heard the sound of a lone guitarist on a park bench, picking out a tune late at night. He'd like to return there someday. He hoped it hadn't changed too much.

Sometime later, he opened his eyes.

His wrists were cuffed together, and they were attached to a rope slung over one of the exposed pipes that ran along the ceiling. The whole thing was pulled just tight enough that his toes barely touched the ground. He looked up at his hands. They had turned purple while he was passed out. He knew he had lost some teeth. In fact, he had seen them come out. It was possible that he had some bruised ribs as well. At least bruised. Maybe broken.

"Hello?" he said.

He felt his Adam's apple bob. Maybe they had left? He was afraid to know, afraid of everything now, afraid of what he had wrought with his own hubris, his confidence. He had played a role, he had pretended to be someone special for so long, and he had come to believe in the role himself. He had lied, and then he had bought the lie.

Stupid. He wasn't special. He was stupid.

Time passed as he hung there. He noticed the shadows had changed. It was brighter in here now. Death would be a relief of sorts. It was Luke Stone, of course. That was why they were here, and it was the only thing keeping him alive. They wanted to know what he had told Luke Stone.

It seemed like an effort even to blink.

There was pain everywhere in his body, and now that he thought about it, that was probably a good thing. They hadn't severed his spinal cord, for instance. If he ever escaped from this, he'd still be able to walk.

129

The three men appeared again. Of course they did. They hadn't gone anywhere.

The tall man stood in front of him. His demeanor hadn't changed at all. Torture meant nothing to him. His eyes were flat and dead, and there was a cruel sense of humor living right around his mouth.

"You're a good sport, Kent, especially for an old man. I'll give you that much. I've seen people cave in much faster than this."

He nodded to the other two. They untied the rope from the ceiling and Kent collapsed in a heap on the floor. The back of his head hit hard, but it was just another pain to add to the list. Still, he faded in and out for a few seconds.

The tall man hunkered down next to him. He stood in a squat like a farmer, like he might run his hands through the deep rich soil. Kent figured he couldn't stand like that now even on his best days.

The man's voice took on a conspiratorial tone.

"We're going to kill you. You know that already. I'm telling you anyway, you know why? Because I don't like to see anybody suffer needlessly, and you seem like a pretty good guy."

"Thanks," Kent said. He made an effort to swallow.

A long pause passed between them.

"I have money," Kent said. "Cash, untraceable."

The man nodded. "Yes, we know. You already told us. You even gave us the locker numbers, and told us where to find the locker keys." He turned to the other men. "How soon they forget, huh?"

They all had a little laugh over that.

The tall man focused on Kent again. His face became solemn.

"You also said you don't know anything about Luke Stone's plans, and that you didn't talk about anything in particular. Oh, just shot the breeze with an old friend. Now, I believe you. But my bosses are not going to. So I have to do everything in my power to make sure you're telling the truth. *Everything*, you understand?

"We're going to cut your teeth out, one by one. We're going to crush your testicles. We're going to break your fingers and toes. We're going to cut your eyes out. We're going to do whatever we want, and whatever we need to do. If Stone told you anything, we're going to find out, and it's going to be a slow process. The way you can forego that fate, and die quickly, is to tell us everything up front, right now."

Kent started to shake. "Look," he said. Abruptly, he began to cry, and that surprised even him. But it hurt. It hurt so much, and they had barely even started yet. It was going to get a lot worse. He

130

knew that. He knew how bad it was going to be—he had seen it done too many times. His body was wracked by sobs.

"I don't know anything," he said. It was the last lie he had left inside him.

He shook his head, the tears still flowing.

CHAPTER TWENTY SIX

12:13 p.m. Eastern Daylight Time
The West Wing
The White House, Washington DC

"He's going to see Dr. Gottlieb," Malcolm said.

Gerry the Shark sat back at his desk, cupping his head with his hands as if he were lying in a hammock. Weak afternoon sunlight streamed in his windows. The light was okay—it didn't bother him. This time of year, the brightest sunlight was never particularly strong.

He stared at Malcolm, who stood in the doorway. It was bad news, and Malcolm's face said he knew it as well as Gerry did. It gave Gerry a sinking feeling in the pit of his stomach—a sensation he was not accustomed to, and one he didn't enjoy.

"The old man said this?"

Malcolm nodded. "Kent Philby. A notorious triple, or possibly quadruple, agent from many years ago. Recruited out of Yale by the CIA in 1959. He was one of the most wanted men on Earth at one time. It appears he'd been living right here in Washington, DC, for quite a while. Who knew?"

"Luke Stone, apparently."

"Yes."

Gerry shook his head. He didn't care about Kent Philby. But he did care about Sid Gottlieb and Luke Stone. These were two people who should never be allowed to talk to each other. In less than five hours, Karen White was going to step down, and Jefferson Monroe would become the President of the United States. Even before that, this afternoon, they would hold their first National Security Council meeting—a session to determine the best way to move forward against the Chinese. This was no time to step backward and have people like Sid Gottlieb and Michael Benn thrown in their faces. Those people were the past, and the future was beckoning.

"Kill him," Gerry said, lowering his voice. He glanced around the office. He'd had it swept for listening devices before he moved in, but how could you know for sure? In this day and age, with all the technology available, how could you know? He plunged ahead anyway.

"This has to stop. I want Stone gone. He's an existential threat to everything we're trying to do here, and I won't stand for it. Make it look like an accident if you can. If not, make it look like what it is, and we'll worry about it later. But I want the trail to go cold, okay? Afterwards… do we still have track of his car?"

"Yes, we do."

"Good. Afterwards, impound his car and pull apart the GPS. I want it analyzed. Get the data and find out where that car has been. That information alone may solve some mysteries for us."

Malcolm was about to duck out again.

"Malcolm?"

"Yes."

"How many people do we have trailing Stone at this moment?"

Malcolm shrugged. "I'm not sure, but I'd say plenty."

"Whatever that number is, double it. I don't care if they make mistakes or if we lose a few of them. But the result I asked for is the result I want, okay?"

"Luke Stone dead," Malcolm said.

That sinking sensation went through Gerry's body again. The walls of this office suddenly seemed alive, like they were breathing, listening, thinking.

He shook his head. He would change offices today, this afternoon. And he'd have his security people pull this place apart all over again. You couldn't be too careful.

He nodded to Malcolm, but didn't say another word.

CHAPTER TWENTY SEVEN

1:55 p.m. Eastern Daylight Time
Old Town
Alexandria, Virginia

Luke caught the smoked glass door as the woman and child exited.

"Hi. Let me grab that, if you don't mind."

The woman was tall and blonde, in a blue designer dress and a white fur coat. She wore high heels and carried a heavy pocketbook draped over her shoulder. The child was a tow-headed kid about nine, and wore khaki pants and a dress shirt under a blue wool sailor jacket. The two of them barely noticed Luke—they lived in a world where if you caught the door, it must mean you were invited inside.

He had timed it perfectly. There had been no extended hanging around in the third-floor hallway, waiting for the door marked Sydney F. Gottlieb, MD, to open, while the cameras videotaped him.

Luke had burned another cell phone and checked in with Swann. Swann had hacked the good doctor's patient database and pulled up today's schedule. Once his one o'clock ended, Gottlieb was free until four o'clock this afternoon. That left them plenty of time to talk, and no patients to worry about getting in the way, getting hurt, or generally confusing things.

Luke felt okay, all things considered. Since he left Ishmael this morning, he had gone back to the hotel, redid the dressing around his mid-section, and popped two Vicodin and two Dexedrines. The Vicodin had turned his pain all the way down. The Dexies had turned his mind, his energy, and his optimism all the way up. It was good to feel optimistic. He didn't like the looks of the entry wound or the angry surgical scar on his torso.

He had used one of the throwaway phones to send Gunner another text. Luke knew that many people had seen him shot on TV, and he wanted Gunner to know he was okay. It was becoming a foolish and pathetic obsession. He didn't even know if he had the right number. He could be sending texts to a complete stranger.

Gunner, he wrote, *if this is still you, please tell me. I am alive, and I am okay. Love, Dad.* Luke planned to keep that phone, on the small chance that Gunner was really at that number and tried to text him back.

Now, Luke slipped in the doorway to Gottlieb's office. Directly in front of him was the front desk, which was empty. Behind the desk, past a small secretarial area, was a large rectangular window, which ran the length of the wall and gave a panoramic view of the harbor and the Potomac River beyond it. It was certainly an arresting view to walk in on.

Apparently, this office stemmed from a time when Gottlieb had a much busier practice, with a receptionist, assistants, and associate psychiatrists and psychologists. But Gottlieb had gotten older, and he was letting his practice go. It wasn't like he needed the money. Most of the time, he was the only one here.

Luke eased the door shut. According to Swann, Gottlieb's personal office was to the left and down the hall. Luke went that way, moving silently on the deep pile carpet.

The door was slightly ajar. Luke pushed it open and stepped into the room.

Gottlieb stood by a wide desk, speaking quietly into a hand-held recorder. To his right was a traditional Freudian chair and sofa therapy set-up. Gottlieb must be the last psychiatrist in America who still did therapy—the better to identify candidates for mind control? Behind him was a window similar to the one out in the reception area.

Luke took a second to absorb the man. He was tall and slim, fit and erect. His lifestyle seemed to agree with him—he was deeply tanned, so tanned his skin was more gold than brown, and trending toward orange. He looked like some kind of rare tropical fruit. In fact, he was beautiful to look at.

He had a big jaw, like a caveman. Through long experience, Luke believed that men with strong jaws were more confident and assertive than most—at least in the normal, law-abiding world. White hair, still thick for an old boy, blow-dried backward. A Breitling watch. This was a guy who seemed to get outdoors a lot—golf and tennis at the club, maybe some sailing. Probably had a weekend place down in Florida. No wedding band. Dr. Gottlieb probably never had much time for a wife.

He noticed Luke there and didn't seem the least bit surprised.

"Hello," he said.

"Dr. Gottlieb," Luke said. He translated the German name into English. "God's love, huh?"

Gottlieb nodded and smiled. "Indeed."

"My name is Agent Stone, and I work for the FBI." Luke shrugged off the lie. He hadn't been an FBI employee in years. It didn't matter who he worked for. What mattered was Gottlieb, and what the man had done.

"I know who you are. I've been waiting for you."

"Me, or someone like me," Luke said. "It was only a matter of time before someone discovered your relationship to Michael Benn, and the mind control experiments you've done on children. Still working with kids, I see."

Gottlieb shrugged and placed his recorder on the desk. He ignored the reference to children. "I've actually been waiting for *you*, Agent Stone. You specifically. Unfortunately, your opponents arrived here ahead of you. I imagine that in your line of work, coming in second place is not much of a consolation."

A door on the other side of the office opened—Luke guessed it was the bathroom—and three large men sauntered out of it. One man was tall and thin. He was older than the others—fifty-five, maybe even sixty. The other two were well-dressed gorillas in informal outdoor wear—utility pants with numerous pockets, heavy black boots, and form-fitting long-sleeved shirts covered with pocketed vests. When you were playing commando, it was important to have a lot of pockets.

One of the men was black, with thick curly hair that stood up in odd tufts. The other was a white man with a bushy mustache. The three men stood in a rough triangle, guns already drawn. The two assistants trained their barrels directly on Luke. All three guns had big, eight-inch silencers screwed onto them—the men were planning to be quiet.

Luke felt nothing about the men, or their guns. He simply watched them, waiting for the mistake. Either they made one, or he died here in this office.

The older man, the obvious leader of the pack, stepped into the center of the room. His eyes were dead and blank. He smiled.

"Well, Mr. Stone, your reputation precedes you. We saw your friend Mr. Philby earlier today. Came straight here from his place, as a matter of fact."

Luke felt a twinge of something—fear, terror. There was no time for it now.

"Let's hope for your sake that he wasn't hurt."

The two gunmen giggled like children.

"Hurt?" the black man said. "He was more than hurt."

The man with the mustache shrugged and smiled. "If he'd been willing to talk, it probably would have gone easier for him."

"Then again, maybe not," the black one said.

"I would have thought the legendary Luke Stone would show us a little more skill," the boss said. "But we've been trailing you all day. Maybe your injuries…"

He gestured with his chin at Luke's mid-section, then shrugged.

"Pain can be a terrible distraction," Dr. Gottlieb said.

The man turned to Gottlieb. "Did I ask you?"

"No. I just—"

"Then please shut up."

"I beg your pardon," Gottlieb said. "This is my office. I'm sure I don't need to remind you who I—"

For the first time, the man raised his gun. He pointed it at Gottlieb's head.

Gottlieb raised his hands. "Wait!" His face curled into a grimace.

CLACK.

The gun made exactly the sound Luke assumed it would—like an office stapler punched especially hard. At the last second, the man lowered his shot and put his bullet into Gottlieb's upper body, just below his neck. Blood and gore sprayed out Gottlieb's back. He dropped to the carpet as if a hole had opened in the floor beneath him.

"Wait for what?" the leader said. He stared down at Gottlieb for a moment, blood pooling around his body, staining the off-white color of the carpeting. The bright red sank into the gaps between carpet fibers and spread out like tentacles.

"The guy has never stopped talking the whole time we've been here."

That was the mistake.

All three men gazed at Gottlieb a second too long.

Luke's gun was out of his holster before that second was over.

Too late, all three men tried to raise guns again.

Luke swung his gun around and fired it before the men got off a shot. One shot—he put a bullet right between the boss's eyes. A red dot of blood appeared on the man's forehead. He stood still for one second, as if realizing what had happened, then dropped to the floor, dead before he reached the carpet.

Luke's gun was loud.

LOUD.

He fired three times at the other guys, but they had already dived for cover—behind the couch, behind the desk. He missed all three shots. His ears were ringing.

137

He ducked back into the hallway.

A second later, a volley of return fire splintered the walls at the threshold. Luke backed away, waited a beat, then wrapped his gun hand around the doorway. He fired three more times into the office.

He took a deep breath. He needed to slow down for a second and think. If these guys called for backup, he was finished. Of course, they were doing exactly that. He could hear them talking in there.

"Throw your guns out and I'll let you live," he shouted.

They answered with another volley, tearing up the doorway and the drywall.

It was all on him. They could sit in there and wait him out. He was the one who had to get out of here. He turned to head back down the hall to the door.

He was already too late. The front door to the suite rattled, as if someone on the other side was trying to open it. Suddenly it burst inward, swinging violently and slamming back against the door stop. The shadow of a man's head appeared behind the smoked glass of the door.

BANG.

Luke shot him right in the Sydney Gottlieb, MD. The glass exploded, taking the man's head with it.

A new volley of shots came from the office behind him, ripping up the doorway again. Luke moved further up the hall, his gun trained on the shattered glass door. The shooting behind him went on for a long time. Finally, it stopped.

They were coming in. He could feel them there.

He ejected his magazine and slammed a new one in.

As he did, a man burst through the front door and dived behind the receptionist's desk, out of Luke's view. Luke didn't even get a shot off.

He hesitated, but only for a second. He was badly exposed in this hallway. Things could only get worse the longer he hung around. If it was time to go, then it was time to go. He turned back to Gottlieb's office doorway, squatted, hearing his knees creak as he did, then rolled into the room. He came up on one knee.

The guy with the mustache leaned against the side wall behind the sofa, like he was hiding. Not much cover there. Who were these guys?

BANG! BANG!

Luke put two bullets into his stomach. The guy fell over, holding his guts. He disappeared behind the sofa. Luke fired three more shots through the sofa.

The third guy was not here. Luke bounced to his feet and darted to the sofa. He glanced behind it. The guy he'd shot lay there, still alive, breathing heavily. His chest gave mighty heaves. He was shot through with holes. His shirt was stained with blood. His teeth were gritted. He looked up at Luke

"Listen," he said, gasping for breath.

"Sorry. No time for that today."

Luke shot him in the head. The skull popped apart like a cherry tomato.

Now Luke glanced around. He should crouch down and take this guy's gun, but he didn't dare do it. He had to finish the job first.

Luke moved through the beautiful office, sleek, gun out, in the shooter's stance he had learned in the Rangers so long ago.

That guy had to be in the bathroom. Either that, or he had magical powers.

Luke kicked in a bathroom door. Toilet, long stone sink, glass shower. In an office?

No one in here. He moved through it. He recognized how important time was—those guys out in the hall were going to be here any second.

He passed an alcove on his left, almost like a closet.

A gun appeared there. He saw it in his peripheral vision, saw it and didn't really see it. He spun, too late.

The black man had hidden inside the alcove—a clever spot. It was amazing that he could even wedge himself in there. He put the gun to Luke's head. Luke reached for it. He was half a second too late.

The man pulled the trigger.

Click.

Nothing happened.

The guy was a kid, maybe twenty-five years old. At most. His face had barely seen a razor. His eyes were hard, but they were lying eyes.

The kid pulled the trigger again.

Click.

What was this, training day?

Luke shook his head, then pointed his own gun at the kid's face. The gun's muzzle was three inches from the kid's forehead.

The kid dropped his weapon.

"You see what happened here?" Luke said. "You got in a gunfight, but you didn't count your shots. You lost your head a little bit. So you ran out of bullets, and you didn't even know it. You've had all this time hiding back here while I've been out in the hallway, and you could have reloaded. But you didn't."

Luke shrugged. "It's the kind of thing that comes with experience. I'm a little surprised they hired you for this job. To be perfectly frank, you weren't ready for it."

The kid smiled. He had some kind of English accent, Luke thought London. "Yeah, but your old friend wasn't ready for me, was he? He was crying before the end. I made him squeal like a stuck porker, okay?"

Luke pulled the trigger, point-blank range. The kid's face imploded. Blood and bone sprayed the white wall behind him. The kid's big body dropped to the floor. The bullet had put a whale of a ragged hole in the drywall.

"No," Luke said. "Not okay."

He padded back into the office. He had some breathing room—maybe ten seconds' worth. He was rusty, but so far he had done okay. Even so, if the kid had been thinking, Luke would be dead now. He was still alive because of luck.

He looked down at the boss, the older guy who had murdered Gottlieb. Sports jacket, slacks, dress shirt, leather loafers. He bent down near the body. He checked the man's jacket for a badge or some kind of ID. Nothing. Just a half-empty pack of cigarettes. He looked for a wallet in the man's pants pockets—also nothing.

These men were ghosts. They weren't government agents—they weren't anybody.

Luke glanced at the ruined doorway to the office. He removed one of the dead man's loafers and threw it out into the hall.

Instantly, the hall was sprayed with automatic fire.

Duh-duh-duh-duh-duh-duh-duh.

The walls and floor were shredded out there. White smoke and dust rose from the shattered drywall

There was trouble coming down that hall, and it would be here any minute. He had to get out of here.

Luke stood and went to the window.

Bingo! There was a fire escape outside. He tried to slide open the window—it wouldn't budge. It had some kind of complicated lock mechanism. It almost seemed like you needed a key to open it, even from the inside. Not much use in a fire.

The reason for it came to him in a split second. The lock kept children from opening the window—children who might want to

140

escape. Luke glanced back at Gottlieb, sprawled on the floor. There was a lake of blood around him, some of it already growing tacky. He had finally gotten what he deserved. It had just taken too long, and when it came, it had happened too fast.

Wrong. Gottlieb was breathing. His breath was a death-rattle, his chest heaving, his lungs gasping for air.

His eyes rolled and found Luke. His face was red and feverish with pain.

He tried to say something.

"What?" Luke said.

Gottlieb gestured with his head at the hallway. "They're going to kill me."

Luke thought about it for one second. Of course it was true. Gottlieb was a loose end, and looser than most. From their perspective, he had to be eliminated.

Luke nodded. "Yeah. I'd say that's right. If you even live long enough for them to get here."

"I'm afraid… to die." It seemed an agony for Gottlieb just to get the words out.

"I'm afraid…"

The air hissed out of him. His eyes unfocused, his chest relaxed, settling to the ground. Whatever he knew, the information had died with him.

There was nothing Luke could do about that now.

He picked up Gottlieb's heavy wheeled office chair, got a good grip on it, and hurled it through the window.

* * *

Just up the street, a chair flew out of a third-story window.

The chair hit the cobblestone street with a loud crash. Glass from the shattered window tinkled down on the brick sidewalk like a rain shower. A woman screamed, as tourists and afternoon shoppers ran for cover.

Ed Newsam's second beer—an IPA brewed in Tennessee—had just arrived on his table at a sidewalk café. As he watched, Luke Stone climbed out of the demolished window and dropped fast down the fire escape—not clambering down the stairs, but falling to Earth along the outside grillwork like a trapeze artist or a chimpanzee.

For Ed, tracking Luke to this place had been easy enough—he had called Swann and asked where to find him. As far as anyone at Quantico knew, Ed was taking a late lunch, and then had an afternoon joint administrative meeting at the Pentagon. Until a moment ago, that still might have happened—although admin meetings bored him to tears.

Even bare seconds ago, he had been enjoying the historic district while he waited for Stone to reappear from his visit to the psychiatrist. The narrow streets of the Old Town teemed with well-heeled, late-season tourists in lime green and sunflower yellow pullovers, peeking in shop windows or laughing as they stumbled out of the restaurants and pubs.

But now Stone had happened, reappearing in typical Stone fashion and upending any other plans or concerns.

The fire escape ended at the second floor. Luke didn't bother opening the ladder. He simply dropped the last ten feet and rolled backward onto the sidewalk. Then he was up and running, the opposite direction from Ed.

Three stories up, more men came bursting out that window.

All over the street, men who were shopping or walking or just standing around, suddenly dropped everything and went sprinting after Luke Stone.

A block away, Ed spotted Luke make a right turn, dart across the street, and disappear down a side street, headed for the waterfront.

Ed leapt up, climbed on top of his table, and jumped over the velvet rope that marked off the edge of the café. His table collapsed to the ground, appetizer plate smashing, beer glass shattering, as he landed on the sidewalk. He was running almost before his feet hit the ground.

Instead of following Luke, he went the other way, cutting down the side street just behind him. He barreled through the crowds, knocking people out of his way. People shouted, their terrified eyes wide as saucers, as the giant black man descended on them at full speed. A young couple tried to get out of his way and fell to the cobblestones, but he kept running.

"Move!" he screamed. "Move!"

A sea of people parted, driven ahead of him like frightened cattle, like daredevils running ahead of the bulls at Pamplona.

He blasted downhill, going very fast. He reached the waterfront and looked to his left. Luke was over there, at least ten men chasing him now. Everything was moving over there, people running, people falling, the entire waterfront district flowing away from him.

Ed crossed to the docks, still pushing people out of his way. A handful of boats were tied up. He moved along the wharf, looking for the right one—he would know it when he saw it. And there it was, just up ahead.

A small Seadoo jetboat—a four-seater with a two-stroke inboard engine. It was a piece of junk, a toy, and probably gave its owner nothing but headaches. But if it went at all, it would go very, very fast.

He pulled his hunting knife as he ran. He leapt across the gap to the boat, cut the lines in a couple of swipes, and let it drift. There was no time for anything. He pulled his gun and hammered the ignition box as hard as he could hit it—one time, two times, three. The box cracked apart, revealing the naked ignition mechanism—he ripped out the key slot with his bare hand.

Now there was no key necessary. He reached in with his thumb and forefinger, turned the ignition, and the engine roared into life. Λ beautiful sound. Music.

He slid into the driver's seat.

"Go, man!" he shouted at himself. "Go!"

* * *

Luke ran down a wide concrete dock. It was a wrong turn.

There were a couple of very large sailboats tied up down here, sails down. No motorboats. Nothing small. By himself, it would take him twenty minutes to get any of these sailboats out of here. He didn't have twenty minutes.

He didn't have twenty seconds.

He stopped and turned. He was breathing very hard, and there was a pain in his gut that did not feel good. It was more than just pain—it felt like he had ripped a couple of his surgical staples out. Even worse—adrenaline was probably masking the real pain.

Not that the pain, or the staples, would matter if he died. Half a dozen men came down onto the dock from the street. Another ten or more were just behind them. The men were no longer running. They walked toward him now.

Tourists, hand-holders, lovers, and strollers of various stripes, flowed along the very edges of the dock back toward the men, squeezing past them, escaping onto the street. The killers weren't interested in them, and let them pass without a glance. Soon, there was no one on the dock but Luke and them.

Who were these guys? They weren't going to kill him in public, in broad daylight, were they?

He supposed maybe they were.

He glanced around. There was a large electrical box to his right. He could duck behind that and try to fight from there. But it probably wouldn't hold up against their guns for long. And once he went behind it, that was it—he was trapped.

He could jump into the water and make a swim for it. But the water was probably very cold this time of year, and they would plug him full of holes before he got far.

He could leap onto one of the big sailboats and try to hold it against them until the police arrived. Surely they must be on their way after everything that just happened. He could duck behind one of the thick mast poles, or climb below decks. The nearest sailboat was all wood, so the bullets would chew it up, but...

It was a long shot, a delaying tactic, but it was the closest thing to a plan he had. If he could hole up, stay safe, even for a few minutes, he might make it. Surely these guys wouldn't hang around and wait for the cops.

Behind him, and to his right, a speedboat was coming in very fast—much too fast. It was bombing hard, bouncing over the river swells. It caught his eye because the man driving it must be insane. He was going to crash into this concrete dock.

The man driving it...

...was Ed Newsam.

The boat cut hard, throwing a heavy swell at the dock. It barely slowed down as it approached, and Luke didn't hesitate.

He ran the last five steps to the end of the dock, leapt...

...flew through nothingness...

...and landed in the seating area just in front of the cockpit.

Ed wore Oakley sunglasses against the glare coming off the water. His face was stern and hard as he scanned the river ahead of them. His big hands gripped the steering wheel. They were zooming, and his eyes were sharp, looking for obstacles—police boats, civilians, anything. His head was on a swivel.

Luke looked back at the dock, quickly fading into the distance. His friends were back there, staring at the boat and drawing their guns. Luke pulled his own gun and looked for a shot.

"Down, Ed! Down!"

Ed ducked, a second before bullets strafed the side of the boat.

Luke leaned over the gunwale and fired several shots.

BANG! BANG! BANG!

The sound was loud, and echoed across open water. Back on the dock, the men were on the ground, taking cover. The dock was dwindling fast, becoming a speck, indistinct against the Old Town waterfront. It was too far to make an accurate shot with a handgun—too far for Luke, too far for them.

Now Luke looked at Ed. His face was about four feet away, on the other side of the windshield.

"Ed, what are you doing here?"

Ed didn't smile or look away from the task at hand.

"I couldn't let you have all the fun, could I?"

CHAPTER TWENTY EIGHT

2:10 p.m. Eastern Daylight Time
The Situation Room
The White House, Washington DC

Ezekiel Harris was reading from the Bible.

"'The law will go out from Zion,'" he said. "'He will judge between the nations and will settle disputes for many peoples. They will beat their swords into plowshares and their spears into pruning hooks. Nation will not take up sword against nation, nor will they train for war anymore.'"

Gerry the Shark sat back in his plush leather chair and stared. Jefferson Monroe's pick for Vice President had once again rendered him speechless.

"Isaiah, chapter two, verses three and four," Harris said.

Gerry looked around the egg-shaped Situation Room. The place was hyper-modern, a far cry from the feverish Cold War doomsday imaginings of Gerry's childhood. Large flat-screen monitors were embedded in the walls every couple of feet, and a giant projection screen on the far wall at the end of the table. Tablet computers and slim microphones rose from slots out of the conference table—they could be dropped back into the table if the attendee wanted to use their own device.

Admittedly, the group was rather sparse today. It was the first time they were using the Situation Room—a preliminary meeting to get everyone on the same page in the China playbook. Robert Coates, former Chairman of the Joint Chiefs and soon to be announced National Security Advisor, was here, along with some of his people. Jeff Monroe was here and a few transition staff from the campaign. And a young Marine carrying the nuclear football—the suitcase with the nuclear codes inside—was here.

But Jeff had also invited Harris, and as a result of that, the whole thing was starting to go off the rails.

"That's very nice," Coates said. "It's a beautiful sentiment. I'm a man of Christ myself, but I think we should be careful. Not everyone agrees on what Scripture teaches about warfare. Also, we're already getting a lot of pushback against our plans, so I think we need to give up this idea that we have the luxury—"

"General," Harris said, "the apostle Paul was echoing Christ's sentiments when he said, *If possible, so far as it depends on you, be at peace with all men.* It's a sin to launch a war simply because you feel like it."

Coates shook his head. "We just don't have time for that. We are on the verge of war, and we need to prepare. There are thousands of people in the streets protesting this presidency, and the upcoming confrontation with China. There are people at the Pentagon who are saying publicly that they will disobey first-strike orders. In this room, we need to circle our wagons, build consensus among ourselves, and get our plan—and how we intend to sell it—right the first time."

"General, I am the Vice President–elect of the United States. I believe I was chosen for that role to bring my experience and my understanding—"

Gerry the Shark clapped his hands, loud, cutting off the conversation. This had gone on too long. It was a joke. Ezekiel Harris had first made his mark on the world as a South Texas used car salesman—EZ Harris. EZ credit. EZ loan terms. EZ no down payment closing—just walk in, sign the paperwork, and drive the car off the lot.

He had amassed his fortune not on all the half-dead beaters he sold, but on the bogus extended warranties that his customers were duped into buying as well. What they didn't know was EZ Harris also owned the insurance companies that wrote the warranties, through a maze of offshore shell companies. What they also didn't know was that the policies weren't worth the paper they came printed on.

Ezekiel Harris was a crook, a thief, and a conman, and he had parlayed his success at selling lemons on TV into a stint in the United States House of Representatives. Somewhere along the way he had become friends with Jesus, and he thought that meant everyone had to drop everything and listen up when he whipped out his trusty Bible.

Not today, man. Gerry had had enough. And the Holy Spirit had finally loosened his tongue.

"EZ, you're here because Jeff Monroe has been married and divorced four times, and has fathered at least three bastard children out of wedlock. Moreover, he doesn't have a religious bone in his body, as far as we can tell. Lightning strikes the doorknob every time he tries to open a church door. We included you on the ticket so that the millions of Christian Taliban out in that great heartland of ours would be able to hold their collective noses and vote for him anyway. Frankly, you were my idea. Jeff wanted to pick somebody real."

Jefferson Monroe raised a hand. "Gerry..." He looked at Harris, shook his head, and laughed. "You know how Gerry gets. He's a maniac, but he's our maniac."

"Jeff, let me finish. I want to get this out there."

Gerry pointed at Harris.

"I'll bet you anything—a million dollars—that I know your own people better than you do. They want this war. You know why? Because the Chinese took their jobs. The Chinese took their prosperity. The Chinese took their future. And not for nothing, the Chinese are pagan idolaters. They worship false gods. This will probably come as a shock to you, but there's no Jesus in Daoism or Confucianism. They *pre-date* Jesus. Ever talk to a Chinese person about the Christian concept of God? They think the whole idea is funny."

Harris shook his head, but he smiled. "Gerry the Shark... I wasn't talking about why you chose me for this position. I know why you think you chose me. I was talking about why the Almighty chose me."

Suddenly, Malcolm was in the room and at Gerry's ear.

"Mr. O'Brien, I've got an update for you."

He said it in a fierce whisper, a tone of voice that suggested the news wasn't good.

Gerry raised his hands. "Okay, okay. I need to take a little break. General Coates, do you have a menu of options for us to pursue?" It occurred to Gerry that Coates wasn't a general anymore, and had in fact been stripped of his rank. Well, they would just have to reinstate him somehow, wouldn't they?

Coates nodded. "The Pentagon has well-researched and longstanding attack plans with regard to China. Many of the scenarios are very good—we just have to get them to agree to implement them. We enjoy vast naval and air superiority. The key is to keep our infantry out of it. We don't want to get bogged down in a land war with the Chinese—they can put far too many boots on the ground."

"Okay, guys." Gerry stood. He turned to Jefferson Monroe, ostensibly the man in charge here. "Jeff, we'll get this all worked out. I promise."

He entered the elevator with Malcolm, and they rode to the first floor without saying a word. Now they walked briskly through the echoing halls of the West Wing. Gerry wished for a closet they could duck into, somewhere they could have a conversation where he knew it would be private. His office was out of the question.

"Talk," he said, under his breath.

148

"Sydney Gottlieb is dead," Malcolm said.

Gerry nodded. "Okay."

"Luke Stone is alive."

Gerry turned to look at him. This was worse than Ezekiel Harris reading from the Bible. Then again, without Gottlieb, what did Stone even have?

Nothing. He was at a dead end.

"But we do have Stone's car," Malcolm said. "And we're retrieving the GPS data now."

CHAPTER TWENTY NINE

3:35 p.m.
Ocean City, Maryland

Luke watched Swann out of the corner of his eye. All the man seemed to do was watch TV and drink beer. That's what he'd been doing when Luke had last left here. Luke didn't relish the idea of Swann holing up in this place the rest of his life—he'd like to get him back out into the world somehow.

The television was gigantic and its flickering screen commanded the vast spaces of Swann's high-ceilinged penthouse apartment. There were no other lights on in the room, and the apartment's big windows were oriented east toward the ocean. The sun set early this time of year, so the light of day was bleak and fading. The shadows were long and growing longer.

Luke washed down two more Vicodin with his own bottle of beer. He glanced around. Swann was on the big white sofa, a computer open on his lap. Ed was in one of the soft chairs, sinking deeper and deeper while nursing a beer.

A woman's talking head appeared on the TV screen, eight times its normal size.

"In just under ninety minutes, Acting President Karen White is expected to step down, effectively handing the Presidency over to her newly announced Vice President, Jefferson Monroe. While political opponents cry foul at this sudden move, many experts suggest there is nothing unconstitutional about the maneuver, and that it isn't even really a surprise. Chuck?"

The screen changed, and a dark-haired man appeared outside in a windbreaker jacket. An unfocused image of the White House loomed in the background. The man seemed to be pressing a headphone to his ear.

"Thanks, Sandra. We're awaiting the transfer of power, the second in less than three days. The ceremony itself will be small and intimate, with no media present. Sandra, political scholars I've talked to say that the move, while certainly unprecedented, doesn't appear to break any laws. And given that Jefferson Monroe would assume the Presidency in two months anyway, it seems prudent to end all the uncertainty and upheaval and allow him to begin his administration now.

"Not everyone will agree, but people I've talked to say that with the President and Vice President murdered just two nights ago, the system our Founding Fathers put into place more than two centuries ago is once again showing its resilience and its robustness in the face of very trying circumstances. From the White House, this is Chuck Shepherd. Back to you, Sandra."

Sandra reappeared, turning toward the camera now as if she had been off doing something else while Chuck was talking.

"Not everyone will agree. That's for sure. Anti-Monroe protests are ongoing in at least a dozen major cities, and despite the midnight curfew in place across the country, police are bracing themselves for more violence during the night."

Sandra appeared to turn a sheet of paper over on her desk and move another into place. The whole thing was a bit of a fake, wasn't it? The woman didn't ever refer to her notes, as far as Luke could see. She spent the entire time reading from the teleprompter. She was less a journalist than a spokesmodel.

"In other news, the body of missing CIA agent Kent Philby was found late this afternoon in a modest Washington, DC, apartment. Philby made headlines three decades ago when it turned out he was simultaneously working for American, Russian, and Israeli intelligence agencies. Today's grisly discovery was a surprise, mostly because intelligence officials had assumed that Philby was long dead. Stay tuned for more on Kent Philby and the legacy of Cold War spies in the next hour."

Luke had to get away from the TV set.

He drifted with his beer out onto the deck. The view from here was wide open, nearly 360 degrees, but it was the ocean his eyes kept coming back to. It spread out vast, endless, and eternal. As the day began to fade, the white foam of the crashing waves stood out against the gathering dark. He placed his beer on the stone parapet.

A stream of images flooded his mind—his mother, Kent Philby, Becca—all dead. He had led them to Philby. In a sense, he had killed Philby. He smiled at all the aliases Philby used to give him. Luke never actually thought of him as Kent Philby—he thought of him as whatever ridiculous alias the old man was toying around with that day. Then he pictured the old man's body lying on the floor somewhere. The TV announcer had called the scene "grisly." Of course it was. Philby wouldn't have handed information over willingly to a bunch of goons.

Luke flashed back to what Swann had told him just a few days ago.

It's like you're superhuman. Even when you get hurt, it seems like it doesn't really hurt. People get too close to you, and they begin to think this thing you have also applies to them. But it doesn't. Regular people get hurt, and they die.

Once upon a time, Kent Philby was not a regular person. But his age made him vulnerable, more vulnerable than Luke could ever understand. Luke had killed four men today—three of them died because they lost their focus for one second, maybe two. It was a gift to be that dialed in, but it was also a curse. No one should be allowed near him. He thought of Gunner, who was probably better off as far away from his father as possible. What would he do if Gunner died as a result of his carelessness?

He looked at the sky, the blue deepening in front of his eyes. Out to sea, it was already turning black. He felt a scream coming on. He was afraid of it—he was afraid of the emotions inside of him—the loss, the anger, the mindless rage. He was alone in this world and he should be alone. It was right and good that he be alone. That way he wouldn't hurt anyone else.

It was like a burst of powerful electricity surged through his body. He raised his arms to the sky, his hands balled into fists. His body stiffened. He opened his mouth and shrieked, but no sound came out. His jaws separated as far as they would go. He stood there, arms outstretched to the empty sky, silently screaming. He was trapped in this position—it was like he'd been hit by lightning.

A small sound escaped his throat. Aaaaaa, glug.

The moment ended. His arms came down. His heart was beating very fast, and his body trembled. His breath came in harsh gasps.

"He was in the game, man," Ed Newsam said behind him. "He knew the risks."

Ed could do what few men his size could do—move in total silence. Luke didn't even know he was back there.

Luke nodded. "I know."

"He was an old, old man, who probably should have died a long time ago. He was doing this stuff before you and I were even born. He used up his nine lives, that's all."

Luke said nothing.

"You didn't force him to meet you. He did it because he enjoyed it. He was addicted to the game, the rush, just like anybody else we've known. You gave him the opportunity to keep his hand in. Well, you keep sticking your hand in the fire, at some point you're gonna get burned."

"It sounds like you're blaming the man for his own death," Luke said.

"I don't blame nobody for nothing," Ed said. "I just try to make sense of things. It seems to me that in our world you have to try to do what's right, you have to stay sharp as hell, and once in a while you have to get lucky. Philby's luck ran out. I get that you loved him, but that doesn't change the facts."

Luke turned to face Ed.

"When this is over," Ed said, "if you want to find the men who did it and go see them, I'll be open to that. But first things first. We're supposed to be on an operation here. I'm risking my job over this."

Luke shook his head. "It's too late anyway. I killed them this afternoon." The futility of the situation landed on him like a bag of bricks. There wouldn't even be a chance to take proper revenge. The guilty parties were already dead.

Ed nodded. "In that case, there's no rest for the weak and weary. I came out here for a reason. Someone just contacted Swann over an encrypted connection. That person wants a meeting with you."

Luke looked Ed in the eyes. The painkiller was kicking in, but so was the beer. He was exhausted, physically and emotionally. He needed to sleep if he was ever going to recover from his injuries. The darkness seemed to be closing in around him. Even four hours of downtime could make a difference. Six would be better. Eight would be like a dream of some fantasy paradise.

"I don't know, man. Can it wait?"

Ed shook his head. "I think you want to take this meeting."

CHAPTER THIRTY

5:35 p.m. Eastern Standard Time
Blue Ridge Mountains, Virginia

The sun had gone down. Night was here.

The assault team closed in.

Twenty men came in five armored SUVs. Two electronics experts blew the high-voltage fencing that surrounded the complex. Eight men approached the entrance to the bunker from the front, five through the woods on either flank. Two men, the team leaders, hung back at the cars as a viewing and command post. There was a helicopter circling overhead, with two sharpshooters leaning out the bay doors.

The men all wore Kevlar body suits and helmets.

Two men crossed quietly to the bunker entrance. The door was heavy metal, double-steel, but it wouldn't hold up to C4 plastic explosive. It looked more like a security door on a Parks Department utility closet than the entryway to an impenetrable nuclear fallout shelter.

The lead man planted the explosive, molding it to the surface of the plate covering the lock mechanism. The second man lit the detonator fuse, and both men ran. Everywhere, the men took cover, slipping noise cancelling headphones over their ears.

BOOOM.

The explosion was bright and loud. When the smoke cleared, the door was still there, hanging on its iron hinges. But fully a third of the door, and the entire locking mechanism, was gone.

Instantly, the assault squad ran for the door. Each man had a flash bang stun grenade. Each man carried a shotgun. The plan was to ride the elevators to the living quarters, then throw the flash bangs in. If the team was lucky, the blasts and the blinding light might disable the subjects, or simply remove their will to fight.

The third in line, a young man named Kevin, wiped some sweat out of his eyes. It was a cold night in the mountains, but he was sweating like crazy. Truth be told, he was nervous. He didn't want to die, not for a job.

He had spent four years in the US Army, two full tours overseas, and he was willing to die for his country. But he was a private contractor now, and taking out the occupants of a private underground bunker—how was that protecting the United States? It

154

seemed like a stretch. He didn't even know who was down there—they told him it wasn't his job to ask questions.

He had a feeling in his bowels, a loose feeling like how it was before he went into a firefight. He smiled. Loose bowels were his good luck charm. He'd never gotten so much as a scratch in combat.

Stop it. Pay attention.

He brought his mind back to the present moment. The line of men was bottlenecked inside the foyer to the bunker complex. There was one elevator here. This had to happen, and already there was a delay waiting for the elevator. Summoning the elevator to the surface was a dead giveaway they were coming.

Already this operation was FUBAR.

Kevin walked over and checked a door at the end of the short corridor. To his surprise, it opened. An iron stairway snaked down into the bowels of the Earth, lit at every landing by yellow sodium lamps.

"Hey, Top!" he said, calling to the squad leader. "There are stairs here. Maybe we should skip the elevator."

The squad leader looked at him. He was a guy in his mid-thirties who had clearly let himself go a bit since Special Forces training, if that was really what it was. Kevin had his doubts. The squad leader shrugged.

"You want to take the stairs twenty stories, be my guest. We'll meet you down there. Personally, I'm going to wait for the elevator."

Kevin came back just as the elevator door opened and the squad piled in. The door closed and the elevator instantly began to descend. It fell fast, zipping past lights he could see outside the tiny sliver of window.

He pictured it in his mind. The door opens, they throw their flash bangs. BAM! Fall back, wait for the explosions, then rush in. He would be second out the door. Hopefully, he wouldn't take a bullet from the defenders as he went.

The elevator stopped abruptly and slowly settled to the ground.

"Ready," the squad leader said. "Look sharp. Ready with those grenades. It's go time, boys."

The door slid open and four flash bangs flew out. Kevin ducked back just as the squad leader shut the door again. The men hit the deck, but the sound and light were muffled from behind the door.

The men stood and got ready for the door to open again.

"Eyes sharp!" the squad leader shouted. "Eyes sharp!"

The door slid open again and they burst out, moving fast, securing the area around the doorway. Nothing moved, no one offered resistance. Within seconds, Kevin was running down a hallway, kicking doors and screaming.

"DOWN! GET DOWN!"

His blood pulsed in his head. His heart hammered. His hands were trembling.

After the third door, he and his partner stopped. The room was a living quarters, with two narrow beds, a table, and a lamp. There was no one here. There had been no one behind any door they'd kicked yet.

Kevin poked his head out into the corridor.

"Clear!" someone shouted from a nearby room.

"Clear!" another person shouted from down the hall.

If the people down here were going to defend their bunker, the smart thing to do would have been to try to stop the invasion at the entryways—in particular, when the elevator had opened. But they didn't do that.

"Clear!" someone shouted from much further inside the complex. The assault squad was moving through very fast, encountering zero opposition.

No one was down here.

CHAPTER THIRTY ONE

5:55 p.m. Eastern Standard Time
Crisfield, Maryland

The dark surface of the water was shrouded in a cold fog.

Luke waited quietly on the rickety wooden boat dock. Behind him, at the very edge, Ed Newsam stood in his brown leather jacket, cradling a shotgun. Nearby, on a different dock, a red fisherman's shack sat inches above the water.

They were on the eastern shore of Chesapeake Bay, in a town known for its tourism and its summer crabbing contests.

Tourist season was over.

It was full dark now, perfect cover for a clandestine meeting. The area was deserted. In the small harbor, moored boats bobbed up and down in the gentle swells.

"Hello, gentlemen."

A man had joined them—he had approached silently along the docks. To Luke, it wasn't much of a surprise. He was beyond exhausted now. The Vicodins weren't making much of a dent in the pain any longer. He was hardly on full alert.

Ed nodded to the newcomer. His relaxed posture suggested he had watched the man coming the entire way.

"Don," he said.

Don Morris, former United States Army colonel and Delta Force commander, founder and former director of the FBI Special Response Team, stood and watched them. In the gloom, Luke could barely make out the lines of his face, but he could see the shock of white hair. Even free from prison, Don hadn't bothered to color it. Once upon a time, it had been mostly black, with gray mixed in. Salt and pepper had become him when he was an authority figure, in command of the SRT. White seemed to become him now that he was… what?

A former hero? A mass murderer?

Luke caught a glimpse of Don's deep-set, penetrating eyes. His body looked as strong as ever—broad arms, chest, shoulders, and legs. He remembered Don telling him about the workout routine he invented, which required no equipment, and which he could do inside his tiny cell in the supermax federal prison. Squats, pushups, chin-ups, yoga, and martial arts. Don had claimed to spend hours a day exercising.

"Ed, how are you doing?"

Ed nodded. He didn't seem interested in meeting his old boss's eyes. "Better than you, I'd say."

"Two and a half years in solitary confinement," Don said. He patted his flat abdominal muscles. "Don't knock it until you've tried it."

"Did you finish the book you were writing?" Luke said. "Your memoir?"

Don nodded. "I did. I'd love for you guys to read it some time. You're both in it."

"I'm sure we'll both look forward to that," Luke said.

The three men stood on the dock. There wasn't much to see in the swirling mists. About a mile away, there appeared to be lights on the back deck of a waterfront bar. Laughter and music came to them through the damping effect of the fog.

"How are Becca and Gunner?" Don said.

Luke shrugged. "Becca died of cancer two years ago. I don't see Gunner much anymore."

"I'm sorry to hear that. Was it a long battle?"

Luke waved that away with a quick swipe of his hand. "Let's save the family updates for another time, Don. You contacted us, and there must be a reason for it. Monroe secured your release. Are you working for him now? Did you come here to ask for some kind of a truce? Because I can tell you, I'm not in a truce kind of mood."

Don shook his head. "Absolutely not. Whatever you think of me, and I remember from the last time I saw you that they are not kind thoughts, know this: I'm an American and a patriot. I'm not interested in working for these people. They are a threat to our country, our way of life, and indeed, the world. You probably felt that way about Bill Ryan and myself, but you were wrong."

Luke didn't know what to say about a man guilty of conspiracy to commit three hundred murders calling another man a threat to America.

Don went on. "They released me for their own reasons, which have not been communicated to me. But I'm out and there are things that I know. If you're fighting Jefferson Monroe, then I'm on your side. And I came here to give you a gift—two gifts, actually."

Luke turned and looked back at Ed. Ed grunted. It could have been the sound of mirth. It could have been the guttural sound an animal makes before it rips out the throat of its prey.

"What are they?" Luke said.

"The first gift is a piece of advice. I was your commander for a long time, Luke. And yours too, Ed. Once upon a time, you would

158

have valued any guidance you received from me, and I hope that's still true."

"Depends on what it is," Ed said.

"It's this: you're moving in the wrong direction. I know what you were after today, and I'm far from the only one. I know about all about the MK-ULTRA mind control program, and the fallout from it. It's not a secret that Sid Gottlieb was killed today, and it's no secret you were there when he died. It didn't make the newspapers or the TV, and it's not going to. But that's because they sent in cleaners to make it go away. Gottlieb's going to be found dead of a heart attack in the next couple of days, alone at home."

Luke nodded. That wasn't a surprise. "Okay."

"No. Not okay. No one knows what Gottlieb told you before he died. This goes beyond Gottlieb, and beyond Jefferson Monroe and his right-hand man, O'Brien. They are minor players. This goes all the way down the rabbit hole."

Don paused and considered his next words.

"The mind control program never ended, Luke, not really. That's what I'm telling you. And if you try to follow that path, I promise you won't get anywhere. Sleeper assassins are the least of it now. Mind control is too deeply embedded in our society for it to end—too many interested parties have too much to lose. You'll make too many enemies, powerful enemies, who would prefer to see Monroe run this country into the ground, or bring on the End Times, than be exposed themselves. You don't have time to sink into that quagmire. World War Three is scheduled to start less than thirty hours from now."

"So Jefferson Monroe didn't send you," Ed said. "But someone else did."

These were Luke's sentiments exactly. Ed just beat him to the punch.

Don ignored the accusation. "When this ends, if it ends, and you want to make stopping the mind control programs your life's work, I won't say a word. It'll probably take you that long—until the end of your lives. But for now, if you want to unseat Monroe, then you have to take a different tack."

"What do you suggest?" Luke said.

Don didn't hesitate. "Election fraud. That was the original investigation, and its validity still stands. He's as dirty as can be—there's no way he won that election. If exit polls are to be believed, he lost by thirty percent. But somehow he won instead. There are people in this world who know how that happened. All you have to do it find those people, and help them go public with what they know."

"Help them, or force them?"

Don shrugged. "Whatever it takes."

Luke thought about it for a moment. Maybe Don was right, maybe he wasn't. Maybe he was deliberately leading them down a false path. Luke would never fully trust Don again—every word the man uttered had to be examined for hidden agendas and motivations.

Don was already turning to go.

"What's the second gift?" Luke said. "You said there were two."

"The second gift is a resource you'll need to prove the election fraud. Wait for it. It'll be here in a minute."

Don disappeared into the dense fog.

Luke looked at Ed again.

Ed shrugged. "It's probably a drone strike. The longer we stand here, the better they lock on to us."

Somewhere nearby, a motorboat engine started. Luke listened as the boat idled, then moved slowly through the no-wake zone, and then opened throttle as it headed out to deep water. At no point did its running lights come on. Gradually, the engine sound faded away. All that remained now was the laughter of the handful of drinkers still on the back deck of the bar.

A figure appeared at the far end of the dock, coming this way. In a moment, it resolved into the figure of a woman. The woman was slim, with long, curly brown hair and a very pretty face. Her nose did a slight upturn at the tip. At one time, she wore funky red-rimmed glasses as part of her style—hipster nerd—but not tonight.

Times had changed and so had the woman in question. She wore jeans, a heavy linen coat, and boots.

Luke thought back to the night he had turned up half-drunk at her apartment in Georgetown. She had answered the door in a long baby blue T-shirt. It hugged her shapely body and barely came down to her thighs.

The shirt had a cartoon of various animals all standing together. A black bear. A moose. A white-tailed deer. A few ducks, and some furry rodents. An elephant. A rhinoceros. Even a small brown boy and a little blonde-haired girl.

Underneath the crowd was a caption: *Too Cute to Shoot.*

At the same time, Trudy herself had opened the door while holding a big matte black Glock. The gun had seemed gigantic in her small hand. Luke had nodded at the gun.

"You gonna let me have it with that?"

Now, two years later, Trudy Wellington stood in front of them on the dock. Life underground agreed with her. She had been young when she disappeared. She seemed even younger now.

"Hello, boys," she said. "Long time, no see."

Luke smiled. It was the first instance when a smile felt genuine on his face in a long time. It was very good to see her.

"Don said he was going to give us a gift. Are you Don's gift to give?"

Trudy smiled and shook her head the tiniest amount.

"Don is a silly old man."

CHAPTER THIRTY TWO

7:48 p.m. Eastern Standard Time
34th Floor
The Willard Intercontinental Hotel, Washington DC

The bedroom was very large, with a gigantic California king–sized bed and a girl draped across it. The stone floors were cool on his bare feet. The room's windows faced the lit up Capitol Building. Wide double doors gave out onto a private balcony.

Room service had left him a cart on rollers with a bottle of spirits, as well as a bottle each of red and white wine. Also, there were some finger sandwiches, a pitcher of water, and a bucket of ice. He barely glanced at the wines or the sandwiches. The spirits were Glenfiddich thirty-year-old scotch, so that was good news. He poured three fingers' worth into a glass, without ice or water, and sipped it, enjoying the taste and the feel of the fire entering his belly.

Evening was here, and his day was done—Gerry the Shark had decided to call it an early night. He was overtired. He recognized that. And being around the White House was starting to make him feel paranoid—he needed to get the entire place swept for bugs. He would do it every day, if he had to.

They had come a long way very fast.

He looked at the girl. Katie the young campaign worker—she of the rich conservative dad who believed so fervently in trickle down economics. She still had the long straight hair, but she was no longer packed into a sweater and a skirt. Now that she was out of her clothes, she had a body with so many curves it was almost an outlandish cartoon of the female form. That body coming free had reminded Gerry of wild horses galloping on a high plateau.

"Wine?" he said.

"Yes, please. Red, with ice."

He grimaced at the thought of it, but uncorked the bottle and poured it for her. She drank it fast and he poured her another. She downed it and he poured yet another. She must be nervous to be in his presence like this. He sipped his scotch.

Gerry joined her on the bed. He ran a hand along her leg, and soon forgot about the many things that were bedeviling him right now. He took his time, even though this was all about him, and not about her at all. Once, he looked into her face and saw that her mind had gone away, maybe running on that high green field with all those beautiful horses. Afterward, they lay on top of the sheets, one of her legs draped across both of his. Gerry picked up his drink where he'd left off.

He was very tired, he realized now. He lay back with his glass propped on his chest and closed his eyes. He could sip his scotch with only the slightest movement of his hand and his chin. His mind drifted from its moorings and began to scan through the past, settling here and there on various memories. It was a pleasant sensation. He smiled.

"Why do you want to start a war?" Katie said.

Gerry took a deep breath. He was feeling so good that he didn't even mind fielding questions from her.

"We have to put a stop to Chinese aggression."

She seemed to think about that for a moment.

"I don't believe you."

He nearly laughed. She was a straight-ahead smart chick, this girl. And not nearly so shy as she acted around the office. She had called his bluff without hesitating. If more people did that on a regular basis, he never would have climbed this far.

"Okay," he said. "Try this on for size. It's a bluff, a giant game of chicken. We have a much stronger military than they do. If we push them, and they back down, it's a huge win for Jeff right off the bat. He will be seen as having delivered for the people who voted for him, and he's only been in the White House a very short time."

She nodded. "Right. But what if they don't back down?"

He thought about that for a moment. This was a more complicated idea, one that he might have to walk her through. She was young, after all.

"War is an organizing force," he said. "It gets the mass of people moving in the same direction, a direction you can choose for them. And it motivates them. It gives meaning to their lives. Having an enemy, especially a threatening one, causes people to stop questioning their leaders. It gets them focused on symbols—like the flag, for example—and on the daily news cycle. They're too distracted by these things to think critically, or make any kind of long-term plans. In particular, symbols are an incredibly powerful way to get people to hand over their minds."

"So starting a war is a power grab," she said. "But a grab for power here at home, and not necessarily out in the world."

He nodded. "Exactly. It's not as if we're going to take over China, is it? Even so, and as difficult as it might be to hear, the best

163

thing for Jeff could be if the Chinese don't back down. This entire country will line up behind his leadership, even most of the people who think they hate him right now. And eventually, we would beat the Chinese—at least in a limited sense."

"What about the people who die?"

Gerry shrugged. "People die in war. Not much I can do about that."

"War is good for Jefferson Monroe," she said. "It's also good for Gerry the Shark. And that's all that really matters."

He did laugh now. "It's also good for Katie the campaign worker."

He took another sip of the scotch. The conversation was making Gerry sleepy. Time passed, and at some point he slept. When he woke again, she was on the terrace, nude in the cold night air, leaning against the stone railing and drinking another glass of wine. A bright quarter moon hung low in the dark sky.

She came back inside, bringing the cold air with her.

"I can't sleep," she said. "I think I'm gonna go."

"Are you afraid?" he said. "What we talked about? The war?"

She nodded. "Yes."

Gerry reached over to the night table and poured himself another small sip of whiskey. "You know what? It's a strange world. You never know what's going to happen next. If I were you, I guess I wouldn't worry about things so much."

She was starting to dress now, picking her things up off the floor.

"You know what?" she said. "I've decided I'm not coming into work tomorrow. I'm done. And I think you should worry a lot more than you do. The things you say could come back to haunt you."

CHAPTER THIRTY THREE

"Girlfriend, where have you been all this time?" Ed Newsam said.

Trudy Wellington shrugged. "Here, there, and everywhere."

Luke was astonished, again, by her beauty. He wouldn't say that he had forgotten about it, or about her. More that he had gone so far into himself, and so far away, that for a long time these things no longer reached him.

"Any place you feel like sharing with the group?"

"If I could blindfold you and slip twelve-hour sleeping pills in your drinks, I would be happy to take you all with me."

It was like a family reunion.

Even more than a family, it was like the reunion of a team that had won the championship some years before, and all the players had gone on with their own lives and their own careers. Now they were back together for a night.

Swann had ordered in a stack of pizzas, and four six-packs of high-class microbrew beers. Pizza and beer for the all-stars. Luke did nothing to discourage the feeling. He was as excited as any of them.

It would be nice to think that something like this could last.

Lights were on throughout Swann's huge apartment—all over the ground floor and upstairs, even crossing the catwalk that loomed above the open living space. Swann was pumping music in, seemingly from everywhere.

Gradually, even with heavy food and beer in their stomachs, talk turned serious, as it always did. They got down to business.

"Where would you start?" Luke said to Trudy. They were both sitting on Swann's long white sofa.

"With this? I'd start at the beginning—a blank slate. Then I'd make a couple of grand, sweeping assumptions and test them to see if they had any validity."

"Make one now."

Trudy nodded. "Okay. Susan Hopkins won that election by a mile. Even if there was voter suppression in minority districts, which I believe there was, it shouldn't have mattered—and at this moment, isn't even worth pursuing."

165

"It's not worth pursuing minority voter suppression?" Ed said. "Trudy, I didn't know you were one of those." He was half-smiling, but only half.

She looked at him and shook her head. "Of course I'm not. The reason we don't pursue that is because voter suppression, even in the most egregious cases, is hard to prove beyond a shadow of a doubt. You have to take it on a case-by-case basis, which means to prove that it impacted an election, you'll want to pull together hundreds, if not thousands of cases. It will become he-said, she-said. Would a reasonable person agree that this new regulation discouraged particular individuals from voting? Even when the evidence is plain as day—for example, when the data is clear that voting in a certain district dropped off the table after a new rule was put in place—the cases can wind their way through the courts for months. We don't have months."

"But voting machines..." Swann said. He had wandered over with a beer in his hand. Luke guessed that it was already his sixth or seventh. It didn't seem to impair him in any way. "They're easier."

Trudy pointed up at him.

"Exactly. For Monroe to have turned this election around at the last minute, there had to have been fraud, and it had to have been widespread. That suggests someone tampering with the machines—not in local polling places, but on a large scale, in numerous places. When we find the evidence of fraud, it will likely be unmistakable. And it will be big. There should be patterns visible all across states that were considered battlegrounds, and even in a few that weren't."

"How do you find those patterns?" Luke said.

Trudy shrugged, smiled, and swigged her beer. "That's what my friend Swann and I are going to find out tonight."

Swann picked up a white remote control off the glass coffee table. He hit a button and to their right, spotlights came on in the only area of the downstairs that had still been in darkness. A glass partition automatically slid away into the wall. A big leather chair sat at a desk with three tower hard drives on the floor beneath it, and two flat-panel screens on top of it. Wires ran all over the floor.

"Remind me of this," Luke said. "How secure?"

"As secure as it gets," Swann said. "Believe me, I don't want anyone tracing anything back to me, so I'm careful. Masking programs run the data all over the world before it comes here through a secure portal. Totally untraceable. And I've got access to everything—hundreds of communications satellites, surveillance satellites, thousands of databases, hijacked network traffic, email servers, you name it. You need information? Here it is."

"Can you hack into the election machines and see if they were tampered with?"

Swann shook his head. "Maybe. But I wouldn't suggest going that route. Even if I got inside the machines, I'd have to pick the right ones, and then I'd have to compare them to ones that were never altered. For all I know, the difference could be a very subtle change in coding that would take a team of investigators weeks to find."

"So how do we do this?"

"It should be simple enough," Swann said. "If you were someone who wanted to alter election results, a campaign, for example, you would want to hire someone who was an expert on voting machines, especially new-fangled digital or network-based ones. More than just an expert—you'd want to hire someone who specialized in these machines, either programming them or hacking them."

Luke nodded. "Sure."

"And that means at some point you had to communicate the exact details of your desires to that person, and that person would have communicated to you how it would work, and what they might want in exchange for doing it."

"Emails," Trudy said.

Swann smiled. "We can expect that the sellers of these services would be very, very careful with their identities and their communications. And we can guess, from prior experience, that the politicians would be almost laughably reckless with theirs."

* * *

"Luke? Let's go, man. It's time to move."

The sun was just rising over the Atlantic Ocean. Luke lay on a lounge chair on the roof deck of Swann's penthouse. He had curled up fully dressed out here the night before—in the night, someone had covered him with a thick comforter.

They hadn't bothered to try and bring him indoors. They knew his tastes—he liked to sleep outdoors.

His eyes were still closed, but he felt the early morning sun warming his face. This time of year the sun was already weak, and its rays barely cut through the chill. He enjoyed the feeling of it just the same. Somewhere above his head, the seagulls shrieked and called.

"Luke?"

"Yeah, Swann. I'm awake. What's the story?"

"The story is we let you sleep. Seemed like you needed it. But it's time to get going. Rachel and Jacob are here."

"Rachel and…" Luke opened his eyes.

They were old friends of his, his favorite pilot tandem back in the Special Response Team days. Both of them were former US Army 160th Special Operations Aviation Regiment. The 160th SOAR were the Delta Force of helicopter pilots.

Standing by the sliding glass doors to Swann's apartment was the whole crew, all of them staring at Luke. Ed, Trudy, Swann, and now Rachel and Jacob.

Neither of them had changed much. Rachel had dark auburn hair. She was brawny like the old Rosie the Riveter posters. Jacob was nearly Rachel's opposite. He was thin and reedy, and looked nothing like your typical elite soldier. Rachel tended to get ramped up and emotional. Jacob tended to stay eerily calm, even while taking fire—especially while taking fire. As pilots, it didn't get much better.

Luke swung his legs off the lounge and put his feet on the deck. To his left, the ocean stretched across the field of vision, a 180-degree panoramic view.

"What are you two doing here?"

Rachel shrugged. "We work with Ed at the Hostage Rescue Team. He called us, so we came."

"Are we taking a helicopter somewhere?"

"No, we're taking a plane."

"But you guys are—"

"We also fly planes," Jacob said. "Just not into combat."

Luke stood. He was glad they let him sleep. He was feeling a lot better. Pain? Sure, but that was a given. He could kill the pain by popping a pill. But his energy, alertness, and ability to think had taken a jump. He also seemed to have more, and better, perspective than the day before.

"Where are we going?"

"Swann and I stayed up all night, running different scenarios," Trudy said. "It turns out that Monroe and his people are very good at keeping secrets. We believe they were in touch with a hacker or team of hackers, but the encryption on their communications is very sophisticated, and could take weeks to break."

"Meanwhile," Swann said, "Monroe's primary opponent wasn't nearly as good, at least within his own campaign. We have internal memos that suggest had he won the primary, he intended to hire a hacker to tamper with voting machines. They never name the person, but it's clear that was the intention."

Luke ran a hand through his hair. "Who was the opponent? I forgot to tip the paperboy and my newspaper subscription got canceled."

Trudy smiled. "Stephen Lief."

The name rang a bell for Luke. He could almost picture the face. Very moderate conservative from an Old Money family. He had been hammered for being weak on a variety of issues, and for constantly falling back on family wealth and family prestige. That guy had been hoping to become President?

"Okay, I'm ready." He moved across the deck in his bare feet. He slipped through the crowd and into the apartment.

Ed was drinking from a white coffee mug. In round black letters, the mug said: *Coffee Makes Me Poop.*

"Nice cup," Luke said as he passed.

CHAPTER THIRTY FOUR

7:45 a.m.
Key Biscayne
Miami, Florida

It was way more house than they needed.

It had belonged to a Colombian cocaine trafficker named Ramon "El Malo" Figueroa-Reyes. *El Malo* meant "The Bad One." El Malo's career had ended abruptly, and his former house— Pierre's people had rented it from a very discreet leasing agency through an intermediary—had some eccentric design flourishes.

Outside, on the entry walkway just before the front stairs, was a three-times-life-size bronze sculpture of El Malo himself with two Doberman Pinschers off their leashes and on the alert. The in-ground pool no longer functioned because El Malo had filled it with salt water—then repeatedly set sharks loose inside of it. The sharks had all died and the pool's maintenance systems had become encrusted with, and eroded by, salt.

However, the design aspects most interesting to Susan's team had more to do with security. There was one road onto the property, which crossed a narrow drawbridge. The drawbridge was currently up. There were deepwater moorings here, but in order to reach them, boats had to pass through a winding channel which ended at a high steel sea gate. The gate was now closed.

In fact, the only way to enter the property at this moment was by helicopter. And a helicopter coming in for a landing would be a sitting duck for gunfire from defensive shooting positions on the second floor of the house. The place was potentially vulnerable to a missile attack, but if it really came to that...

All bets were off.

Susan padded down the grand spiral stairway in pajamas and a pair of slippers. Chuck Berg and another Secret Service agent shadowed her every move. They followed her through the great room and into the industrial kitchen. There were a dozen work stations in here, pots and pans hanging from hooks overhead.

Susan found some instant coffee packets in a drawer and put on a small pot of water. She turned and the two Secret Service men were still there, right behind her.

"Don't you guys know that I'm already dead? They're supposed to put me in the ground today. Or tomorrow. Or whenever they get around to it."

Chuck almost seemed to smile. "That's what we're trying to avoid."

She mixed her coffee with a fake creamer packet and a couple of sugar packets. She sipped it. It tasted awful. She carried it out of the kitchen with her and shuffled along down a long hallway toward the sound of a television.

The hall emptied into a large living room with sweeping views of the bay, a large causeway, and downtown Miami toward the northwest. Embedded in a white entertainment system was a massive seven-foot flat-panel TV. Kurt Kimball and Kat Lopez, both already dressed, stood and stared at the screen. Susan plopped down on a plush sectional pit sofa—it must have had twenty separate pieces. If she was already dead anyway, she wasn't going to stand at attention—she was going to relax a little, if she could. She had been through the wringer these past several days.

"What's new in the world today?" she said.

"They've postponed your state funeral again," Kat said.

"Why do you suppose they're doing that?"

Kurt shrugged. "They know you're alive, or they suspect it. Pierre's people sent us satellite imagery of a raid conducted on the bunker complex last night. I think the last thing they want to do is claim they have your body, hold a funeral for you, and then have you turn up on CNN an hour later."

"It's a good thing we got out of there," Kat said.

"Well, we have Luke Stone to thank for that," Susan said. They hadn't heard a word from Stone since he had left two nights ago. Susan found herself hoping he was still alive.

On the TV, a commercial break ended and Karen White appeared on the screen. She was dressed conservatively in blue slacks and matching jacket. Her hair was trimmed and styled. She looked almost… professional.

"So is today Karen's victory lap?" Susan said. "The shortest term as President in American history? She looks pretty good. Being President upgraded her wardrobe, in any case."

Kurt put a finger in front of his mouth to shush her. "Listen."

"Tell us more about Gerry O'Brien," the host of the show, a middle-aged man, said to Karen.

"Gladly," Karen said. "I think people on the outside recognize that Gerry is the brains of Jefferson Monroe's operation. But it goes much deeper than that. Gerry is in charge. He's a modern Rasputin.

He's a master manipulator, and he orchestrated events to get them into this position."

"Give us an example," the host said.

"Okay, Tom. You asked. And it pains me to say this. I could have kept quiet about it, but after a night of heavy soul-searching, I'm not going to do it. I would have remained Acting President until Monroe's inauguration. But Gerry forced me to name Monroe my Vice President and then resign immediately."

"He forced you? Come on, Karen, you're a big girl. You've been a survivor in the rough and tumble of politics for a long time."

Karen's voice started to shake. "He threatened me, Tom. He has damaging information on me, and he told me he was going to release it. He said he was going to destroy my career."

"So you're saying the President's policy advisor, his closest aide, blackmailed you into stepping down?"

She nodded. "Yes." Tears began to stream down her face.

"He also told me he was going to control my votes in the House of Representatives with the dirt he has on me. And he was going to control my public statements. That's why I came on your show this morning. And I'm going to go any other show that will have me. Because I can't let him do that. And the American people need to know what kind of criminals are occupying the White House."

"Do you want to tell us what kind of dirt O'Brien has on you?"

She hesitated. "Yes. I have to put a stop to this. Gerry O'Brien threatened to leak to the media that I am a prescription drug addict."

"Are you?"

"Yes."

Susan watched Karen White weeping now on national television. It was as though she were seeing Karen for the very first time. These early-morning news shows were watched by millions of people getting ready for work. Karen had just made a whale of an admission.

"Wow," Susan said. "That was brave."

"And it just about torched Gerry O'Brien," Kat said. "Monroe must be having a stroke."

"Careful," Kurt said. "They've weathered worse storms than this. We don't know how much legitimacy Karen White has in the eyes of the public. If I'm not mistaken, people generally see her as a fool, a sort of comedy relief. That's usually how I've seen her. Although I'll admit she's a lot better without the funny hats."

"What will you do now?" the TV host was saying.

"I need to go away for a while and get some help," Karen White said. "I know that. I've been running and running for years, working too hard, and what I never realized was I wasn't running toward my goals, I was running away from myself. I need to stop doing that. If it takes three months to get better, or a year, or eighteen months, so be it."

"And if your job in the Congress is no longer there when you return?"

Karen nodded, as if she expected the question. "Then I'll do what I should have been doing all along—raising awareness about this terrible problem that I have, and that so many millions of other Americans also have."

The host looked directly into the camera. "Karen White, Speaker of the House of Representatives, and briefly, Acting President of the United States. We wish her the best in her battle with drug addiction. More after this."

"I don't know," Susan said as the next wave of commercials came on. "I for one am taking her a lot more seriously today than I was yesterday."

Outside the house, a sound caught her attention. Suddenly, Chuck Berg and the other Secret Service agents were on the move. One agent stayed behind.

"Susan, hold tight," he said. "If I get the word, we'll go straight to the panic room and lock ourselves in."

The sound resolved itself into the whirr of helicopter blades.

In the doorway, Chuck Berg was holding a large black walkie-talkie. He looked back into the house and nodded. "It's okay. It's Pierre."

Susan rushed to the doorway. The chopper was small and white—not at all the kind of helicopter Pierre normally rode in. The words CHANNEL 6 NEWS were stenciled in red on the outside. Quite a disguise.

The chopper landed on the pad, and before the blades had even stopped, Pierre jumped out. A moment later, Susan's heart leapt as Lauren and Michaela, her two beautiful twin daughters, climbed out after him.

Not for the first time, the thought occurred to her: there's more to life than being President of the United States. A lot more.

And yet…

"I think we should announce that I'm alive," she said to no one in particular.

CHAPTER THIRTY FIVE

8:05 a.m.
Palomino Ranch
Ocala, Florida

"I've been waiting for someone like you to come," the man said.

Luke and Ed stood in the front yard of the sprawling ranch house, looking up at the man on the porch. The man was middle-aged, owlish in round glasses, with a vaguely pear-shaped body. He was Stephen Douglas Lief, former United States Senator from Florida, former primary candidate for President of the United States.

Luke worked to focus on the man, but he had to admit he was distracted. When the plane had landed, Luke had a new text message on his throwaway cell phone. It was from Gunner.

Dad, it said. *I'm glad you are alive. I was worried. I want to see you. Gunner.*

No mention of the word "love" in there, but it was real progress. His son wanted to see him! His heart raced at the thought of it. He would see Gunner – as soon as he could, just as soon as this operation was over.

Now, Ed was holding his badge up. "Sir, I'm Agent Edward Newsam with the Federal Bureau of Investigation. This is my associate, Agent Luke Stone."

Luke didn't say a word, or offer a badge. He didn't have one anymore.

Lief waved all of that away. "Yes, yes, of course you are. Please come in. Would you like some coffee? If you haven't eaten, I'm sure our cook would love to whip you up some bacon and eggs, or anything you want. The food is very good here."

"Coffee is fine," Ed said.

"Sure, coffee would be nice," Luke said.

They followed Lief through the house to a large veranda in the back. Rolling green pastures extended as far as the eye could see. It was shaping up to be a warm day. The sun was bright and hazy. Half a dozen horses galloped and played in the near distance.

"Won't you please sit down?" Lief said, offering them seats at a rough wooden table.

They did as he asked, and a moment later, a young black woman in a domestic uniform brought their coffee on a silver tray, with cream in a decanter and sugar cubes. Once the coffee was on the table, the woman evaporated as fast as she had appeared.

Lief indicated the horses with a tilt of his head.

"We raise them. Quarter horses. Chargers. Also, sometimes thoroughbreds come and retire with us after racing, and sire the next generation. It's really a wonderful place to be a horse."

Luke nodded. The man's small soft hands told him everything he needed to know about who raised the horses around here. "That's nice."

"I assume you aren't here to arrest me," Lief said. "I imagine there'd be a bit more fanfare for an arrest. Anyway, my security team would never have let you come up the driveway if I thought it was that."

Luke pictured the driveway—it was a mile-and-a-half-long dirt road.

"We're just here to talk," Ed said.

"In that case, please do," Lief said. "I'm all ears."

"You were Jefferson Monroe's opponent in the primaries," Luke said.

Lief nodded. "Naturally."

"And we understand it was a vicious campaign."

Lief's owl eyes opened a little wider. "You understand that, do you? Did you not follow the campaign?"

Ed shrugged and offered a ghost of a smile. "Agent Stone and I both spend quite a lot of time on assignment. We can be out of the news loop for long periods."

"Of course," Lief said. "I understand. In that case, I'll tell you a little about it. I've been in politics my entire life, and it was the worst thing I've ever seen. Jefferson Monroe and his right-hand man, Gerry O'Brien, are the two dirtiest campaigners in modern American history. Monroe doesn't open his mouth without lying. And O'Brien…" Lief shook his head. "Suffice to say that's a man who knows where the bodies are buried."

"So there's no love lost between you?" Luke said.

"Love lost? That's putting it mildly. I hate Jefferson Monroe. He has brought politics in this country to a new low. His rise is a tragedy for the United States. I was raised to believe that civility in the public sphere was important. We're all Americans, and as much as we might disagree on issues, we're all trying to do the best for our country. Monroe doesn't care about things like that. He doesn't care about honor or tradition or mutual respect. He didn't call me by my name, not once, during the entire campaign. He referred to me at various times as Mr. Nice Guy, The Sellout, and The Trust Funder. His supporters ate it up. Ate it up.

"Monroe represents a strain of anger and resentment that rears its head from time to time. His version of it is the worst I've seen. I understand that there are people who feel they've been left behind. And as a country, we need to do better for them. But the United States is, and since its inception has been, a nation of immigrants. My family has been in this country since the 1600s, but even we came from somewhere else. And because I believe immigrants inject new energy and innovation into this society, and because I believe that free and open trade can bring prosperity to all people… this makes me the Sellout?"

"In that case," Ed said, "I wonder if you wouldn't mind telling us how Jefferson Monroe won the election?"

"The primary?" Lief said.

Ed shook his head. "The general election."

Lief's eyes became very wide indeed. "How he won…"

"When we first arrived, you thought we might have come to arrest you," Luke said. "There was a reason for that. We believe it's because you know how Monroe beat Susan Hopkins, despite the odds against him. You know a lot about certain techniques he used. Inadvertently, you might even have helped him win."

Lief looked at Luke, then turned to Ed, then came back to Luke.

"Ah," he said.

Ed nodded. "Yes."

"Care to take a walk?" Lief said.

* * *

They let Lief tell it his way, and in his own time.

They walked with him through the fields. Many of the horses knew him and came close when they saw him approach. He patted them and called them by name. When the horses came to him, he slipped them each a large sugar cube from a bag he kept in the pocket of his riding pants.

"When you're Stephen Douglas Lief," he said, "not becoming President of the United States means you're a failure."

"Tell us," Luke said.

"My great-grandfather owned all the land you see here, and much, much more. A hundred thousand acres, much of it citrus farms. My grandfather was sent north to East Coast private schools, and became a Wall Street titan. He was one of America's first billionaires, back when a billion dollars was a lot of money. My father went to Harvard Medical School, and he practiced as a doctor for a little while, but found politics more to his liking. He was in the Senate for thirty-six years. He became a fixture in Washington for nearly four decades. So who was I to become, if not President?"

"Pablo Picasso," Luke said.

Lief laughed. "You have to have some talent to do that."

Luke didn't bother to mention that he had worked directly for the President, and she was one of the most talented people he had ever met.

"No, I was going to become President. And until Jefferson Monroe appeared, it really seemed like there was just one person I needed to beat."

"Susan Hopkins," Ed said.

"Yes. Susan was popular, certainly, but our polling against her was strong. In a head-to-head match-up, it looked like it could go either way. The election would be about the battleground states, as it always is, but the margins would probably be so slim that victory would come down to a handful of key districts in just three states. And even in those places, the difference would be a razor's edge. To gain the Presidency, you had to somehow tip the scale in those districts."

"Or put your thumb on it," Luke said.

Lief shook his head. "More subtle than a thumb. At the last second, a housefly had to come and land on your side of the scale."

"Hack the voting machines," Luke said.

"Yes."

"Turn the votes in your favor by the narrowest of margins in just a few crucial districts, and make it impossible to detect that you had done that."

"Yes."

"You'd need a pretty sophisticated hacker for that," Ed said.

Lief nodded. "I had one."

"And after you lost the primary by a wide margin, he introduced himself to Jefferson Monroe."

Lief nodded again, but said nothing.

"We need to talk to that man," Luke said.

"I'm afraid that won't be possible," Lief said. "He died two days ago."

CHAPTER THIRTY SIX

8:50 a.m. Eastern Standard Time
The Situation Room
The White House, Washington DC

"Mr. President, make no mistake," the man said. He was a former four-star general, slim and fit, with a flattop haircut, a man named Sanford Walters. "We will win a war with China. There are several ways we could play it, one of which is markedly preferable to the others."

Jefferson Monroe stared at the man, but was having trouble focusing on his words. Walters was another cast-off from the Susan Hopkins days—he'd had some trouble with her, been forced into early retirement, and now they were bringing him back. He was old cronies with General Bob Coates, who had brought him in, touting him as some Asia expert.

What Jeff Monroe didn't want was a bunch of has-beens that had been drummed out of service by the previous administration. When things settled down, he was going to get some real generals in here.

"Can you explain our options to me, please?" Monroe said.

Walters nodded. "Of course, sir. And glad to do it." He stood and went to the large projection screen at the far end of the room. An image of China and the South China Sea appeared. Icons of missiles and warships came and went. Walters droned on about missile systems, strike forces, payloads, and megatons.

They sat around the conference table, Monroe at the head. He had Walters, Coates, numerous members of their staffs in the outer ring of seats, and Gerry the Shark. The young Marine with the nuclear football was gone. Sometime during the night, the Pentagon had taken him back—it was an astonishing breach of protocol, but they no longer trusted Jefferson Monroe with the nuclear codes.

Monroe shrugged that off. He could only handle one problem at a time.

Gerry was the major distraction today. Karen White was all over the TV news, telling the whole world that Gerry had extorted her into quitting. Monroe himself had watched her act on three different shows, beginning at 6:30 in the morning.

By the time he had finished dressing and eaten his breakfast, she was hinting about something quite a bit darker than blackmail—she seemed to suggest that Gerry O'Brien was somehow involved in the Hopkins and Horning assassinations. If that story got legs, it was going to be very hard to put the lid back on it.

Almost as bad, as far as Jeff Monroe was concerned, was he had taken a call from one of his earliest and best supporters this morning. Abe Becker was the president of Becker Industries, which was involved in infrastructure services for the energy industry—drilling rigs and ocean platforms, logistics like shipping and trucking, pipelines, heavy earth movers. Jeff had been friends with Abe's dad, who had founded the company, and over the years he had also become good friends and partners with Abe. Becker Industries was on board with Jeff's campaign almost before anyone.

Abe's young daughter, Katie, had been a campaign aide, and had stayed on board right into the White House—until this morning, when she'd resigned. She had called her dad last night in tears, saying that Gerry O'Brien was mean to her personally, deliberately intimidated and bullied staff members, and told her point-blank that they were instigating a war with China so they could seize more power here in the United States.

"Jeff, what's this war about anyway?" Abe had said over the phone.

"The people want it," Jeff told him. "The people who elected us."

"Are they still going to want it when their kids start dying? And if they don't want it then, who are they going to blame? Themselves?"

"Abe, it's not going to—"

"Jeff, when you set off on this adventure, what were you and I talking about? If you don't remember, let me remind you. Business-friendly environmental and workplace policies. A lower effective tax rate for corporations and top-tier personal incomes. A tough but realistic negotiating stance with our adversaries. Basically, a return to the Reagan years. We said those two exact words over and over again, as I recall: Ronald Reagan. An older statesman with a firm hand. Since then, somehow this whole thing has morphed into talk of nuclear first strikes and goon squads attacking Chinese people in the streets. What happened?"

"Abe, I'm late for a meeting. I need to call you back."

"Jeff, I've got a daughter sitting in her apartment crying this morning. I've got an ex-wife calling me, accusing of backing a lunatic and getting our daughter in over her head."

Monroe shook his head. "This isn't a sheltered workshop, Abe. Katie is welcome back any time, but please understand that Washington politics are hard-hitting. I've seen some thick-skinned people get their heads handed—"

"She's my little girl, Jeff. And I was there for you when everyone else thought this was a joke."

Monroe rubbed his eyes. "I know it."

Now, in the Situation Room, he watched Gerry the Shark watching the general's presentation. Gerry looked fresh and alert, dressed sharp in a three-piece suit. His shoes were so highly polished, the reflection of the overhead lights could practically set paper on fire. Gerry had been an asset to the campaign, there was no doubt about that.

But Gerry had also pressed for security fences around the Chinatowns—a project that was stalled, first because construction workers were walking off the job sites, and now because a federal judge in California had declared the whole thing unconstitutional late last night, and issued an injunction against it. As events stood, the Chinatown initiative was looming as a colossal failure and an embarrassment. It was going to be a major challenge to get it back on track—an easier, more effective approach might be to cut bait on the whole thing and move on to other agenda items.

Gerry was being accused of blackmail—and possibly murder—on national television by one of the highest ranking politicians in the country, the former Acting President and Speaker of the House.

Gerry had somehow made Abe Becker's daughter cry and quit her job. Gerry had abruptly removed all the remaining Secret Service from the building this morning, and replaced them with private military contractors—he claimed he had evidence that the Secret Service were loyal to the previous administration. And Gerry was the driving force behind war with China. This thing was his baby.

Monroe didn't want to think of Gerry as a liability. He didn't want to consider throwing him overboard. But he had to admit events seemed to be headed in that direction. Only they couldn't go there, could they? Jeff Monroe and Gerry O'Brien made an odd couple, but they were inextricably linked now. The things they had done, the things they knew about each other, had cemented their relationship in blood.

There was no way out, and there was no going back. The walls were starting to close in, as Jeff supposed he had always known they would. If he and Gerry the Shark were going to win this, they had to win completely. Utterly. Destructively.

There couldn't be any compromises. It was absolute power or nothing. And war with China was the way there.

War would sweep any lingering questions of election fraud or murder investigations off the table.

War would allow them to jail their enemies and crush dissent.

War would mobilize their supporters to new acts of violence and intimidation.

War was a good reason for widespread surveillance.

War, if it were dangerous enough, could lead to suspension of the Constitution, especially the Bill of Rights.

War was the answer.

Monroe raised his hand. "General Walters? I'm sorry, I lost the thread. Can you give me this one more time—the bullet-pointed version, not the master's thesis."

The general nodded. What else was he going to? Tell the President no?

"Of course, sir. As I indicated, there is a lot of reluctance at the Pentagon about a war with China. Privately, the Joint Chiefs are saying they will not act on attack orders from the White House."

"It's treason," Gerry the Shark said.

Monroe nodded. "Treason indeed."

Walters went on. "Mr. President, we have what I think is a pretty solid workaround. We have an Ohio class submarine, the USS *Alaska*, currently operating at the eastern edge of the South China Sea—the submarine is outfitted with twenty-four Trident II tactical nuclear missiles, each carrying eight warheads. The commanding officer on that ship is Captain Reginald Harlow. I'm old friends with Reggie Harlow. We are on the same page, so to speak, with regard to the Chinese."

Monroe nodded. "Good. Sounds good."

"Reggie is willing to make a first strike against the Chinese artificial islands at Fiery Cross Reef, Johnson South Reef, Mischief Reef, and Subi Reef. Chances of success are close to one hundred percent, and should totally destroy those islands. Reggie is actually more than willing—he's eager to do so, at our command. And once he does, the most dangerous moments of the war will commence."

"Dangerous?" Monroe said. "How so?"

The looks on the faces around the room made it clear what everyone thought: Jeff Monroe had drifted off during the general's presentation. So be it. Monroe was President—he could drift off if he wanted to.

"China has a no first-use policy," the general said. "But once attacked with nuclear weapons, they reserve the right to not only respond, but respond against high-value civilian population centers and infrastructure targets."

"In other words," Gerry the Shark said, "once we hit their fake islands, manned by a few hundred soldiers and sailors, they will feel free to hit our cities, with a population in the millions."

"Well," Monroe said. "That doesn't sound good."

Was it odd that Gerry was smiling about that?

"It gets worse," General Walters said. "Our intelligence suggests that the Chinese have fifty-four intercontinental ballistic missiles capable of hitting the United States. Our Asia-targeted missile defense shield has only thirty-seven interceptors—thirty-three based at Fort Greeley, Alaska, and four based at Vandenburg Air Force Base in California. Each interceptor is designed to shoot down enemy warheads after they've separated from their missiles, about halfway through their flights."

Monroe was liking the sound of this less and less. "So let me get this straight. A best-case scenario is that every one of our interceptors hits one of their warheads, and seventeen Chinese nukes make it through and hit the mainland of the United States?"

The general shook his head. "It would be comforting to think that, but no. Testing suggests that each of our interceptors has about a fifty percent chance of hitting its intended target."

Monroe did the math in his head. "So about thirty-six Chinese warheads will hit us? Son, I've always said I want to transform this office into a strong Presidency, but to do that, I'm going to need some people left to rule over."

"I wish that was the worst of it, sir."

Monroe's shoulders slumped. "Do tell."

"An unknown number of the Chinese missiles are the so-called Dong Feng 41. They have the longest effective range of any missiles on Earth, and can hit anywhere in the United States. Each missile carries a dozen warheads. Five minutes after launch, but before our defense shield would kick in, the missile falls away and the warheads separate. In other words, each Dong Feng becomes a dozen projectiles. A handful of these missiles will easily overwhelm the defense shield."

The general raised his hand in a STOP gesture.

"One good thing here is that the Chinese don't have enough fissile material to make dozens and dozens of nuclear warheads, so at least some of the warheads will be decoys, or conventional weaponry. But again, we won't know which is which until they hit."

Monroe glared around the room. Was this a joke? "I want to know the name of the man who designed this missile defense shield," he said. "And I want you to bring me his head on a plate."

"Sir, the defense shield was designed more with a rogue state like Iran or North Korea in mind. Not a great power like China."

The Situation Room settled into an awkward quiet. Downcast eyes studied the conference table, the video screens, anything but the President of the United States. Only Gerry the Shark was smiling. His eyes were gleaming with mischief.

"Okay, Gerry, out with it."

"Jeff, I think you're overreacting. The plan was never to attack the South China Sea islands and expect that to be the end of it. We have more than four hundred Minuteman missiles sitting in silos in Wyoming and North Dakota, all of which target China. If we launch them, we will destroy mainland China—their cities, their military bases, and any chance they have of counterattacking."

"But what good does that do, unless we launch them—"

Gerry nodded. "First, yes."

Finally, the plan began to crystallize in Jeff Monroe's mind. "But the Pentagon said they won't…"

General Coates finally spoke. "It's a high-stakes game of chicken, not so much with the Chinese, but with the Pentagon. They have all the information we've presented to you here. If we inform them that we have the ability to strike the South China Sea islands without their input, and that we are going to do so, they'll have no choice but to calculate the blowback from that, and take appropriate remedies."

Monroe still wasn't convinced. "What if they reach different conclusions?"

"Mr. President, both General Walters and I worked at the Pentagon for decades. We are very familiar with their thinking, and we have the channels to communicate with them. Once they know how serious we are, they will have no choice but to come to our conclusions. We will all be on the same page very quickly."

"Casualty assessments, based on your scenario?" Monroe said.

Walters nodded. "Of course." He leafed through some papers on the desk in front of him. "Between three hundred million and half a billion Chinese will die during the attacks. Many more in the weeks and months after that—of radiation sickness, dehydration, starvation, and exposure to the elements. On our side of the fence, we can assume some of their missiles will be launched and make it through. A worst case is that twenty million Americans could die in the initial exchange, with another ten million over time. A best case is that five million Americans will die."

"So our hair is going to get mussed, no matter what we do?" Monroe said.

Generals Walters and Coates looked at each other. "Our hair will indeed get mussed," Walters said.

"But you should see the other guy," Gerry the Shark added.

CHAPTER THIRTY SEVEN

9:35 a.m. Eastern Standard Time
The Skies over Georgia

"Albert," Luke said. "Albert Helu?"

"This is Albert," Swann said.

Luke shook his head. The Albert Helu thing was wearing a little thin. They had maybe twelve hours to get Monroe out of office before he started a war with China. Maybe they didn't even have that long. Since they both knew the deadline was coming, either China or the US could pull a preemptive strike at any time. Tripping over Swann's alias was chewing up precious seconds.

"I need you and your female friend to find something for me," Luke said.

Luke and Ed sat in the operations theater at the front of the FBI plane—a round table with four seats embedded around it. Ed sat across from Luke, talking into one of the air-to-surface phones. Luke was speaking into another one.

Luke stuck a finger in his free ear, partially drowning out Ed's conversation. He took a deep breath and dove in.

"A man named Dak Pearl was found dead in his apartment in Durham, North Carolina, sometime during the past couple of days. His place was looted of thousands of dollars' worth of computer and home entertainment equipment. They also took his car, a late-model BMW. It looks like a robbery, but it wasn't."

"Okay," Swann said.

"I need you guys to get me everything there is to know about Dak Pearl. Where he was from, what he appeared to be doing, known associates, bank accounts, real estate, anything at all."

"Who was he?" Swann said.

"He was the hacker who changed the course of American history."

There was a pause over the line.

"Give us thirty minutes."

"Twenty is better," Luke said.

"Naturally," Swann said. "I can't remember a time when I heard you say, take your time, uh... Albert. Go slow, be thorough."

"Fast and thorough," Luke said and hung up.

He sat back and stared out the window. The skies were clear. Far below them, a sea of white clouds billowed. They looked soft, like cotton candy. A vague wisp of memory floated across Luke's mind—a daytime jump when he was young. The clouds looked just like that, fluffy like a mountain of pillows. Then he passed through them, free falling, and they were cold and wet inside. They never seemed to end, there was no visibility at all, and he thought:

My God, am I going to hit the ground?

When he came out, he was still 10,000 feet above the ground, and it was a beautiful, beautiful day.

"I need a tactical unit," Ed said. "And I need it in the air." He paused, shook his head, and made a face. "No, I don't know where it's going yet. If I knew, I would tell you. I want it in the air over the southeastern United States, ready to land basically anywhere." He glanced at Luke and rolled his eyes. "Here's what you need to know. I'm with the Hostage Rescue Team, and I'm on a classified domestic operation. I am going to need a TAC unit to back me up. Today. I don't know where I'm going, but when I get there, if I don't have that backup, you are going to find yourself in a very hot place." He paused, the nodded. "Good," Ed said into the phone. "No, I don't need to vet the unit. Give me the best available, people with experience, and I'll just assume you did me right."

He hung up and looked at Luke.

"You'd think I was asking for the invasion of Normandy."

Luke smiled.

"Sure. What could possibly go wrong? You just need a bunch of SWAT guys, in the air, ready to risk their lives making a tumultuous entry... somewhere. No idea of the operational environment, no idea of the opponent."

Now Ed smiled. "That's right. They should be used to that by now."

He gestured at Luke's phone with his chin.

"What did Swann say?"

Luke shrugged. "He and Trudy are on it. Hopefully, they find us something we can work with."

The two men stared at each other for a long moment. Luke didn't feel it as awkward. It just was. A lot had passed between them, and then... it ended. There was nothing unusual about it. People were in your life, and then they weren't. Time moved on, and so did life. It hurt a little that it didn't have to go that way in this case, and he had been the one to blame. But there wasn't much he could do about that now.

"How's the job?" he said.

Ed shrugged. "Parts of it are good. Parts are... I don't know. I'm making the best money I've ever made. I've got the most responsibility I've ever had. But you know? They're moving me up and out of active operations. That's the price you pay—you reach a point where you're supposedly too valuable to be boots on the ground. You're too old, you've got too much experience, and they've put too much time and money into training you. So you sit at headquarters and watch young men die on a video monitor—over something you sent them to do."

He shook his head. "That ain't me, man."

"But that's where you're going," Luke said.

Ed nodded. "Like it or not."

The phone rang and Luke picked it up. Trudy's voice came over the line.

"Luke? We've got some stuff for you."

"Put her on speaker, man," Ed said, indicating a button on the phone.

She launched into it without preamble.

"Dak Pearl, twenty-seven-year-old African-American. Born in the Algiers section of New Orleans. Raised on welfare, living with his mother and three older sisters. He was identified as gifted at a young age—157 tested IQ, aptitude with both musical instruments and programming languages. He graduated from high school at the age of sixteen. Entered the Computer Science and Engineering program at Louisiana State University on a full scholarship, but dropped out after one year."

Luke did the math. That history brought Dak to seventeen. "What's he been doing the past decade?"

"He drifted for a bit. His rental history shows apartments in San Francisco, Seattle, and Somerville, Massachusetts. There are big gaps, which could mean he was in roommate situations and not on a lease. His job history indicates short-term programming jobs at various tech industry temporary agencies. There are large gaps there as well. It looks like he was either trying to break in somewhere, or just making fast money between his hacking efforts.

"About four years ago, he seems to settle down. He incorporated a North Carolina LLC called Crystal Clear Consulting. Two years ago, he purchased a condominium unit in an upscale building in Durham, which is the same apartment where his body was found. Around the same time, his mother left New Orleans and

187

bought a small home in Destrehan, Louisiana. Whatever Dak was doing, he was starting to move up in the world."

"What was the crime scene like?" Ed said.

"He appears to have been murdered in the shower. He was found nude with the water still running—shot once in the head. Neighbors didn't report hearing anything out of the ordinary, which suggests the shot was silenced. The police found his body because of an anonymous tip.

"According to news accounts of the murder, people in the building knew that he worked in the computer industry, but didn't know what he did. People did know that he had thousands—possibly tens of thousands—of dollars' worth of computer equipment in his unit, along with a collection of guitars and other instruments with an estimated worth of around a hundred thousand dollars."

"And all of that stuff was gone?" Luke said.

"Yes."

He looked at Ed. Depending on how much he talked about it, and to whom, the man really could have been murdered for his stuff. Ed's eyes said he was thinking the same thing.

"Known associates?"

"That's the thing. Dak Pearl appears to have been a loner who kept a very low profile. Cell phone records suggest that he called his mom a couple of times a week. He had no land-based telephone, and Crystal Clear Consulting operated from his address. We haven't been able to find a client list."

Ed shook his head. "I'm not buying that, Trudy. A young black man with money burning a hole in his pocket? He knew people, and they knew him."

"Uh, guys?" Trudy said. "Hold on a second. Looks like—"

Suddenly, Swann was on the line.

"Luke? Ed?"

"Yes. We're here."

"It's Albert. Listen, I went on a funny detour here with Dak Pearl. Actually, I went down the rabbit hole. Dak was a member of a local fitness place in Durham, something called Soul Studio. It's a place that does stationary cycling, yoga, other kinds of classes. Okay, not very exciting, except this. When he signed up, he had to fill out a waiver. I have a scan of it. Under emergency contact, he put someone named Pris Roy. Under relationship, he wrote girlfriend."

"That sounds like a known associate," Luke said.

"It gets better," Swann said. "Priscilla Roy, age twenty-five, owns a cabin in Foscoe, North Carolina. It's near Grandfather Mountain, in the middle of nowhere in the northwestern part of the state. A town called Boone is the closest thing they have to civilization out there. On the property deed, her permanent address is Dak Pearl's condo in Durham."

"It's his cabin," Ed said. "He put it in her name to hide it."

"Here's the best part," Swann said. "The cabin's electricity is on a smart meter system. All the power companies are going that way, and the data is on the internet—it's about the easiest thing in the world to break into. So I took a peek at the cabin's power usage—it's nuts. They're either growing a couple of acres of marijuana inside that house, or they're running a stack of computer servers twenty-four hours a day."

Ed and Luke stared at each other now.

"Looks like we have a destination," Luke said.

CHAPTER THIRTY EIGHT

10:15 a.m. Eastern Standard Time
The Oval Office
The White House, Washington DC

"Where are you on all this?" Gerry the Shark said.

Jefferson Monroe gazed out at the window at the November version of the White House Rose Garden. Nothing, he imagined, like it would be come spring.

There was a terrible power in his hands—the power to destroy the current order and remake it in an entirely new way. What would the world look like after the total nuclear annihilation of the most populous country on Earth? Which way would the fallout blow? Would there be a nuclear winter? He had to admit that he didn't know, nor had he thought to ask the generals.

What would life be like in the United States afterward?

It stood to reason that the Constitution would be suspended, and he would become the absolute ruler. Of course it would be meant as a temporary arrangement—someone had to be in charge during a crisis of that magnitude. But why, once the power was in his hands, would he ever give it back?

"Where would you suggest I be?" Monroe said, without turning around.

"On board," Gerry said. "One hundred percent."

"Is there any other way forward?"

There was a long pause before Gerry answered.

"I don't think so."

Monroe nodded. "Did you blackmail Karen into stepping down?"

This time Gerry didn't hesitate. "Yes."

"Did you have Susan Hopkins and Marybeth Horning murdered?"

Gerry didn't respond.

Monroe still didn't turn around. He found that he didn't want to look at Gerry. "Son, this office was swept for bugs two hours ago. We can't sweep it every ten minutes. At some point, you just have to accept that it's clean. Did you or did you not have those two women murdered?"

"Jeff, you know I did. Just like I had Patrick Norman murdered. Just like I had Dak Pearl murdered. There's no sense pretending you didn't know what I was doing in your name. We got here, but it wasn't pretty. I never promised that it would be."

Monroe nodded. He had known what Gerry was doing all along. He never knew the details, of course, but he always knew the general gist of it.

"Incidentally, Susan Hopkins is alive," Gerry said. "We don't have her body. Her people rushed it out of here that night. She was pronounced dead, but the body never turned up. I'm concerned that she's going to resurface at some point, and that's going to put another dent in our legitimacy."

"How do you know she's alive? How can you know for sure?"

"Her pet secret agent Luke Stone is investigating us. Our people have been following him the past couple of days. He's partnered up now with an old co-worker of his from the FBI Special Response Team. They commandeered an FBI airplane this morning, flew down to Florida, and had breakfast with Stephen Lief."

Monroe felt his heart skip a beat at Lief's name. He despised Stephen Lief, his country club upbringing, and everything he stood for. One of the great delights of his life had been giving Lief a sound thrashing in the primaries. But still, he and Lief had something in common...

"Dak Pearl," he said.

Gerry sighed. Monroe didn't think he'd ever heard him do that.

"Dak is dead. All his equipment has been destroyed. The money was placed in numbered offshore accounts. There's nothing to tie him to us—at least, nothing they'll find between now and when we go to war. After that, I doubt it'll matter."

Monroe finally turned and faced Gerry. He was surprised by the sight of him. Gerry looked fresh and relaxed, youthful even, as though the stress of these events was aging him in reverse. Was he bothered that right this minute his name was being dragged through the mud on all the television networks? Did he mind that newspaper reporters were bombarding their media staff with endless unfriendly questions about him? Did he even know that the White House comment line was inundated with thousands of phone calls demanding that he be fired immediately?

Monroe would have to guess that the answer, in every case, was no.

"What should we do in the meantime?" he said. "About this man Stone and his partner?"

Gerry shrugged. "We're tracking them. They're currently flying north, and we assume they'll land in the Raleigh-Durham area, trying to purse more information about Dak. Wherever they go, we have two security units from Blackstone Recruiters on standby. They're going to converge on Stone's location. If we can get him and his partner in an isolated place, we'll have the security units eliminate them. If we can't get them somewhere isolated, we'll have our guys eliminate them anyway."

Monroe nearly laughed. Gerry had missed his calling. He should have been a comedian.

"And us?" Monroe said.

Gerry nodded. "We should get underground. They tell me that Site R in Pennsylvania is our best bet. Once inside, we'll be safely tucked away, not just from the Chinese, but also from anyone in this country who might try to stop us. Then we can launch the attack."

Another long pause passed between them.

"Are you still ready for this? Nuclear war? The clash of civilizations?"

Monroe didn't hesitate. He'd been thinking about almost nothing else.

"I am. Yes."

"Do you want to make accommodations for your children or ex-wives?"

It seemed a strangely sentimental question, coming from Gerry the Shark. Monroe waved his hand at it.

"Eh. None of them speak to me anyway."

CHAPTER THIRTY NINE

11:28 a.m. Eastern Standard Time
Foscoe, North Carolina

For a moment, Luke didn't think their car was going to make it.

The driveway was a steep dirt road, pockmarked and rutted, which wound uphill through dense woods—the trees were already barren for winter.

The road dead-ended at the cabin. Their car was a rental sedan—it wasn't made for climbing. Somehow, it crested the hill and they parked it in the dusty dooryard—right next to the four-wheel drive, open-air Jeep already there.

Luke and Ed climbed out of the car and walked slowly toward the small cabin. It was fairly new, tidy, of log construction. Behind the house, a higher mountain gradually rose off in the distance. They stepped onto the front porch and approached the door. There was a modern doorbell with an internal nightlight.

Ed pulled his badge from inside his jacket, reached out, and pressed the button. The bell made a very homey *ding-dong* sound.

"Somebody's home," he said. "If that Jeep is any indication."

A woman appeared from around the corner of the house. She was to their left and a little bit below them. She was young, blonde, and pretty, and she held a shotgun pointed at them. Luke glanced at it. It was a large gun, probably a twelve-gauge, with a revolving cylinder that would hold about a dozen rounds. It was a combat shotgun, what people used to call a "street sweeper."

"Put your hands in the air!" she shouted. "High up there. If either one of you moves, I swear I'll kill you both."

Ed's hands snaked into the air. "That's a big gun for a little lady," he said.

She nodded. "Yeah, it makes a big sound, too. And it puts big holes in things."

Ed pushed it one step further than necessary. "You sure you can handle the kick on that thing?"

"Test me and find out."

Ed shook his head. "Ma'am," he said, "let's start over. Can we do that? I'm Agent Edward Newsam of the FBI. My identification is in my right hand. This is Agent Luke—"

"Don't even joke," she said. "I don't care what you say your names are."

"We know what Dak Pearl was doing."

"Of course you do. You killed him. Now you want to kill me, but it's not going to happen that way."

"Pris?" Luke said. "I know you're afraid, and that it's hard to think at this moment. But I want you to consider something, and take all the time you need to do so. I think you'll see the truth in it. The thing I want you to consider is this: when the killers come for you, they're not going to ring the doorbell."

The woman stared at them. A long, long moment passed. In the trees somewhere nearby, a bird started to chirp.

"Who did you say you are?"

"We are the FBI. I'm Agent Newsam, and this is Agent Stone. We aren't here to kill you. We're investigating Dak's murder. We believe he was involved in tampering with the results of the Presidential election, and that he was killed because of it. But if we want to prove that, we're going to need your help."

Ever so slowly, she lowered her gun. "Dak was such a fool," she said.

* * *

"He died for nothing," Priscilla Roy said.

She sat on a futon couch in the open living space of the cabin. It was a pleasant enough room—couch with matching futon-style chairs, a stone fireplace so clean it looked like it had never hosted a fire, a couple of stand-up lamps, a shaggy white throw rug covering about half the wooden floor. Mounted against one wall was a large flat-panel TV—the sound was off, but it was airing some talking head news show on cable television. The furnishings looked like they had been ordered online after about ten minutes of deliberation.

On an end table rested a TEC-9 semi-automatic. A long magazine extended from the bottom of it—Luke guessed it held thirty rounds or more.

The girl indicated the TV. "I keep it on in case Dak's face turns up. I figure he has to sooner or later. The man that threw the election to the bad guys gets murdered—that should be national news, right?"

Luke and Ed glanced at each other. The people who operated in the shadows rarely turned up on TV. When they did, it meant they were doing something wrong.

Pris shook her head. "He barely even made the local news in Raleigh. Just some tech guy who got killed because somebody wanted his nice toys."

There was a long pause. She stared at the white rug beneath their feet.

"He thought that because he grew up in New Orleans that meant he was tough and could play with the big boys. He was harder than everybody else. He was smarter than everybody else. He could run circles around anybody."

Tears welled up in her eyes. She closed her eyes and the tears rolled down her cheeks. She shook her head.

"He was kidding himself."

"He worked for the Jefferson Monroe campaign," Luke said.

She looked at Luke, her eyes glowing red now. "Yeah. He did. His plan was to do what he was supposed to do for Stephen Lief—flip a few close districts at the last second. But once he got started with Monroe, it was clear he was going to have to do a lot more than that. He was going to have to throw dozens of districts across probably eight or ten states. He would even have to do it in places where the vote wasn't going to be all that close. It was going to be impossible to do that without leaving evidence behind. That's when he started buying these guns."

"He thought they would try to kill him," Luke said.

She nodded. "To cut the evidence trail. But he was in too deep to stop. They had already paid him the front third of the agreement. It was a lot of money. I would get on him about the toll this job was taking, on him, and on us. And he'd say *What do you want me to do? Give the money back?* Of course I didn't want that. We had a nice life. I didn't have to work. I spent most of my time at the gym."

She shook her head, looking into deep space. The tears began to stream down her face again. Her body trembled the slightest amount. "If I had known then what I know now, I would have said yes. Give it all back."

"Do you have any evidence of what he was doing?" Luke said.

She shrugged. "I have all of it. I have everything and more. I have all the data files, and tons of screen captures of the work he's done over the past three or four years—he used to obsessively take screen captures. Finish a section, take a picture of it, save the file, keep going. He did it all with keystrokes. It was like he didn't even realize he was doing it—Dak could be like a robot sometimes. He also kept records of the people he worked for—Jefferson Monroe wasn't the only one, believe me. I have the aliases Dak used, and records of the bank transactions. Most of the money transfers took place outside of the country."

Luke looked around at the cabin—there wasn't much to it beyond this room. A kitchen and dining area. A bedroom and bathroom. This place was like a weekend getaway. Swann said it was sucking a lot of electricity, but if it was, Luke couldn't see where it was going.

Priscilla sighed. Her entire body shuddered, and she hugged herself.

"I guess I should show you guys the evidence."

Ed nodded. "If you don't mind. It'll help."

She shrugged. "It won't help Dak."

She stood, and with a violent yank, pulled the white throw rug back into a corner. A trapdoor was outlined in the wooden floor, with a lock mechanism near the top. She took a set of keys from her jeans pocket, inserted one in the lock, then pulled up the trapdoor. It was a thick door and Ed helped her with it. She threw it back and it landed on the floor with a heavy THUNK.

A ladder led down into the darkness.

She indicated the hole. "Be my guest. The light switch is to your left when you get to the bottom."

Ed went down first. Luke followed. For a split second, he imagined the girl slamming the door down on top of them and locking them in.

It didn't happen.

Ed flicked the light switch. A bank of overhead fluorescents twitched and flickered, then came on. The light was almost too bright. It revealed a room of solid concrete—concrete floors and walls. A row of tall computer servers stood on racks, lights blinking. Three tower CPUs lay sideways on racks extending from the wall. There was a bare table, with two monitors and a keyboard, and an executive-style desk chair. It was cold in here, noticeably colder than upstairs—a large air conditioning unit was embedded in the far wall. Luke could hear it running.

The man had hidden a tech center beneath his rustic mountain cabin. Clever.

"Okay," Ed said. "Let me go call this in. We'll get that tactical unit out here to secure the house, then we'll bring in some systems folks to—"

Luke interrupted him. "Are you sure that's a good—"

Ed looked at him. "I trust my people, man."

"Guys!" Priscilla shouted from above their heads. "FBI men! We have visitors outside. A lot of visitors."

Luke glanced up at the hole in the ceiling.

"Yours?" he said.

Ed shook his head. "I doubt it. I haven't called anyone yet. They don't even know where we are."

Luke stared at Ed.

"Oh man."

CHAPTER FORTY

A large gray Sikorsky helicopter came in low across the bay from Miami, an executive chopper which could carry eighteen or twenty passengers.

Susan stood near the front doorway to El Malo's house, watching the chopper land. She felt a nervous tickle in her stomach. She was flanked by three large Secret Service men—people who were loyal to Chuck Berg, and who had kept their mouths shut about this situation since the White House shootings.

Chuck himself stood just outside the door on the stone porch. The super-size bronze statue of El Malo and his dogs was just down the stairs from him.

"Who are they, and why do they think they're here?" Susan said.

Chuck didn't move or change his posture. He just kept his eyes on that helicopter touching down.

"They are TV reporters from the Miami affiliates of the national networks—ABC, CBS, NBC, and FOX. There's also a CNN person on there, usually does hurricanes. Each one of them has a camera person with them, and no one else. They think they're here because I'm going to act in my capacity as your former head of White House security, and make some announcement about your remains. They have no idea why we're doing this at the mansion of a drug lord, but it's probably piqued their interest."

"Have we checked them?" Susan said. "For weapons?"

She didn't want to embarrass Chuck or his men, but it was a sensitive issue right now. She had almost been killed by someone who had made it into the White House briefing room with a gun.

Chuck took the question in stride. "Oh, yeah. They've all been searched, right down to their undies. If any of these people has a weapon on their person, it's really *on their person*, if you take my meaning."

Susan raised the STOP sign hand, but then realized he couldn't see it.

"Okay, Chuck. That's more information than I need."

There was a briefing area set up about halfway between the house and the helipad. There was a podium with a microphone on a low platform, facing about a dozen white folding chairs. There were a couple of small speakers mounted on metal stands. The backdrop of the podium was sweeping views of the bay. It looked rather more like the setting for a small, intimate wedding than a press conference.

Already the first of the reporters were settling into their seats. At the back of the briefing area, there was a table with water bottles, a coffee dispenser, and some pastries—the camera people were helping themselves.

"I'm going to make this short and sweet," Chuck said. "Thirty seconds or less. When you hear me say your name, that's your cue."

Susan hung back while Chuck went up to speak. She took her hand-held mirror from her pocket and tried to get a sense of her look. Hair pulled back and neat. Blue suit—it looked okay. Decent shoes. She had done her makeup on her own, which was better than it sounded—she had learned to do makeup like a pro in the early days of her modeling career.

She gave herself a B on the overall look. The sense was of someone who had survived an attack on their life, went into hiding, and was doing their best to look presentable. Which was more or less exactly what had happened.

"So here's President Hopkins," Chuck said. "She's going to give a few formal remarks, and then I'm sure she'll be happy to answer some questions."

Susan walked out, flanked by the Secret Service.

The cameras attempted to move in on her, but other Secret Service agents kept them boxed in the press briefing area. The news reporters were all standing, craning their necks to see her. It seemed to take forever to reach the podium.

She stepped to the microphone.

"Thanks, everybody, for coming. First things first: I'm alive. And I can tell you that the reports of my death have been greatly exaggerated."

The reporters, who had been blank-eyed and confused a moment ago, now began to clap and cheer. The sound of it was not overwhelming—there were only six people involved. But it went on for what seemed like a long time.

"Susan, we are so happy to see you," one young woman said.

Susan smiled. She was already on familiar footing. This had been her wheelhouse her entire career—standing up front and giving her remarks. She had knocked more than a few of them out of the park in her time.

"I want to share a message with the American people, and having you folks come out here seemed like the most direct way of doing that. By law, I am the President of the United States, and will continue to be until January twentieth. I assure you that I am fit and competent to lead, and I plan to return to office immediately.

"There's been a great deal of confusion about the events of November twelfth, and I believe I can clear up some of it. For one: yes, I disappeared right after the shootings, and have remained in hiding until this moment. This is because my White House security detail, themselves members of the United States Secret Service, were convinced that the murder of Vice President Horning, and the shooting of myself, was an assassination planned and carried out by the incoming organization of Jefferson Monroe. They were, and remain, further convinced that the Monroe organization remains a threat to my life."

Gasps went through the small crowd. Susan could imagine the effect this was either having, or about to have, nationwide. If they hadn't been carrying this event live at first, they were almost certainly preempting everything to get it on live now.

She smiled. Let Monroe deny it.

"I would have been tempted to stay in hiding, possibly for the rest of my life, but for the courage this morning of the former Acting President and House Speaker, Karen White. If she isn't going to let Monroe and his thugs bully her, then I'm not going to either."

That was an applause line. Susan watched the reporters fight the urge to break out in spontaneous clapping. They did a good job.

"Further, a terrible danger confronts us now. The danger is that sometime in the next several hours, Jefferson Monroe intends to launch a completely unprovoked and unprecedented nuclear attack on the People's Republic of China. His flimsy justification for this is the Chinese threats to call in their debt, and their island-building activities in the South China Sea. Are these activities a concern? Of course they are. Do we, the United States, agree with the Chinese about the activities? No we don't, and we will continue to voice our opposition to them until the Chinese come to their senses. However, these activities are barely enough cause for a breakdown in diplomacy, never mind an existential war that threatens all of humankind."

200

She paused. Those lines would be red meat for Monroe supporters, the very people who thought she was soft on China. So be it. They weren't the majority of the American people.

"As I indicated, I am returning to the White House this very evening. I call on Jefferson Monroe to vacate the premises immediately, and formally step down from his role as Acting President. I call on all branches of the United States military, its leaders at the Pentagon, and all servicemen and women deployed anywhere on Earth, to refuse further orders from Mr. Monroe or his organization."

Microphones and cameras were pointed at her like guns. All eyes were on her. She could feel them—millions of them, not just here, but everywhere. This was going out live in many, many places by now. She remembered chatting with a veteran journalist once upon a time about how they decided what to cover.

If a dog bites a man, he'd said, *it's not news. But if a man bites a dog, it is news.*

The President had returned from the dead. If that wasn't a man biting a dog, she didn't know what was.

"And finally, I call for a resumption of the formal investigation by the Federal Bureau of Investigation and the Justice Department into the fraudulent activities that led to the election of Monroe in the first place."

She took a deep breath. Here came the first and only lie of the day—and she wasn't even sure it was a lie. In fact, she was hoping it was true. It all depended on Luke Stone and what he'd been doing since he left her bunker.

"My staff have uncovered significant evidence of Monroe's tampering with the election results, as well as evidence to suggest that his organization was behind the murder of Marybeth Horning. We will be happy to share that information with both the FBI and the Justice Department when the time is right."

Susan signaled she was done.

The air erupted with questions, the reporters shouting over one another as they stood. There was nothing she would have loved more than to answer all of them.

But Chuck and his men surrounded her and ushered her off, and she had to admit, thinking of what was to come, she felt safer being whisked away.

CHAPTER FORTY ONE

12:15 a.m. Beijing Time (12:15 p.m. Eastern Standard Time)
Central Military Commission
August 1st Building, Ministry of National Defense
Beijing, China

"The attack could come at any time."

Xi Wengbo sat at the head of the large oval conference table in the meeting room of the Central Military Commission. Perhaps thirty people sat around the table with him, and another hundred fifty in seating that lined the outer rim of the room. Of the many people in attendance, it was understood that few were empowered to speak.

Xi was a slight man with prematurely thinning hair and glasses. His eye doctor had recently confided to him that his vision was failing—a defect that ran among males in his family, and for which nothing could be done. He was only thirty-six now, and he could expect to be mostly blind by the age of forty.

Xi was the most powerful person in the room—indeed, one of the most powerful on Earth. He held several official positions simultaneously: he was President of the People's Republic of China, he was the General Secretary of the Communist Party of China, and he was the Chairman of the Central Military Commission.

It was an informal position that he relished the most, however—that of Paramount Leader. The term suggested the most important person in Chinese political and cultural life, and the undisputed leader of the country—in the eyes of both the Chinese and the rest of the world. In recent months, more and more indications hinted that he had grown into and held that role—the youngest person ever to do so.

Of course, with recognition came heavy responsibility. The people in this room were looking to him to guide them through the dangerous waters of conflict with the United States. This was the reason he was here after midnight, when he would much prefer to be at home with his wife and three children.

He had played chess since he was a small child, however, and had reached the Grandmaster level by his mid-twenties. His political career had superseded chess, and he no longer played with any regularity. He regretted that fact. But this—this was much like a chess game, only on a much greater scale.

"In what form do we anticipate the attack?" Xi said.

The Defense Minister was Wu Fenghe. He was a small man in his sixties, very intelligent, himself a ruthless political player, who had joined the People's Liberation Army as a young man, and over long decades had maneuvered his way to the very top. He was in command of the largest military in the world, and had a vast storehouse of knowledge, both of Chinese capabilities and those of its opponents.

"We anticipate a nuclear rocket attack or attacks, likely from enemy Ohio-class submarines operating near the South China Sea or in the Western Pacific Ocean. The stealth technology in use by American submarines will make it difficult or impossible for us to detect the attack until it is already underway.

"The American Trident II missiles deploy warheads with a destructive power of roughly one-half megaton. One strike by such a warhead will be enough to completely destroy any one of our installations on the South China Sea islands, render such places uninhabitable for decades if not centuries, and disrupt the delicate underwater ecology for an equal amount of time. All personnel will of course be killed. The Trident missiles are famed for their accuracy and reliability, and it is likely that once launched, each warhead will find its target nearly one hundred percent of the time."

Wu turned a sheet of paper over on the table in front of him. He looked up and his owlish eyes gazed around the room. They settled on Xi Wengbo.

"Mr. Chairman, each Ohio-class submarine is outfitted with twenty-four of these weapons. This suggests that just one such submarine can launch attacks that will destroy all seven of our island-building projects, as well as the large installation long-established at Woody Island. In addition to military personnel, there are hundreds of women and children—family members—living on Woody Island.

"We believe that as many as six Ohio-class submarines are currently operating within range to make these attacks—four of which can best be described as whereabouts unknown. Our best guess is that once the attacks commence, they will be completed within minutes."

Xi settled deep into his seat. Why would the Americans make these attacks now? This was much too soon.

203

It had long been clear to him that American power and American influence were in decline. He was a student of history. He knew that the 1800s were considered the British Century. But the British Empire waned, as all empires eventually must do. Then it became clear that the 1900s were the American Century. And that power was waning. Now, in the 2000s, China was on the rise.

But the dissolution of the previous dominant empire must be managed, and managed carefully. In retrospect, Xi considered it remarkable that the Russians, when faced with the dissolution of their own once-powerful empire in the recent past, acted with such restraint. A nuclear-armed power, watching its own influence and prestige collapse, might be expected to lash out violently, and with terrible consequences. The Russians, to their credit, had done quite a good job of managing their own demise.

Would the Americans do the same? It was beginning to appear that they would not.

"What is our response?" Xi said.

"Mr. Chairman, you are a chess player, and a good one," Wu said.

Xi nodded, not accepting or rejecting the praise. Modesty forbade him from articulating his true feelings—he was much better than good.

"So please allow me to think several moves ahead."

Xi nodded again. "Of course."

"Our policy is, and has always been, no nuclear first strike. Once attacked, however, we reserve the right to attack *counter-value* targets. In other words, even if only our military is attacked with nuclear weapons, we will counterattack against civilian targets. This policy is well known and well understood, and it helps us to mitigate the effects of the superior nuclear arsenals of our most likely aggressors, Russia and the United States."

"Yes," Xi said. The policy was so well understood in this room that it might have been beside the point to state it again.

"American intelligence knows this policy well, and we assume has a very good grasp of our retaliatory abilities. We have seventy-two nuclear-armed missiles that are operational, and can reach the continental United States. Certain design elements of the missiles, including stealth technology, supersonic speeds, and the ability to carry multiple warheads, suggest that once successfully launched, they will overwhelm American missile defenses, and a high percentage will reach their targets.

"We will likely be able to destroy major American cities, including New York and Philadelphia, Washington, DC, Miami, Chicago, Houston, and the entire western seaboard of the United States, from San Diego north to Seattle. In most scenarios, Vancouver, Canada, and Tijuana, Mexico, will be destroyed as collateral damage.

"Further, we have thousands of conventional rockets that can destroy the American military presence in Japan, South Korea, and on the Pacific islands—the major American installations on Guam will be completely eradicated. Our bombardments would likely kill much of the Japanese and South Korean populations, and both Tokyo and Seoul would cease to exist as we know them today."

Wu paused and looked around the room again. "The Americans are aware of these capabilities. We have analyzed this situation as logically as possible—our arsenal is meant as a deterrent. If the Americans are undeterred—and they have publicly stated that they intend to attack our islands with nuclear weapons—this suggests they have a much larger attack in mind."

The room, which a moment ago had been filled with ambient sound—papers shuffling, shoes scuffing on the floor, the occasional cough—went completely silent. All eyes were now on Wu.

"We believe that the Americans plan to commence a massive and coordinated first-strike attack on the Chinese mainland, delivering a knockout blow to our defense systems, our ability to respond, and murdering hundreds of millions of our citizens in the process. We believe this attack is imminent, and there is little or nothing we can do to stop it."

Xi had a feeling in his stomach. It was a feeling he associated with childhood, and with being unprepared for the demands his schoolwork was making on him. He had rarely felt it as an adult, and only in the most fleeting way. It was a vague sense of nausea. An unsettled feeling.

He had heard people call it "butterflies."

He thought of his family, asleep at home in their beds.

He thought of the Chinese policy—often stated—of friendship and open trade with all. He believed in it totally—in a dangerous world, it was China's best and surest path to its rightful place at the top of the power structure. The Chinese Century would not come about through military dominance.

And now he thought of more than a billion people, and their dreams and aspirations for a prosperous future.

"What do you suggest, Minister Wu?"

"We have but one hope," Wu said. "We must rescind our no first-strike policy, and launch the largest preemptive attack we can muster, using all of the resources at our disposal. At the same time, we must immediately mobilize the people and direct them to the fallout shelter and tunnel system developed during the Cold War. We understand much of that system has degraded through decades of neglect, but parts of it are still fully operational, and much more of it can be restored quickly through heroic effort."

Several audible gasps went through the room, as each new bad idea was announced. The plan sounded like the fever-dreams of a madman.

"None of this will stop an American attack," Wu said. "But it may degrade their ability to respond, thus tempering the level of destruction they are able to unleash upon us. Further, if we can get millions of people safely into the tunnels, at a future date those people can emerge and rebuild."

A feeling of unreality settled over Xi. This meeting now seemed like a hallucination. A nightmare. He looked around the room, but the heads of the gathered officials seemed indistinct. They could be helium-filled balloons attached to strings. He had no reference for the things he was feeling, none from childhood, and none now.

The people, attacked by some remnant of the devastating American nuclear arsenal, crawling like rats from holes in the ground at some unknown distant time.

Civilization in ruins. A world in flames.

The Chinese Century indeed.

CHAPTER FORTY TWO

12:23 p.m. Eastern Standard Time
Foscoe, North Carolina

Susan Hopkins's gigantic head was on the muted television set in the cabin's living room. She was standing somewhere warm, with palm trees and wide open blue waters behind her, and a large city looming in the far distance.

Luke stared at Susan's head and then at the caption across the bottom of the screen.

LIVE: Key Biscayne, Florida.

"Susan is on TV," he said. "What is she doing in Florida? The last I knew, she was in Virginia."

"Man, we've got more pressing issues than Susan's whereabouts," Ed Newsam said.

That was true. Outside the cabin, four black unmarked SUVs had pulled up, each one ejecting four passengers. There were sixteen men out there, quickly staging for what looked like an invasion—shrugging into ballistic vests and putting on helmets, loading up shotguns and rifles, digging through boxes of flash bang grenades. Two men had a heavy spring-loaded battering ram. At least one man had gone by with a tear gas gun.

They were coming in.

Ed had tried to call his people, but there was no cell phone coverage here. There was no landline in the cabin, and Ed's satellite phone was out in the car.

"Really?" he had said to Priscilla. "You have no way to make a phone call? What if there's an emergency and you need to call nine-one-one? Like now, for example?"

She shrugged. "There's one cop around here. He's sixty-seven years old, works part-time, and has astigmatism. He worries that they're going to take his driver's license away one of these years. I'm not sure how much help he would be in an emergency."

Now Priscilla was busying herself by bringing out all the guns her boyfriend Dak had stored here. So far there were three TEC-9s and a stack of loaded magazines for them—thousands of rounds. There was the street sweeper shotgun and several boxes of shells for it.

207

The extra shotgun ammo was probably useless—in a firefight, there would be no time to reload that thing.

Luke picked up a TEC-9. He had real distaste for this gun. It was a cheap piece of stamped together sheet metal. When he was in the military, guys who had handled it called it the "Jam-o-Matic."

"Why do you suppose a young guy with money would buy these things instead of something good?" he said.

Ed shrugged. "You didn't grow up in the ghetto, so you don't understand. Kids in your old neighborhood probably wanted a Camaro when they grew up. Or a surfboard. God only knows. Kids in my neighborhood dreamed of their first TEC-9. You want to be a bad dude? You get yourself one of these. Dreams like that die hard—logic doesn't figure in. It's all about passion and emotion."

Ed held up the other two TEC-9s, one in each hand.

"Are you going to use both of those?" Luke said.

Ed smiled. "I have two hands, don't I?"

"Full auto?" Luke said, inspecting the gun.

"Nah," Ed said. "You have to modify it for full auto, and it looks like he didn't. Doesn't matter. The action on these things is crazy fast. Just keep pulling the trigger. And when you slide in a new magazine, make sure you ram it home hard and clean. Otherwise it'll jam."

He paused, thoughtful for a second. "And it might jam anyway."

"Terrific."

Pris came out from the bedroom, carrying what looked almost like a big sawed-off shotgun with a wooden stock, along with a couple of boxes of ammunition.

Luke stared at it. It couldn't be.

"You've got to be kidding me," Ed said.

He took the gun, an M79 grenade launcher, from Pris. He ran his hand along the barrel—his touch was that of a lover. To say this was Ed's favorite weapon would be akin to suggesting that the Grand Canyon was a large hole in the ground. It was much more than that—Ed was a master artist, a Rembrandt of destruction, and the M79 was his preferred medium.

"I guess great minds think alike," Luke said.

Pris looked at him, confused.

Luke indicated the gun. "He likes those."

Ed slid a grenade into the chamber. "Okay," he said. "I think we—"

"PEOPLE INSIDE THE HOUSE," someone on the outside said. The voice, amplified by a megaphone, sounded like a demon emerging from the netherworld.

"YOU HAVE NO CHANCE OF ESCAPE. EXIT THROUGH THE FRONT DOOR WITH YOUR HANDS IN THE AIR."

All three of them stared in the direction of the voice.

"What if we do what they say?" Priscilla said.

Ed shrugged. "They shoot us down like rabid dogs."

He noticed the look of alarm on her face.

"Probably," he said. "Not guaranteed. I mean, they haven't said who they are. That's not usually a good sign."

Luke indicated the hole in the floor. "Pris, it's about to get hot up here. You better go downstairs. Can you lock that thing from underneath?"

She nodded. "Yes."

"When we close it, you lock it. Then turn the lights out and get down on the floor."

"Wait a minute," Ed said. "You have internet down there?"

"Of course."

"Video conferencing?"

"Yes."

Ed slapped himself in the head. He took a business card from his wallet and scribbled two addresses. "Contact these people. Tell them exactly where you are, and tell them you're with me. Tell them I need immediate emergency assistance. A helicopter, paratroopers—it doesn't matter. State troopers, National Guard, anything at all. Whatever is closest and whatever is fastest."

She took the card. "What are you guys going to do up here?"

Luke sighted down the length of his TEC-9. "We're hosting the party."

* * *

The front door was open a crack.

Ed crouched near the opening. "This is Agent Edward Newsam of the FBI!" he shouted. "Either identify yourselves, or throw down your weapons and surrender! We don't want to hurt you."

Luke was positioned near the window. Across the yard, from behind an SUV, someone fired a projectile.

"Incoming!" Luke shouted.

Ed slammed the door and dove backward onto the floor.

209

Luke watched it come. It hit the door with a hard THUNK, then bounced back onto the porch. Smoke rose from it.

"Tear gas canister," Luke said.

Ed was sprawled face down on the floor. He looked up and shook his head. His eyes were hard. "That was unfortunate. As far as I'm concerned, they brought this on themselves."

They had gone through the tiny cabin, assessing their situation. Verdict: bad. The place had a lot of windows, which made it a nice, sunny weekend getaway—and difficult to hold against an all-out assault.

They had done what they could. The narrow kitchen was a bright spot—they had toppled the refrigerator sideways, wedging it between the back door and the counter space. It would be difficult, if not impossible, to come in through that door. There was one large window in the kitchen, which was above the sink and countertop. They had pulled the louvered blinds shut, reversed the sink fixture, and turned on the water—it was now spraying all over the countertop.

Someone coming in that way would have to shoot the window and the blinds out, then crawl in across the slippery counter. Anyone who tried it would waste precious seconds navigating the obstacles. Luke hoped that the first man through would get shot down in the attempt—and after that his corpse would block the way.

The rest of the house was not nearly as good.

Together, they toppled over the futon couch and slid it against the front door. That battering ram out there would blow the lock off the door in one or two shots, but pushing the couch out of the way while under fire should present a problem for them.

"When the shooting starts," Luke said, "I'm going to take out all these front windows with the TEC-9. That'll give you room to operate with the M79, and there'll be less flying glass coming our way. Then I'll take that left corner and rip up anything I see. They should draw on me, which will buy you some time on the right side, and give us a little bit of triangulation. I'd suggest the first thing you do is take out those SUVs—all of them. Deny them their cover and their operating base."

"Then the fun starts," Ed said.

Luke shrugged. "Such as it is."

He backed up and readied the gun. Bare seconds later, a projectile came crashing through the window. Another tear gas canister. Smoke began to rise.

Instantly, Luke opened up the TEC-9. The action was fast, and he controlled the recoil easily. DUH-DUH-DUH-DUH-DUH.

The gun was loud.

LOUD.

He sprayed the three front windows, the glass falling in shards like rain.

"Get it out, man! Get it out!"

Ed picked up the canister and threw it back out the now missing window.

Luke went to his corner. Ed crouched and went to his window. Luke picked a sharp angle and started firing, not aiming at anything, just hosing the outside with bullets.

The shriek of the gun was deafening.

His cartridges ejected and tinkled on the wooden floor. He emptied his magazine and dove to the ground.

Ha! Didn't jam at all.

They lit him up. In seconds, his corner of the house was shredding to pieces. The wooden logs splintered and fell apart. Sharp pieces of it sprayed down on him. His ears were ringing. He covered his head with his hands. His eyes were squeezed shut.

"Ed!" he screamed. "Ed!"

Doonk!

The telltale sound of the M79 came to him. It was a benign sound, like something from Pong-type video games of the 1970s—a sound perfectly out of synch with the destructive capacity of the weapon.

Luke held his breath.

BOOOM!

Seconds passed and there came the sound of rending, burning metal, and the screams of people caught in the inferno. Something—a car door, a roof—landed somewhere with a heavy thud. There was a crinkling sound, like sheet aluminum being balled up and crushed by a big angry hand.

A second later, a smaller explosion: Ba-booom! As a gas tank on one of the cars went.

Then everything went silent.

Soon, there was nothing but the sound of crackling flames.

Luke got up and crept close to the window. There were men all over the ground out there, crawling away from the burning wreckage. Two out of four SUVs were on fire.

He scanned his left and right—eyes sharp, head on a swivel—no one was setting up for a shot.

Ed ran low toward the window on the other side of the door. Smart man—never pop up in the same place twice.

They had the initiative now, and they couldn't afford to lose it. Luke grabbed a new magazine and rammed it in, pushing it until he felt it settle home.

He moved to the window and sprayed three of the crawling men, instantly taking them out of the game. They shivered from the bullets and lay flat, face down.

A second later, Ed fired again, this time from a new angle: *Doonk!*

BOOOOM!

He hit a gas tank directly. The explosion was enormous, apocalyptic. It sent a ball of flame thirty feet into the air, followed by a jet of black smoke. All the SUVs, the girl's Jeep, the rental sedan—everything was on fire now. The first SUV hit looked like a flaming skull.

Luke crouched low. No one was visible out there. Somewhere behind the inferno, a person was screaming in agony.

No one was returning fire.

Ed crawled over. He lay on his back and slid another grenade into the chamber.

"Anything moving?"

Luke shook his head. "No. But I doubt they're done yet."

Behind them, the back wall of the cabin suddenly blew in.

The noise was so loud, so close, it didn't make sense as sound. For a split second, Luke thought his ear drums had burst. He didn't even try to turn around – he knew what had happened without having to see it. Someone had sneaked around back and planted explosives on the side of the house.

Luke ducked, and curled into a ball at the base of the front wall, beneath the shattered window. He pulled his knees to his chest and covered his head with his arms – he was like a turtle pulled into its shell. He gave the explosion nothing to hit but his back.

He was pummeled with debris. Something hard and heavy hit him – a chunk of wood maybe. It struck him with the force of a car crash. The breath went out of his lungs, and everything went black.

He was swimming, swimming in deep dark water. It seemed that everything above him was turmoil and rage. He wanted to dive deeper, into the black. Someone was calling his name – it sounded like his mother's musical voice. Then a strong hand seemed to grab him, and drag him toward the surface, through the roiling sea, into the light.

"Luke!" Ed was screaming. "Wake up! Wake up, man!"

The room was filled with smoke. Dense particles hung in the air. The ragged hole where the back wall had been was on fire – flames licked at the edges.

Ed, laying against the wall five feet from Luke, fired his M79.

Doonk!

The projectile sailed through the hole on a sharp, low trajectory. It hit something out there – woods, a shed, who knew? – and a backdraft of flames hit the rear wall of the cabin. A man stumbled in through the hole, his upper body on fire.

Luke shot him with the TEC-9. He hit him five times and mercifully dropped him – few fates were worse than burning to death. But now the gun was empty.

He glanced around for the reload magazines. The smoke was thick – it made it hard to see, hard to breath. And everything had changed. There was heavy debris, fragments of the wall, all over the floor.

Quiet had settled in – nothing but the crackling of flames and somewhere outside, screams of pain.

"Luke!" Ed said. "More trouble!"

Luke got on his knees and glanced out the window.

Six men in black armor ran toward the house. They all carried Uzis. One man spotted Luke's head in the window and aimed for him.

Luke dove for the floor just as the bullets flew. They ripped up the sturdy log construction, raining more splinters of wood on top of him. He reached for a fresh TEC-9 mag… didn't have one. Where were those things? There had been a pile of them right… where?

He crawled like a snake over sharp, jagged edges, feeling through random junk for the magazines. If those guys made it to the house…

A new sound came, shattering the relative quiet.

It was the sound of a gun – big and fast, 30 millimeter armor-piercing rounds at ten rounds per second.

DUH-DUH-DUH-DUH-DUH-DUH-DUH.

Behind that was another sound. It took a moment to come closer and resolve into something familiar. Once it did, Luke looked into the sky. A US ARMY Black Hawk helicopter was up there, camouflage color, a mix of dark and light greens and tans.

"ALL COMBATANTS DROP YOUR WEAPONS," a female voice said over the speaker system. "ALL COMBATANTS DROP YOUR WEAPONS. THIS IS YOUR ONLY WARNING."

The chopper hovered some distance from the flames, and now men in full combat gear began to rappel out either side. Luke spotted an M230 chain gun mounted beneath the chopper. On the ground, the men in black armor were dropping their guns, rather than risk another burst from that M230.

"Looks like the cavalry is here," Luke said.

From his vantage, Ed rolled and gazed out the window at the sky.

"Did you hear that voice?" he said.

"Yeah," Luke said.

"That was Rachel."

As Luke watched, the black armored men were thrown to the ground and disarmed by the newcomers. He glanced around the cabin. Smoke still hung in the air, though it was starting to clear. The dead man's smoldering corpse lay near where the back wall used to be. Luke's back felt like it had taken a swing from an aluminum baseball bat.

Outside, the chopper touched down, and Rachel and Jacob climbed out. They made an odd pairing – she was short and muscular, he was tall and slender.

"They must have gotten tired of waiting," Ed said.

Luke nodded. "Good thing, too. We were just about dead in here."

CHAPTER FORTY THREE

1:35 p.m. Eastern Standard Time
Site R—Blue Ridge Summit, Pennsylvania

"Gentlemen, this is where the rubber hits the road," Gerry the Shark said.

Gerry didn't like being underground. He had never thought of himself as claustrophobic before, but this place could get him leaning that way. What if they had to stay down here for months?

Or years?

He sat in a chamber deep beneath the surface of the earth. The chamber was mostly bare, with a large conference table in the center, a poured concrete floor, and rounded stone walls and ceiling. White, long-lasting LED lights were mounted in recessed ceiling fixtures. Oxygenated air was pumped into the room through several small vents. The complete lack of windows gave the room the sense of being the dead end of a cave, which was exactly what it was.

The chamber was behind a double-thick steel door at the end of a metal catwalk. The catwalk teetered three stories above a dim and cavernous command and control room operated around the clock by a skeleton crew of technical personnel—augmented now by the dozens of private security contractors who had become the de facto protection unit for the President. This was the deepest part of the sprawling Site R facility.

A half dozen men sat in padded leather office chairs around a conference table that could seat four times that many. General Walters was here with an aide, as was General Coates. Jefferson Monroe was here. And Gerry himself.

The former Vice President, Ezekiel Harris, was not here. He had resigned from office an hour ago, when the news about Susan Hopkins broke. Susan was alive and well, and accusing Jefferson Monroe on live TV of trying to murder her. She even insisted she had evidence to back up her claims.

The news got worse.

Fifteen minutes ago, Malcolm had called him and told him that Luke Stone and his FBI agent friend Ed Newsam had emerged from the North Carolina backwoods. They were touting supposedly irrefutable evidence of election fraud, along with powerful circumstantial evidence pointing to the idea that the Monroe campaign had murdered a hacker named Dak Pearl.

They had even unearthed a girlfriend who was ready to testify that Dak had worked directly for Monroe, that he was highly skilled at hacking voting machines, and that he feared for his life in the days before his death. All of this, and they had more or less wiped out two assault teams sent to kill them. Five of the sixteen men on those teams had survived, and two of the survivors had been airlifted to a burn unit in Charlotte.

Gerry shook his head. The walls really were closing in this time, and this room did nothing to combat the feeling.

He thought for a moment of Dak. He was a good kid—young, smart (at least when it came to computers), and enthusiastic. If life were different, Gerry could imagine mentoring a kid like that—Gerry could even see a little of himself in Dak. They both had rough and tumble upbringings, they were both smarter than the people around them, they were both like rocket ships taking off for the stratosphere.

What Dak didn't have were eyes in the back of his head. If they'd had more time together, Gerry could have taught him that. Instead, Dak didn't realize he was doomed until it was too late. For Gerry, it was a cruel irony that he was the man who could have taught Dak to save himself, and at the same time was the man who had him killed.

"General Walters, can you give us that intelligence report you mentioned?"

The general nodded. "Of course. My networks operating inside the Pentagon tell me that during the last hour, there has been a massive and sudden movement of people within mainland China. An unprecedented movement. Hundreds of thousands, possibly millions, of people are leaving their homes and gathering in rendezvous points. From those points, they are being bused to Cold War–era fallout shelters and tunnel systems."

"What does that mean to you, General?"

"I think it's clear. The Chinese are anticipating a nuclear attack, and are moving their people underground, as many as they can, and as fast as they can. At the same time, there's been an explosion of chatter across Chinese military networks. The code language is one we are not familiar with—likely kept in mothballs until this moment so we wouldn't have a chance to break it. But satellite data suggest they are preparing to launch everything they have, both nuclear and conventional weaponry, from land, sea, and air."

"Why do you suppose they're doing all this?"

The general shrugged. "They did the math. They knew we were planning a tactical nuclear strike, and they saw how quickly that will escalate. They might have even considered that we planned an all-out decapitation strike. So they've decided to beat us to the punch."

Gerry sighed. "What will happen if they *beat us to the punch*, as you say?"

The general shook his head. "I'd prefer not to think about it."

"Is your friend Captain Harlow still ready to launch his attack?"

"I spoke with him just thirty minutes ago. He's ready. On our order, he will launch."

Gerry nodded. "Good."

It was an odd symptom of this situation that the only way out seemed to be through a nuclear war. If war broke loose, and millions died, and vast parts of civilization were destroyed, questions of a computer hacker that got murdered, or some votes that were stolen… things like this would become rather quaint. He looked at the other men—outside of Jeff Monroe, did any of them realize what this was about?

At one point, pitching a war with China was a good way to rile up the base. But now it had become the path—possibly the only one left—to keep Gerry O'Brien out of prison, and Jefferson Monroe in office. It had also become a looming existential apocalypse.

"Have we alerted the Pentagon to our plans?"

"Yes. They are fully aware, and not happy about it. We told them only that we have the capability to launch the attack—we didn't mention Reggie Harlow by name."

"Good," Gerry said. "Perhaps we should talk to them now, and see if they've finally come around to our way of thinking."

CHAPTER FORTY FOUR

2:30 p.m. Eastern Standard Time
The Skies over Florida

The dark blue Secret Service jet zoomed north against a blue sky, carrying the President back to Washington.

"It is two thirty in the morning in China," Kurt Kimball said. "Reports from the Pentagon indicate that enormous numbers of people have been roused from their beds, and are being bused to fallout shelters. The CIA reports air raid sirens are being heard across Beijing, Shanghai, Chonqing, Hong Kong, and a host of other cities. The NSA has intel of communications indicating full mobilization of rocket units, fighter squadrons being scrambled, and naval strike groups pushing out of port."

He looked at the small group gathered in the cramped meeting area at the front of the plane. "All indications are that they are preparing for a nuclear war."

Susan sat in a leather-backed swivel chair bolted to the floor. If this were a happier time, she could spin the chair to her left and gaze out the window at the passing sky. It was not a happier time, and she knew what she would see if she did that now—a full escort of F-18 fighter planes.

She knew Luke Stone had resurfaced with evidence that Monroe had tampered with the election results. The FBI had begun digging into the data and had already discovered records of altered outcomes in voting districts in Michigan, Ohio, Pennsylvania, Florida, New Hampshire, and Wisconsin.

She knew that Stone also had evidence Monroe's people had killed the hacker who carried out the tampering. Monroe's days in the Presidency were numbered—there might only be hours left. And in the days ahead, if a full investigation were to go forward, it would probably find evidence of widespread crimes, including collusion with white supremacist groups, the murder of Patrick Norman, and the assassination of Marybeth Horning.

The only problem? It seemed like it was already too late to do any good.

"Jefferson Monroe and the remains of his staff have evacuated the White House," Kurt Kimball said. "There have been many defections throughout the day, including Ezekiel Harris."

A small cheer went around the table.

Kurt raised his hands.

"If only that were good news. They've gone to the Site R shelter complex. They are holed up deep inside, with private security contractors guarding the entrances. They claim to have the loyalty of one or more nuclear-armed submarine commanders willing to attack the artificial islands in the South China Sea. They are trying to pressure the Pentagon into launching a full nuclear assault on the Chinese mainland."

"Why are they doing that?" Susan said.

"Simple enough," Kurt said. "Our nuclear capabilities are vastly superior to theirs. If we strike first—a surprise attack and total war—the Chinese will be unable to respond."

"It seems a little late for a surprise attack," Kat Lopez said.

"What does he want?" Susan said.

"He wants to be President of the United States," Kurt said.

"Not much hope of that anymore, is there?" Chuck Berg said.

Kurt nodded. "And he wants to attack China. Don't ask me why someone would want to attack China. But he's been saying for months that he intends to do so, and I think we need to take him at his word."

Kurt paused.

"We have some other shocking news. In the past two days he has gathered certain dead-enders to himself, ones that you forced out of the military in years past. These include former general Sanford Walters, and former Chairman of the Joint Chiefs Robert Coates. They are both eager war hawks. All indications are that they are with Monroe at Site R, and are participating in the negotiations with the Pentagon."

"Can we retake Site R?" Susan said. "Or destroy it with them inside?"

Kurt looked at Chuck Berg.

"Almost impossible," Chuck said. "It's a hardened facility designed to withstand direct hits from Soviet-era nuclear weapons. A conventional bombing attack wouldn't hurt it much. And a troop assault would likely end in disaster. The defenders enjoy tremendous advantages at a facility like Site R. There are heavy machine guns and mortars operated remotely from inside the communications center. Even if we took those out with an air assault, it still doesn't get our people inside. Estimates suggest that invaders would lose personnel at a ten to one ratio compared to defenders."

He paused. "By the time we reached their command center, they would already have launched whatever nukes they control."

"Can we knock out their communications?" Susan said. "If we stop them from communicating with the—"

Kurt was shaking his head. "The facility is designed to withstand an apocalypse, and operate independently afterwards. Everything within it has multiple redundancies. We can't cut off their power or their communications."

One last idea occurred to Susan. After this one, she was done, and it was a desperate Hail Mary pass. She didn't know if it could possibly work.

"What if I talk to Xi Wengbo?" she said.

Kurt looked at her. "Okay, I'm listening. And tell him what?"

Susan shrugged. "I don't know. We've found common ground in the past. I could ask him—nicely—not to attack us first. Then I could suggest to him that if one of our submarines launches nuclear missiles at his artificial islands, maybe he could simply allow it to happen."

"That's hard," Kurt said.

"I know it," Susan said. "But we could pay reparations. We could do the environmental clean-up afterward and rebuild the islands for them. Anything. If we break it, we'll fix it."

"And if we end up launching a full-scale nuclear strike?"

Susan shook her head. "I guess all bets are off at that point."

Kurt looked at Kat Lopez. "Kat?"

Kat shrugged. "I imagine he's awake. I'll see if we can get him on the phone and route the call to this airplane."

* * *

"How's it going out there?" Pierre said.

He, Michaela, and Lauren were in the tiny living quarters at the back of the plane. The three of them were sprawled across the Murphy bed that extended out from the wall. The girls—beautiful girls, soon to be young women—stared intently into their hand-held devices. Pierre had reading glasses on and was thumbing through an old Anthropologie catalogue. He was still a design freak, after all these years. He peered at her over the top of his glasses.

None of them had shoes on, and they were all wearing matching socks, even Pierre—Bugs Bunny eating a carrot.

"As good as I can make it," Susan said.

She dove onto the bed with them. The girls smiled and laughed, but barely looked away from their devices. Susan sighed, mostly to herself. That's how it was with the kids nowadays—they were addicted to those things.

She imagined there were worse things a couple of thirteen-year-olds could be addicted to.

"What's happening?" Pierre said.

"I'm going to be talking to the President of China in a few minutes."

"Wow, Mom," Lauren said absently. "That's cool."

"It's all worked out now, though," Pierre said. "You're going to be President again, at least for the short term, and that whole attack idea of Monroe's is off the table."

He said it as though it wasn't a question.

"Sure," Susan said. "Of course. He and I just need to work out a few details." Susan fought the urge to burst into tears in front of them. "Whatever happens, now or in the future, I just want you guys to know that I love you all very much."

Pierre raised his eyebrows at that. His face darkened. "I love you all very much" tended to set off alarm bells in people's minds.

"We love you too," he said.

"Mom," Michaela said. "Why do you still want to be President if people keep trying to kill you?"

Susan shook her head. "Sweetheart, I have no idea. I guess your mother is just crazy."

"But we knew that already," Lauren said.

The door opened and Kat Lopez poked her head inside.

"Susan, we're ready for you."

* * *

She picked up the slim black telephone on the table in front of her. It was an oddly cheap-looking phone, made out of hard plastic, and it was attached to a receiver with large glowing buttons. It looked like something from the 1990s—the interregnum period when rotary phones were dying out and smartphone technology hadn't come roaring in yet. The big advance in those days was touch-tone dialing.

"The President of the United States is on the line," a male voice said.

"The President of the People's Republic of China is on the line," came another voice.

221

Susan had a brief nervous moment. There had been a time, early in her administration, when she was afraid to make these calls. She had felt like a fraud in those days, a second-rate player who had somehow wandered into the big leagues.

"Hello? This is Xi Wengbo."

"Mr. President," Susan said. The feeling dropped away almost instantly. She was who she was, and she did what she did. And sometimes what she did was ask for enormous favors. "This is Susan Hopkins."

"Madam President," the Chinese leader said. "I am very glad to speak with you. I can tell you we are overjoyed here to learn that you are still alive."

"Thank you," Susan said. "I feel the same way."

"Will this mean that you have returned to power?"

Susan took a breath. "It's complicated. I am returning to the White House right now, but my powers have not yet been fully restored. The situation with Jefferson Monroe is that he has barricaded himself inside one of our fallout shelters, with his followers. He claims to have maintained control over elements of our military—the truth of this claim is uncertain."

"It is difficult," Xi said.

"Yes, it is."

"Do you believe he has control over nuclear weapons?"

Susan looked out the window as white clouds streaked by. "We believe he might. That is the claim he's making. But if there are units loyal to him, he has not revealed what they are."

"Very unfortunate," Xi said.

"Yes." A pause stretched between them. "Mr. President, are you mobilizing for nuclear war?"

"I regret that I'm unable to discuss activities of that nature with outsiders. As your people would say, such activities are considered top secret."

"I would like to run something by you," Susan said.

"Of course. Please do."

"I think it possible that Jefferson Monroe may be able to launch a small tactical strike against your island-building activities in the South China Sea. Such an attack would be very limited in scope. Yes, people would die and there would be a great deal of damage. But this wouldn't necessarily demand a counterattack."

"Madam, our policy has been clear for decades. We reserve the right to a massive counter-value response to any nuclear attack."

"Yes, I understand that. But we would make reparations, both to the People's Republic of China, and to the families of any individuals harmed in the attack. We would rebuild the islands for you, and—"

"What you ask is impossible," he said. "I'm afraid you overestimate me. I am not superman. I cannot unmake a policy with a wave of my hand, and I cannot ask our people to not retaliate against an historic crime. Nor can I ask our people to stand by and watch an incoming missile attack—the scope of which we will be able to measure only after the bombs hit their targets. I'm sorry. Against the formidable American arsenal, our only hope is massive and immediate retaliation. Madam, your Monroe has put us, and the entire world, in a very awkward position."

"Mr. Xi, I would just ask—"

"Mrs. Hopkins, it is very late. I'm sure you will understand that I would like to get home to my family and children. I hope we can speak again, under more pleasant circumstances. Good night to you and yours, Madam. I pray that your ancestors and your gods keep you safe."

The line went dead.

Susan stared at the phone.

Here's where I say something sarcastic and funny.

She looked up at Kurt. She couldn't think of a single thing to say.

CHAPTER FORTY FIVE

3:05 p.m. Eastern Standard Time
The Skies over Virginia

Luke and Ed sat at the table near the front of the plane. Ed was drinking a celebratory beer from a cooler on the floor. Luke would do the same, only…

Even when something looks like it's over, it isn't, Kent Philby had once told him. *It's never over.*

"Things are bad," Swann said, his voice crackling through the phone.

"Bad?" Ed said. "The data records Dak Pearl kept, all by themselves, should be enough to get Monroe out of office."

"They are, and they already did. Monroe has left the White House."

"Good," Ed said. "And there's some heavy murder allegations coming down the road. Dak's girlfriend's testimony—"

"Sure," Trudy said. "It's going to be more than enough. And once the investigation really gets rolling, there should be a cascade of evidence and testimony about other murders—Marybeth Horning, Patrick Norman, Kent Philby, and Sydney Gottlieb to name a few. That's not the problem."

"What is the problem?"

"Monroe and his policy advisor Gerald O'Brien, are barricaded inside the Site R facility. They've got a couple of real war hawk former generals with them, and they're trying to launch a strike against China. They claim to have control over a nuclear submarine."

Luke and Ed stared at each other. It never ended with this guy. Kent Philby was right again.

"Should we go there?"

"Even you guys will never get in to Site R," Swann said. "The approach is all concrete walls, electrified fences, razor wire, surveillance cameras and machine gun nests. You'd never make it to the bunker entry, and even if you did, you'd get chopped to pieces before you managed to open it. The intel we have suggests it would take hundreds of men to storm that entrance."

Luke looked around the plane. It was too small, too slow. He felt trapped all of a sudden. He wanted to punch his way out of here. Then he wanted to punch his way into Site R.

But a thought occurred to him. It wasn't even as if he had the thought – it was like a quiet voice whispered the words in his ear.

Don Morris.

Don Morris the traitor. Don Morris the terrorist. Don Morris the mass murderer.

Don Morris, his old mentor…

…could get inside Site R.

It was risky. Don was hard to know. He claimed he wasn't on Jefferson Monroe's side in all this, but then again, Monroe did spring him from prison. In Luke's mind, he saw an image of a firefighting helicopter flying above a gigantic wilderness fire… and dumping gasoline on it.

"What about Don?" he said.

"Don…"

Luke nodded, but of course Swann couldn't see that. "Yeah. Don Morris."

"If you guys can't get in, how is Don is supposed to do it?"

Luke shrugged. "Don is some kind of hero or symbol to those guys. If he shows up there, they might just let him in."

"Or they might not," Swann said.

Luke glanced at Ed. "Yes. True enough. He'll have to charm them."

Trudy spoke up. "Luke, I don't think it's fair to ask Don…"

"To do what?" Luke said. "Risk his life for his country? For the world? It's the kind of thing he used to do on a regular basis when I first met him. And considering the crimes he committed a couple of years ago, I'd say he owes everyone a pretty big favor."

"I spoke to Don today," Trudy said. "As soon as he heard Susan was coming back, he started getting ready to leave the country. He knows the writing is on the wall. Even if Monroe or Karen White had the right to release him - a legal question which is up in the air - there are a host of crimes he can still be charged with and convicted of. He plans to disappear and keep his freedom."

"Trudy, if there's anyone who can convince Don to change his plans, I think it will be you."

"You're asking a lot," Trudy said.

"I understand that, but please understand that Don is all we've got right now."

A moment passed. "Trudy?"

"Okay," she said. "I'll try, but I'm not making any promises. And I'm not going to push him. I'm going to let him decide."

"Trudy…" Luke began. He was about to start in on one of his patented inspirational challenges: "Don't try, Trudy. Just do it. Do it all the way. Sometimes you have to push people. Sometimes people have to risk everything."

He was about to start, but he didn't get there. Trudy knew him too well.

"It's the best I can do," she said, and hung up.

Luke looked at Ed again. Ed passed him a beer from the cooler, and Luke opened it. Might as well.

"Charm?" Ed said. "Don is supposed to get in there by using his charm?"

Luke sipped his beer. He shrugged. "Don Morris is about as charming as an infection."

CHAPTER FORTY SIX

3:14 p.m. Eastern Standard Time
Site R—Blue Ridge Summit, Pennsylvania

Don Morris was a rock star.

Jefferson Monroe had seen the security footage of him arriving at the security gate to the bunker complex. He had driven up in a white Mercedes, parked the car, and simply walked to the guardhouse. He wore a black leather jacket, jeans, and heavy boots. His hair was perfectly white—he didn't even look real.

He walked calmly, hands in the air. All around him, above him, from pillboxes along the wall, machine guns were trained on him. He could die anytime.

He went to the gate and spoke one sentence to them:

"I'm here to see Jefferson Monroe."

Would Monroe see him?

Would Monroe see the man who had practically invented Delta Force, and later, the notorious Special Response Team? Would he see an American hero who had spent nearly his entire adult life in combat at one time or another? Would he see the man who risked his life, his legacy, and his freedom to unseat Thomas Hayes, perhaps the most dysfunctional President of the past hundred years?

Monroe would be honored to see him. He remembered years ago, when Morris would appear at Senate hearings—his testimony was the most colorful Monroe ever heard. It would get his heart racing and stir his pride. The object of a Jefferson Monroe Presidency—the organizing principle—was to give men like Don Morris the latitude to do the things they needed to do.

Monroe looked around the room. There were a bunch of pinched faces in here. They were shouting at the black speakerphone device at the center of the table. Even Gerry the Shark seemed to have lost his composure. Having Don Morris come on board was going to make a big difference. He would cut through these problems like a hot knife cut through butter.

They were bringing him down here now.

"We are going to launch the attack," Gerry said to the phone. "That's the given. Those islands are going to be destroyed, and the

227

Chinese are going to retaliate. If you don't launch a preemptive strike—"

"We are not going to launch a strike," some general at the Pentagon said. His voice squawked out of the box. "Mr. O'Brien, you have no military experience. You have no understanding—"

"I understand plenty," Gerry said. "I understand that the Chinese are preparing to launch their own preemptive strike, and if they do—"

"If they do, we will launch a retaliatory strike at that time."

Gerry shook his head. "And be responsible for the deaths of millions of Americans."

"No, sir. You will be responsible for the deaths of millions of Americans. None of this would have happened without your lunatic saber rattling."

"Mitch," Robert Coates said to the phone, "this is Bob Coates."

"Bob, what are you even doing there? This is insane. You're retired. You're a civilian. Why are you trying to launch a nuclear war?"

"Cut it off!" Gerry said to one of the aides. He made a slashing gesture across his throat. "Cut it off. I'm tired of listening to this guy."

The call ended. A moment of silence passed as everyone took a deep breath.

"I say we go forward," Gerry said. "We launch the attack and let these guys play catch-up. Let's get the submarine commander back on. There's no time to waste. The Chinese could launch their own attack any minute."

He looked around the room. "You guys okay with that?"

The generals murmured their assent.

"Jeff, you okay with that? It's getting to be zero hour here in a minute."

Gerry's eyes were sharp and red. It was almost as if a fire was going on in there, and Gerry himself was burning inside of it.

To Monroe, it looked as if Gerry's soul was on fire.

"Sure, let's get him on the horn."

An aide was at the phone system, bringing the submarine back.

Behind them, the door slid open with a clang. Don Morris stood there, flanked by two black-clad security guards with shotguns. He stepped in—broad-shouldered, big-chested, thick-legged. He had steely eyes in a face as cracked and weathered as his

228

old leather jacket. His white hair was like a rude shock. He looked every minute of his age. No, he looked like he was a thousand years old—but fit and vigorous and ready for a thousand more.

Monroe stood and stepped to the man. He reached out and Don Morris shook his hand.

"Don, it's great to have you here."

"Jeff, what in the name of God do you think you're doing?"

Monroe stared into those eyes. Their hands were still clenched. Monroe had a moment when he wondered if Don Morris was going to let him have his hand back. And he realized something during that long moment—he really had no idea what he was doing. The things he had hoped for… well, this was quite far away from them.

It was over. And maybe that was for the best.

"Reginald Harlow," a voice squawked over the phone box behind them.

"Reggie, this is Don Morris."

"Don… Hey, Don, how are you doing?"

Don smiled, still holding Monroe's hand in an iron grip. Monroe almost smiled himself. Don Morris enjoyed instant legitimacy with the sub commander—of course he did. Few men had survived as much warfare as Don Morris. Few men had put their lives on the line as many times. He was a legend.

"I'm good, Reggie. But I need you to do something for me. I need you to trust me. This situation is in flux, I understand that. But I need you to reconnect with your chain of command, and I need you to stand down immediately."

"What's going on, Don?"

"There's a lot to sort out, but we're pulling this thing back from the edge, at least for the time being."

"Don, I—"

"Reggie, your commanding officers don't know it's you, do they? They know someone out there has gone rogue, but they don't know who it is. Am I right?"

"Yes."

"Well, they know now. I know, so they know, and I'm sure they have your coordinates. And I can tell you that they will sooner see you at the bottom of the ocean than allow you to start World War Three. You understand that, don't you?"

The man hesitated.

"Reggie?"

"I guess I do, Don."

229

"Good. Then please do me and everyone else a favor. Bring that hunk of junk to the surface and pull into port somewhere."

"Roger."

The call ended and Don finally released Monroe's hand. He looked around the room at the men gathered there.

"Okay, men, what else? Can we wrap this up? Prison isn't so bad, and most of you haven't actually killed anyone. For the ones who did…"

He shrugged.

Suddenly, Gerry the Shark was standing. Monroe wanted to tell him to sit back down, that whatever play he was going to make was pointless, that the game was over anyway. They had been driven into a hole in the ground—no one was on their side anymore. He wanted to say these things, but Gerry had pulled a handgun.

"Gerry…" was all he said.

Gerry pointed the gun at Don. The two guards moved to draw their weapons, but Don stopped them. "Wait."

He stared across the table at Gerry. It was a moment frozen in time—Gerry with his gun, Don Morris with his hands up, the others in their spots around the table.

"What can I do for you, son?"

"It doesn't end like this," Gerry said.

Don nodded. "Yes, it does. You want to fire that gun, you know where you need to put it first."

Gerry's eyes grew very wide.

Suddenly, he stuck the barrel of the gun in his mouth, pointed up. He took a deep breath and pulled the trigger.

BANG.

Jeff Monroe watched his mastermind's brains blow out through the top of his skull. For a split second, Gerry's body didn't seem to understand what had happened. It remained standing one second too long, then slid sideways and fell, hitting the table on its way to the floor.

A puddle of blood began to spread out like a halo around Gerry the Shark's ruined head.

"What do we do now?" Monroe said.

"We call the Chinese," Don Morris said. "And apologize for the inconvenience."

CHAPTER FORTY SEVEN

November 19
1:00 p.m. Eastern Standard Time
Mount Carmel Cemetery
Reston, Virginia

REBECCA ST. JOHN
To Live, to Laugh, to Love

Luke bent and placed a dozen fresh roses at the base of the grave marker.

Then he stood beside Gunner, staring down at the gleaming black marble. Once upon a time, he might have put his hand on his son's head and tousled his hair. The urge was still there. But it would have been awkward now, at least in part because Gunner was a lot taller than he used to be.

"Do you miss her?" Luke said.

Gunner nodded. "I miss her a lot. I pray to her every day. Sometimes I feel like she's talking back to me."

Luke almost envied him his feelings about her. His mother was perfect in his eyes, and would always stay that way. For Luke, so much had happened before the end. She had hardened against him, not just when she was dying, but for years before that. He still loved her, but that love was tempered by confusion, by anger, and by regret.

If he had it to do over again...

But it was a lie. You never got to do it over, and even if you did, you'd probably do it the same way.

They walked the grounds of the cemetery for a little while. It was a bright, sunny day, and warmer than it had been all week. Luke's injuries hurt a bit, but not too bad—the painkillers were keeping them tamped down. The surgical scar on his torso itched a bit. In general, he was comfortable enough walking.

Across the hillsides, thousands of grave markers stretched away from them. Here and there, people dotted the landscape, visiting their deceased love ones. There was something undeniably pleasant about this cemetery.

"What did your grandmother say?" Luke said. "When you told her you were going to see me?"

231

Gunner shrugged. "She told me not to do it, that I'd be sorry. She said you were a deadbeat dad and were going to break my heart."

"And your grandfather?"

"He didn't really say anything. He just kind of looked up from his newspaper, shook his head, and grunted. He was reading the *Wall Street Journal*."

Luke suppressed a smile and shook his own head. There was a lot of truth in this kid. Those were about the most accurate depictions of Audrey and Lance that Luke had ever heard. Becca never once described them like that.

Gunner was looking at the ground as they walked. Luke fought the urge to tell him to keep his head up, his eyes sharp. Situational awareness, kid—that's the key. It was the key in sports, the key in politics of any kind, the key to life or death. Did a deadbeat dad have the right to tell his son that?

"She said you were going to disappear again," Gunner said now. "She said you always disappear."

"What did you say to that?"

"I told her you were planning to stay this time."

They kept walking.

"Are you? Are you planning to stay?"

Luke nodded. "Yes. I am."

"That's good." Gunner's tone said he was noncommittal. Luke could prove himself, or not. It wouldn't matter as much this time.

Luke hoped—really hoped—that he could make good on it. He had people here. Gunner was the anchor, of course. But Ed was also around—they'd made a plan to go deep sea fishing next weekend. Swann was hiding out in his apartment over in Ocean City. And Trudy was… who knew what Trudy was going to do? It seemed like she had already dropped out of sight again.

After a few minutes, Luke and Gunner came to another grave. The marker was simpler than Becca's, the words hewn into white stone.

Kent Philby

Beneath the name, in smaller characters, there was a long epitaph:

May the sun shine warm upon your face;
the rains fall soft upon your fields
and until we meet again,
may God hold you in the palm of His hand.

Luke stood there perhaps a moment too long.

"Who was he?" Gunner said.

Luke shrugged. "I don't know. Just some guy, I guess. I like the poem, though." He should like it. He was the one who paid for it to be there.

He looked at Gunner. "You want to grab a bite?"

Gunner's eyes narrowed. "I'd love to, Dad."

CHAPTER FORTY EIGHT

November 20
7:10 p.m. Eastern Standard Time
The White House Residence
Washington, DC

Susan was dressed like a teenager.

She had changed into a favorite pair of old blue jeans, faded and ripped and sprung in all the right spots. She wore a hooded yellow sweatshirt. She was in bare feet.

She was living in the White House again, a place that frankly creeped her out, and her family had gone back to California. So she might as well make herself as comfortable as she could.

It had been a whirlwind couple of days. Hundreds of calls of congratulations and well wishes had come in from across the globe. Susan had taken the most important world leaders—and would try to respond to the secondary ones over the coming days. Yet, to her surprise, even rebel groups had also called. Dissidents, terrorists, and rogue states—even avowed enemies of the United States clearly preferred that the American President not be unhinged.

Criminals had checked in. The fugitive Russian mobster Victor Balhurin had called from wherever he was hiding to offer his best. And Ramon Figueroa-Reyes—El Malo himself—had called from the federal supermax prison in Colorado. He was delighted to hear that she got some use out of his house, and hoped that she enjoyed it. Funny—she might even call him back. It was a great house. Maybe the FBI could seize it as a drug asset and it could become the Winter White House.

She smiled at that thought.

She sat at the small round alcove table in the Family Kitchen. Just across from her sat Luke Stone. There was a bottle of red wine on the table. She was drinking it, and in fact was on her second glass—he had barely touched any.

She took a bite of the chicken salad the chef had made at her request. Over the years, the chicken salad had become one of her favorite quick and informal meals here. She probably ordered it too much. It was the best chicken salad in the world—the smallest bit tart, with unsweetened cranberries and tiny almond slices embedded in it. They often served it with crusty French bread and a nice green salad on the side, just like they had done tonight.

Boy, it was good.

"What about the guy in Florida, Stephen Lief?" Stone said.

They had been talking about who might make a good Vice President.

"He's in the other party, Stone."

"I know, but he has a pretty good way with horses. Gentle. He can't be all bad."

She sighed. "I'll put him on the list."

The doors to the kitchen were closed, one Secret Service agent right outside, listening in on this conversation through an earpiece. That's how it was. It was always going to be that way, and she was used to it by now.

But would they still listen if Susan and Stone…

Susan stared at him. He had let his beard grow again in the past few days. His hard blue eyes peered out from atop a blond beard and mustache. In the past, letting his beard grow would suggest to Susan that he was about to disappear again.

Why don't you stay this time?

Do it for your boy.

Do it…

for me?

Luke Stone was elusive, maddening, a hard person to figure, and still… she was attracted to him. Maybe that's why she was attracted to him. He was the international man of mystery character that Hollywood made movies about—like James Bond, only more rugged and weathered. Less polished—she had trouble picturing him wearing a tuxedo at a casino in Monaco.

James Bond meets the Marlboro Man.

Also, he had saved her life. And her daughter's life. And the entire world. Stone had saved everybody's life now too many times to bother counting.

I wonder what he thinks about that.

His eyes were watching her. He had barely touched his food.

He was nervous, she decided.

"The food's really good," she said. "The chef here makes the best chicken salad on Earth. I'm kind of an expert on chicken salad, so I should know."

"I'm sure it's great," Stone said.

"Then why don't you put some of it in your mouth? That would be the polite thing to do."

"I don't know. I'm not sure I want to get filled up."

She rolled her eyes. "I know. People often get filled up on chicken salad. It causes a lot of trouble."

He smiled and shook his head.

"Do you remember," she said, "when we were in the bunker?"

He nodded. "Yes."

"We got pretty close in there."

"I agree," he said. "We did."

"And you said to me something like, 'I've always wanted this.' What did you mean by that?"

Now he laughed, and he blushed like a little boy. His face turned as red as a delicious apple. He turned away. "I'm pretty sure you were the one who said that."

Suddenly, Susan felt like a predator, a lioness, moving in for the kill. Maybe it was the wine. Maybe it was everything that had happened between them. Maybe it didn't matter what it was. She had him right where she wanted him. And with that realization, the heat began to rise within her.

"I need to show you something," she said.

"Now?"

She nodded. "Yes."

"What is it?"

"It's the bed where the President sleeps."

She stood and took him by the hand. His hand was large and rough against her soft skin. But he held her gently. He stood, but made a move as if to head toward the hall.

"Not that way," she said. "There a Secret Service man out there."

"Which way?"

She indicated the door that went straight to her quarters. They passed through the doorway. The door to the bedroom was down a narrow hall.

"Uh, it's been a while," Luke said.

"Same here," she said.

"Also, I've been shot recently. I'm still recovering. Take it easy on me, is what I'm saying."

She glanced back at him and smiled.

"Not a chance."

OUR SACRED HONOR
(A Luke Stone Thriller—Book 5)

"One of the best thrillers I have read this year. The plot is intelligent and will keep you hooked from the beginning. The author did a superb job creating a set of characters who are fully developed and very much enjoyable. I can hardly wait for the sequel."
--Books and Movie Reviews, Roberto Mattos (re Any Means Necessary)

OUR SACRED HONOR is book #6 in the bestselling Luke Stone thriller series, which begins with ANY MEANS NECESSARY (book #1), a free download with over 500 five star reviews!

When China bankrupts the U.S. economy by calling in its debt and by shutting down the South China Sea, Americans are desperate for radical change. President Susan Hopkins, running for re-election, is floored as she watches the returns come in. Her rival, a madman senator from Alabama who ran on the promise to deport all Chinese and to nuke China's ships out of the South China Sea, has, inconceivably, won.

President Hopkins, though, knows she cannot yield power. To do so would be to spark World War Three.

Knowing the election was stolen, President Hopkins needs 48 hours to prove it, and to stop the escalating war games with the Chinese. With no one left to turn to, she summons Luke Stone, the former head of an elite FBI para-military team. The stakes could not be higher as she commands him to save America from its greatest threat: its own President Elect.

Yet as one shocking twist follows another, it may, even for Luke Stone, be too late.

A political thriller with non-stop action, dramatic international settings and heart-pounding suspense, OUR SACRED HONOR is book #6 in the bestselling and critically-acclaimed Luke Stone series, an explosive new series that will leave you turning pages late into the night.

"Thriller writing at its best. Thriller enthusiasts who relish the precise execution of an international thriller, but who seek the psychological depth and believability of a protagonist who simultaneously fields professional and personal life challenges, will find this a gripping story that's hard to put down."
--*Midwest Book Review*, Diane Donovan (regarding Any Means Necessary)

Book #7 in the Luke Stone series will be available soon.

BOOKS BY JACK MARS

LUKE STONE THRILLER SERIES
ANY MEANS NECESSARY (Book #1)
OATH OF OFFICE (Book #2)
SITUATION ROOM (Book #3)
OPPOSE ANY FOE (Book #4)
PRESIDENT ELECT (Book #5)
OUR SACRED HONOR (Book #6)

Jack Mars

Jack Mars is author of the bestselling LUKE STONE thriller series, which include the suspense thrillers ANY MEANS NECESSARY (book #1), OATH OF OFFICE (book #2), SITUATION ROOM (book #3), OPPOSE ANY FOE (book #4), PRESIDENT ELECT (book #5), and OUR SACRED HONOR (book #6).

ANY MEANS NECESSARY (book #1), which has over 500 five star reviews, is available as a free download on Google Play!

Jack loves to hear from you, so please feel free to visit www.Jackmarsauthor.com to join the email list, receive a free book, receive free giveaways, connect on Facebook and Twitter, and stay in touch!

Made in the USA
Coppell, TX
21 June 2021